Pride Publishing books by Logan Meredith

Single Books
The Story of Us

I0681394

THE STORY OF US

LOGAN MEREDITH

The Story of Us
ISBN # 978-1-83943-872-1
©Copyright Logan Meredith 2019
Cover Art by Cherith Vaughan ©Copyright September 2019
Interior text design by Claire Siemaszkiewicz
Pride Publishing

Published in 2020 by Pride Publishing, United Kingdom.

Pride Publishing is an imprint of Totally Entwined Group Limited.

THE
STORY OF US

Introduction

This is the love story of two men. One of these men —
that's me — is an ordinary part-time college student.
And when I say ordinary, I mean utterly normal. So, let
me dispel any misconceptions you may have. I am not
straight. I didn't start college thinking I was straight,
meet a hot roommate and discover I'm into dicks, nor
did I seduce my straight roommate. I don't even live on
campus. So, I didn't go from acknowledging I might
enjoy dick to power bottoming for some well-endowed
jock in a span of three weeks. There's nothing wrong
with those stories. They're just not ours.

I became a — *gulp!* — forty-something last December.
Around puberty, my gay gene activated and I couldn't
ignore it, although I tried. Like most gay men, my
coming-out story was a process. I lost friends...but
nobody close. Most of my family, my parents included,
recognized and accepted my attraction to men. So, I
didn't put off college because an ultra-conservative,
homophobic mother disowned me and neither was I

cut off by a wealthy father. I delayed college because I couldn't afford it and neither could my parents. Like most of my peers, I found a job after graduation and learned a trade—construction, in my case. Now I'm a manager for a custom home builder in Central California.

Perhaps you're saying to yourself, 'Aha—a blue-collar gay man.' This must be the story of a hot, hunky construction worker who rocks my world and fucks me while I operate power tools. Don't get me wrong, I would have fucked a sexy, hunky construction worker if they'd offered. Although not on a job site because I don't relish the prospect of being unemployed and I've never been so turned on that I couldn't avoid taking my dick out around machines that might sever it from my body. I'm sure other gay construction workers exist, but the twenty men I work with are all as straight as they come. So, this will not be the story of me trying to resist an inked-up jock who works for me.

I'm out with the guys I work with. Not in a 'Hi, my name's Kyle and I'm gay' sort of way. But I don't do pronoun gymnastics when describing my most recent weekend blind date disaster. Trust me. They all know what team I bat for. While this doesn't get me invited to many weekend barbecues, it doesn't get me beaten up either. To lay it all on the line… I won't be raped, outed, discriminated against, extorted, blackmailed or otherwise emotionally damaged in this story and neither will the other man.

How can this be, you wonder? How can an average, forty-year-old construction manager tell a romantic story without drawing on any of these clichés and keep it interesting? You may ask, "Kyle, will there be sex?" Of course. Just not the unlubed, drill-me-hard-with-your-ten-inch-dick anal sex that is so prevalent in gay erotica. Gay men don't enjoy anal sex without lube. Well, I should say, this gay man doesn't, and none of the fifteen — give or take a few — men I've had sex with over the years did. Despite what you might have seen on *Queer As Folk*, we don't carry around packets of lube everywhere we go. So, I'll concede that I'm no Brian Kinney — promiscuous uber-top with an anaconda between my legs, ready to fuck whenever and wherever the mood strikes.

So, you're probably wondering why should you read this story? It sounds like a boring gay romance. That's fair. After all, I've only told you everything this story is not. I should say what happened and let you make up your own mind.

This is the story of how I, Kyle McMillan, came to meet, date and subsequently fall in love with Lucas Cass. You already know I'm a forty-year-old, blue-collar, part-time student and a versatile gay man of average intelligence, sexual experience, dick size and financial means. So perhaps it would be a good time to mention that Lucas is better known as Tommy Bruiser. Yep, that's right. My boyfriend is a gay porn star.

Got your attention now, didn't I?

Chapter One

Years before

I never stood a chance. All the ingredients for a true romantic comedy meet-cute were present and accounted for. Seriously. If Julia Roberts and Tom Hanks themselves had been in the library during our encounter, I wouldn't have been surprised.

Let me paint the picture.

Rainy spring day... Check.

Accidental collision of two handsome strangers... Check.

Sexual tension... Double check.

What started as a slight drizzle strengthened into a wallop of a springtime shower midway from the parking lot into the building. I had two hours between the end of my workday and my algebra midterm. My faded navy-blue sweatshirt covered my head while I powered through the pounding horizontal rain.

A revolving door marked the entrance to the main library at Simmons University. Midterms had packed the two-story building and a steady stream of students flowed in and out, keeping up a constant whirl-whishing-click sound I used to time my entrance into an open wedge. Lucas approached from the opposite direction. I kept pace, entering at the precise moment the opening became available — only so did Lucas and his oversized umbrella.

Two full-grown men both with loaded backpacks proved too much for the small space and the whirling of the door came to an abrupt halt with the stem of Lucas' umbrella in his hand and the opened top still outside. The student in the other wedge hit the glass in front of her with a hard whack, and since I had entered our side before Lucas, I did the same. I couldn't turn around. We were squeezed in tight. Between the hysterics behind me and the laughter from the students inside the library, I determined what had happened. I gathered we were a comical sight.

"Fuck, my umbrella is stuck," Lucas said, laughing too hard to do much about it. I could hear him cycling through attempts to push the handle out and retract the top in. Nothing worked. The force of the door and the unamused girl trapped next to us who inexplicably kept pushing on her side wedged us in further. "Stop pushing," Lucas hollered. "See if we can back up enough so I can free this."

I wiggled my arms out of my backpack and turned around. The three of us coordinated our efforts to work against the natural direction of the door.

"Push it out," I said when enough space opened to heave the umbrella outside. He did, and the girl next to us shoved the door hard enough to send Lucas and me flying into the library. I fell over my backpack and Lucas fell on top of me. His weight jammed the corner of the calculator I kept stashed in my bag into my balls.

"Fuck me." My anguished groan echoed in the quiet confines of the library. Snickers from several students bounced back. All eyes shifted to me as I writhed, grabbed my crotch and muttered every swear word I'd ever learned and a few I invented in the moment.

Lucas scrambled off me, scarcely able to breathe. His contagious hilarity infected me and forced me to smile, despite the excruciating pain of having a TI-83 calculator smack hard against my scrotum. Through my wincing, something resembling a laugh escaped. We lay together on the library floor and recovered our breath while students who had resumed using the revolving door stepped over us into the library.

Following a stern look from the librarian, Lucas regained enough composure to stand. He offered me his hand and assisted me to my feet.

"Man, I'm so sorry. Tell me how I can make it up to you," Lucas said, handing me my sopping wet and muddy sweatshirt from the library floor.

I took my sweatshirt and sized him up for the first time. Shorter than me by two inches, Lucas had a blond Southern California surfer boy vibe going on — shaggy hair curled on the ends fell into perfect place with the shake of his head and blue eyes roughly the color of the Pacific Ocean. *And young... Oh, so young.*

"You owe me something after that." The words could have come out sexy if I had bothered to lace them with any innuendo. Instead, they came out like the grumpy old man in the Scooby-Doo cartoons. I'd essentially called him a pesky kid.

His smile yielded to a conciliatory grimace. "Sorry, sir."

Sir? Damn if that didn't hurt worse than being hit in the nuts. "Don't worry about it. I'm fine. It's not like I need my balls to take an algebra test." *Oh my God. Shut up, Kyle. What the fuck am I saying?*

His gaze dropped to my pelvis and my sweatshirt-covered crotch and traced back up. A blush flushed his cheeks. "Yeah, I guess not," he said. "I should let you study." He entered the revolving door again, and I followed him, my mouth opened wide in case the remaining fragments of my brain wanted a chance to escape.

I noticed it had stopped raining seconds before Lucas swooped to retrieve his umbrella. He stood and once again shook his head, silently commanding all of the golden strands back to their proper place. He repeated the motion twice more when one blond wisp refused to fall in line.

With his halo back in place, he looked at me, breaking the hypnotic spell of his hair-flip ritual. Lucas' focus re-acquainted me with a level of mortification I thought reserved for puberty. Not only was I blatantly staring at him, but I also had no explanation for leaving the library we'd spent an exorbitant amount of effort to enter. I knew it, and by the bemused expression on his face, so did he.

"Cool. Cool." My spectacular conversation skills displayed once again.

Lucas' lips curved upward. "What's cool?"

Oh, for fuck's sake. I turned to leave. *That's it. Walk away and pretend you've got somewhere else to be.*

"You're leaving?" he hollered, laughter escaping in the same breath.

Desperate for any plausible explanation, I turned toward him and stopped at the edge of the covered entrance. I opened my mouth, but only random, meaningless sounds came out. I couldn't hide how flustered I was, and his expression told me he'd determined precisely what had caused my reaction. He checked me out again, that time with all sorts of lascivious intent, and grinned. "Don't you need to study?"

"Um. I... Um." I pointed and gestured but said nothing intelligible. *Maybe I contracted an acute case of brain damage from my fall?*

Like a lifeline, he offered his hand. "I'm Lucas."

I stopped rambling long enough to shake it. Lucas' satiny-smooth palm in my clammy, calloused hand fired off inappropriate urges. "Kyle," I returned, still flustered. "I'm sorry," I added, although I had no idea what for. *Blatant ogling?*

He shrugged off my apology but kept my hand in his and adjusted his mane again with another small shake of his head. "So, Kyle, would you like to go find a private enclave and...um...study with me?"

Fuck. Now that's how you say something with innuendo. *Why couldn't I have done that earlier?* "Oh. Um, sure. Yeah, I guess you owe me that." The rest of the English language escaped me and I bobbed my head to convey my enthusiasm. Saliva pooled in my mouth and I gulped so hard my throat ached.

As I followed Lucas to the staircase, my brain seemed to catch up to what was happening, leaving me momentarily panicked. I paused. *Am I really doing this? Me?* The rise and fall of Lucas' steps and the spellbinding bounce of his ass steadied my nerves, and suddenly I was poised to take the first step toward the most outrageous thing I'd ever done.

At that moment, Lucas glanced back and delivered a filthy challenge with nothing more than a smile and a wink. I missed the step and gripped the handrail to keep from falling on my ass again.

With an amused laugh, Lucas backtracked, took my arm then slid his fingers down my forearm and laced them with mine. "Careful," he smiled and squeezed my hand.

He led me with more confidence than any man had a right to own toward the private study rooms that flanked the outer wall on the second floor of the library. Before I could warn him that the rooms would be booked solid so close to midterms, he stopped and flung open the door. "I reserved this last week," he said, gestured me inside and closed the door behind us.

The room was small, scarcely large enough to hold the table and four chairs. I studied the carpet pattern, intricate geometric shapes on a black background. It was old and slightly musty, as though the carpet hadn't dried after the last cleaning.

"Kyle." Lucas' voice was just above a whisper, but commanding nonetheless. "Come here."

I swallowed again and gathered the words to explain how out of character our little rendezvous would be for me, but Lucas' cockiness had turned predatory, and storm clouds settled over his ocean-blue eyes. Physically he was almost too perfect to be real. At the first step toward him my knees buckled and he took hold of my waist and deftly moved me. Once again, I fell dumb.

A thud resounded from the table I found myself crowded against. Startled, I twisted. Lucas swept my bookbag and tossed it on the floor next to his. He latched on to my chin, edged me back until the table dug into my thighs and, for lack of a better word, took ownership of me. *Jesus!* I am *not* a small guy, but Lucas had a presence I could never fully explain, and the way he kissed me lit me on fire — full-fledged 'take-me-now, holy shit, what is happening' fire.

I freed my mouth long enough to draw a deep breath, squeezed my eyes shut and recited the alphabet backward — in my head, of course, because it had been a while. And, well...I refused to be *that* guy. Sometime around M or Q — who can say the alphabet backward, anyway? — I opened my eyes. Lucas moved down my neck, and slid his hands under my shirt. My pulse raced and my chest pounded so hard that I briefly considered I might be in the midst of a heart attack. It was too much, and I gripped his hips and tried to signal my desire to slow it down a bit.

Lucas paused and appraised me. The intensity in his eyes stole my breath. And not in a good way. He looked, not angry, but different. "Isn't this what you had in mind?"

I nodded, not knowing what about the last thirty minutes had given him the impression I held any capacity for rational planning.

"So, this is the fantasy then? Is this what I owe you?" His dark tone was far more biting than seductive, as though we were role-playing but with two different scripts. He resumed kissing me, aggressively sucking on a spot low on my neck and kneading my ass in a desperate, almost painful way I loved. I tried to close my eyes and enjoy it until he bit my earlobe hard and muttered something else about not wanting to disappoint me.

"Hey, wait." I summoned all my self-control and stopped his fingers from unzipping my fly. Another uninterpretable comment about giving me what I expected accompanied his hand shoved down the back of my pants. I reached behind me and stilled his wrist. "Wait," I snapped.

"What's the matter? Can't stay hard under pressure?" He jerked away and wiped his mouth with the back of his hand, leaving a perplexed expression under it.

"No, I'm plenty hard but confused as hell." I searched him for clues. "I was kidding when I said you owe me. This is… Wait… Is that what you're doing with me?"

Lucas gave a noncommittal shrug and reclaimed the air that separated us. The sweet kisses along my neck made my insides swim, but something was still off. He moved to my lips and dialed up the aggression to a ten again. The fog of hormones cleared, and my erection wilted with the way Lucas kissed me — like a roadblock he had to remove. I stayed him gently, straightened my untucked and half-unbuttoned shirt and regained composure. My balls groaned in protest, but Lucas' weird vibe had clicked my real brain back on.

"Seriously, I'm attracted to you, but I… Shit, I'm sorry. I think we've had a misunderstanding. You don't owe me anything, and I have no expectations of you. I would never take advantage like that."

His dumbfounded gawking did not provide the assurance I'd hoped for. I was quite sure he never got turned down, especially not by a guy like me, but even I wasn't pathetic enough to accept a pity fuck for an apology.

"Um, it was nice to meet you, Lucas."

Bewildered and acutely aware of the protest formed in my now-twice-insulted testicles, I left the private enclave. With barely an hour of study time, I gingerly took a seat at one of the small tables in the open section of the second floor, hauled my algebra book out and reviewed my notes, my concentration on par with an attention deficit child left in an arcade after downing a triple espresso and eating their weight in cotton candy.

My scribbled notes about linear inequalities were less confusing than what happened next. Someone joined my table uninvited. I glanced up long enough to confirm my suspicions. The sexy smirk on Lucas' lips told me I'd fallen short of my intended subtlety. Annoyed and embarrassed, I gave him my full attention and projected as much confidence as I could muster. *Yes, hot men always approach me in the library.*

"I want to ask you a question and your answer will have everything to do with our future."

Our future? I nodded, although, again, clueless.

He continued, "Before today, had you ever seen me?"

"Do you have mental health problems?" I whispered.

He howled so loudly that the students at the other tables aimed dirty looks at us. "Answer me."

"No," I whispered, trying to encourage him to lower his voice.

Lucas' mysterious enthusiasm blossomed. "That's what I thought."

Beyond confused, I waited for an explanation that didn't come. Lucas remained in front of me, a broad, stupid smile still plastered on his face.

I returned my attention to my notes, because even in a parallel universe, I was pretty sure I still had a midterm to take. Lucas continued to stare at me, flabbergasted by my feigned disinterest or perhaps mulling over why he even cared. The silence was laced with an unnerving current of anticipation.

"Okay?" I tossed my pencil down and peered up to meet his eyes. "Was that all?"

"No," he replied. "Kyle, would you like to have dinner with me? I'd like to make you dinner."

Either I had been transported to an alternate reality where hot men *did* ask me out in the library or he was completely fucking with me. The latter seemed more plausible, which annoyed and disappointed me at the same time. With a sarcasm infused, "Yeah right," and a dramatic eye roll, I dismissed him—or so I tried.

"I'm going to take that as a yes." He produced an iPhone, tapped at the screen and stared hopefully at me. "Give me your number," he prompted.

"Are you serious?" I asked.

Lucas nodded, smiling.

"But you don't owe me anything."

"I know. I asked you because I wanted to." He looked around at the students who were now not-so-subtly watching us. Lucas lifted a hand to the side of his mouth and stage-whispered, "It'd be awesome if you didn't turn me down in front of an audience." He turned to face the other table, drawing embarrassed laughter from the gawking students.

"Say yes," a random girl fake-coughed, and about twenty students nodded, adding a chorus of agreement with a few murmured, "He's hot" and "I'd go out with him in a second."

Lucas turned with an appreciative smile. "See?" Lucas gestured to the girl at the table next to us. "C'mon. Look at her. She has an advanced physics textbook. What's your name?"

"Monica," the girl offered with a giggle.

Lucas smiled warmly, "See? Listen to Monica, Kyle. Monica, should Kyle go out with me?"

"If he doesn't, I will."

Lucas grinned and gestured, as if to say, 'See? Monica thinks I'm hot.'

Monica and her entire table stared at me with their breath held, waiting for my answer. What was I supposed to say? The whole exchange was surreal. "Sure, yeah. Dinner is great." I rattled off my cell number, and a few seconds later, a text message caused my phone to vibrate against the wooden table. I stared at it like the device would explode if I touched it.

Lucas laughed again. "You're cute, Kyle. Good luck on your test." He kissed my cheek before leaving and a small smattering of applause broke out. My math studies notwithstanding, I couldn't have put two and two together to save my life.

Chapter Two

The day of our first date, my body seemed hell-bent on reminding me that men my age had no business going to a college kid's apartment for dinner. I wasn't doing anything remotely manly at the time. Nope—bending over to pick up a goddamn piece of litter on the job site of a McMansion is what had me popping Advil like M&M's. If that weren't bad enough, my testicles and left thigh displayed seriously unattractive bruising from the calculator.

From the landing of an outdoor metal staircase, I checked the address in my text messages again. Lucas lived on the third floor of an apartment complex with no elevator. I closed my eyes and pictured his abdominal muscles. I hadn't seen them in the library, but he'd pushed against me, so I could imagine them...vividly. I'm a sucker for abs, and Lucas' would be worth every bit of the next few minutes. So, with my mind focused on three to four ripples of muscles and a picture-perfect innie belly button I'd surely want to dip my tongue into, I put one foot on the first stair and braced myself for the shooting pain to course up my back. It did, and I winced with each agonizing step.

Loud music greeted me at the top. *Was that...?* "Fuck," I muttered.

Dining to Eminem? I couldn't have pulled that off ten years ago. Lucas would take one look at me and send me packing. I debated options, but I'd climbed the Everest of staircases, so running away held as much appeal as hearing the rejection straight from Lucas' actual mouth. Before I could decide if pretending to like Eminem would be more or less painful than rolling down three flights of stairs, a door opened. Lucas stood there, holding a large box of cookware. He stuttered hello, clearly surprised to see me.

"Hey, you're here."

Panicked, I reached for my phone to check the date and time. "Yes," I said frantically checking our text messages. "You said Friday at six." I held up my phone. "It's five-fifty-nine."

"Oh. You're punctual, huh?" He laughed in a way that said my old man ways amused him, like how I laughed when my dad told corny jokes. *Is punctual a bad thing now?*

"It's fine. I'll take this to the dumpster later." Lucas' smile eased my anxiety, and he ran his hands through his hair.

"You cut your hair," I blurted.

He tossed the empty box next to his door and smiled wider. "Yeah, I let it get too long during midterms, but I figured a hot date was a good reason to get my mop cleaned up. Come in, Kyle." He motioned me inside.

Lucas lived in a standard student apartment. A small family room, dining area and kitchen were visible from the doorway. Toward the back, a short hallway contained two closed doors, which I assumed led to his bedroom and a bathroom. I couldn't identify dinner by the aroma in the air, but it smelled delicious and heavy on flavors—lemon, garlic and something earthy like mushrooms. I loved a man who could cook, and that realization sent a fluttering of anticipation from my stomach to my heart. I clung to that feeling. I didn't know how to label it precisely. *Potential, maybe?* A chance that something beyond the promise of great abs had compelled me to climb Lucas' stairs.

I had envisioned bean bag chairs and a PlayStation, but Lucas had actual furniture, and any video games were tucked away behind a decent quality entertainment system. Art adorned the uncolored walls—very geared toward gay men, but still, original framed art, not posters, and a few select decorative touches that helped me forget I was in campus housing.

"Would you like something to drink?" Lucas shouted over the music and shut the door behind us.

"What?" I motioned to the stereo speaker, grateful that it drowned out my awkward laughter.

He grimaced, hastened to the coffee table and grabbed a remote control to turn the music off.

He smiled back apologetically. "Drink?" he repeated and led me toward the kitchen. Cookware, still wrapped in plastic, lay on the counter. If he caught the questioning look on my face, he did an excellent job of ignoring it.

"Beer, if you have it." He plucked out two kinds and offered me a choice. I pointed to the Belgian-style wheat ale from a local brewery and he produced a frosted mug from the freezer and poured it.

"Want an orange slice?" He searched the fridge and located a container. Since he already had them cut, I nodded. Discreetly, I wiped my sweaty palms in my pockets and accepted the drink.

"So how was your test? What was it again?" Lucas asked and grabbed a second beer for himself.

"Oh, fine. The scores aren't back yet. It's algebra."

His nose crinkled, and I chuckled. "Not a math fan?"

"Not my favorite. What are you studying?"

"Mechanical engineering right now. I'm still getting the basics out of the way."

"Yeah, this was my first year too. I'm a business marketing major, so I have to take accounting courses for my math requirements." I groaned audibly.

"Something against business marketing?" Lucas chuffed and poured his own beer, twisting the orange slice before tossing the rind into the glass and licking the juice from his fingers.

I hated myself before the words left my mouth. "Should you be drinking that?"

Lucas glanced at his beer, appearing momentarily confused by my question. Suddenly, he clutched his chest with a dramatic gasp. "Are you insinuating I can't afford the calories?"

A smile. *Goddamn, that smile.* Wars could have started over it. Also, he was fucking with me again.

"No, I'm insinuating that you're underage. Well, under twenty-one, anyway."

"Insinuating or asking, Kyle?" He sucked briefly on his bottom lip.

Obscene. His smile was obscene.

"Um, asking?" I didn't know. And honestly, his lips mesmerized me.

"You're in algebra, right?"

I needed to understand the sorcery of his lower lip. He scraped it between his teeth and rewet his lips in slow motion. *One perfect freckle dead center. Magical.* "Uh-huh?"

"That's a freshman-level class?"

"Um." I took a sip and tried to coordinate my throat muscles to swallow, which isn't as automatic a reflex as one would think.

"Exactly. First year doesn't mean I'm underage. I'm old enough."

Not for me, I thought. "For?" I asked instead. I'm only human.

"For whatever...." Lucas shrugged noncommittedly, then for no reason whatsoever, he stepped toward me. His lips crashed into mine, and I gasped. Literally, I gasped into his mouth. He pulled back, and I shook my head.

"What's wrong?"

"Umm... I can't... I'm not sure I should...."

"I'm twenty-three, well out of jailbait territory, so relax."

I shook my head because his age had surprisingly little to do with my reaction. All day I'd been psyching myself up with thoughts of Lucas wanting to get to know me, but that kiss advertised a much different agenda. *I am the biggest idiot. Of course, this isn't an actual date. This is a hook-up.* "I'm forty," I admitted because the rest seemed like a moot point.

Quite sure that would be the end of the evening, I set my beer down and eased back a step with an eye toward the door. I sighed. "Listen. I think I should..."

Lucas' face fell. "Please don't go," he said. "I knew you were older when I invited you to dinner. The age difference doesn't bother me at all. I'm sorry for launching myself on you. I just... You were staring at my lips. I thought you wanted me to."

"Oh, um, yeah. It's fine. Just... I'm not really into hook-ups, so I don't want to give you the wrong impression. That thing in the library... You should know that was way out of character for me."

Lucas stepped toward me and cupped my cheek. He focused on my lips with laser precision, but he leaned in slowly and pressed his lips softly to mine. The kiss was nice. Gentle, even. He tasted sweet from the orange. I couldn't have held back the sigh of relief if I'd tried, thankful that we'd connected on a setting other than raging lust.

He pulled away, smiled and said the words that reassured me enough to stay. "Come sit down with me. I want to know everything about you." Time seemed to disappear while we talked. Or I guess Lucas asked me questions and I rambled answers in my half-coherent, not-sexy-at-all way.

Dinner wasn't homemade. I would have gone through with the ruse because — first date and all — but Lucas' commitment didn't extend to transferring food from the takeout containers he'd stashed in the oven to the new cookware.

I assured him I appreciated the dinner regardless... and I did. His blush, though... That gift I loved even more. Even if I was the water boy to his starting quarterback, somehow Lucas' aborted scheme had put us on the same field. That he'd tried to impress me and failed placed him back on earth with us mere mortals, and I started to recognize myself during our interactions.

By the end of our meal, I'd approached an acceptable level of charming, and Lucas had gone from captivating to downright enticing.

We returned to the family room, resettling on the couch much closer to each other than we'd sat previously. His knee brushed mine, and he flirted his hand across my thigh and lingered as he situated himself. My mind began to form possibility out of the earlier potential. Following a longing stare, he leaned in to kiss me again—just a brush across my mouth before he pulled back and bit his lip.

"Ready for dessert?" he asked shyly. For the first time since we'd met, I thought Lucas might have been more nervous than me.

Lucas placed a crème brûlée still warm from the oven on the coffee table in front of me. He switched on the stereo low, something I found easy to ignore, and sat on the floor, inviting me with his eyes to join him. Carefully, I lowered myself, and Lucas grabbed a pillow to stick behind my back. Grateful, I smiled when he held a spoonful to my lips.

Lucas waited for me to swallow and chased it with a kiss. Leaving his hand resting on my thigh, he sighed happily and took his own bite with the same spoon. With each taste from our shared spoon, the evening grew more intimate. I began to touch him more—a thumb over his lips to wipe away some crème brûlée, a squeeze of his hand, a bump of our shoulders. The anticipation built steadily until I finally braved a brush of my hand over his hair. *Exactly as silky as I'd imagined.* "I like the haircut, by the way."

Lucas smiled and ran a hand through it. "Yeah? I wasn't sure."

I nodded and brushed the hair away from his face. "I liked it long too."

A faint nod and another happy sigh. "I might grow it out again then."

Ugh. I was smitten. I caressed the silky strands. "It's soft. It's the first thing I noticed about you."

Lucas preened, but my candor embarrassed me. I glanced around the room, avoiding the intensity of his eyes and found my change of subject. Motioning to our dish, I asked, "What was the plan here?"

"What do you mean?"

"I mean…" I leaned in to kiss the concern off his lips. "Did you have a blowtorch at the ready?"

He seemed confused, so I explained. "The sugar on top. It's melted with a small propane torch. I guess you didn't think that far ahead."

Lucas chuckled. "I'm still learning."

"How to fake it?"

"No, I had planned to cook for you, but I expected to be home all day, and I asked my mom to help me."

"Well, that's" — *sweet, adorable, amazing and, oh-my-God, his-mom* — "nice."

"All day I kept thinking, 'I still have five hours' then, 'three hours should be enough,' but before I knew it, I had less than an hour and my mom had to go to work, so I panicked. But this is nice, right? The food was good? I didn't know what you liked. She told me I should text you to ask about allergies, but…" Lucas peered up, and I caught his smile. "I'm rambling."

"Dinner was delicious." I smiled and touched his hand in what I hoped was a reassuring gesture. "And I understand about timelines. Sometimes I'll ask what idiot came up with a build schedule. Of course, it's me who always underestimates how long things will take, so I have no one but myself to blame. I'm in construction. Did I tell you that already? What do you do?"

Lucas took a slow sip of his drink. He smiled oddly — mysteriously, perhaps, or uncomfortable, but it didn't fit right on his face. "Well, now I mostly go to school. So what aspects of construction do you manage?"

Lucas' expression shifted back toward neutral while he waited for my response. I launched into the highlights of my job and his natural smile blossomed again. Ignoring his cagey answer paid dividends in pure sunshine.

We bounced from subject to subject, winding through safe, first-date topics. Before I realized it, I'd spent thirty minutes detailing my dream project — designing my own house on the same Oregon lake where I'd spent my childhood summers.

"Do you like to travel?" Lucas asked. He turned toward me and propped his elbow on the seat of the couch. He trailed his other hand down my arm and it came to rest over mine. He danced his fingers over my skin and, without thinking, I turned my palm face-up and let him continue to touch me while we talked.

"Travel? Sure. I can't say I've done much. If I have the time and money, I'd like to see more of the world someday. Matt and I used to…" My thought trailed off when I realized I'd inadvertently introduced ex-boyfriends into our conversation.

Lucas' eyes widened in question. He sat up and removed his hand. "Who's Matt?"

"Um…just a guy."

"Oh? So, is he the one who got away, the one who broke your heart or the one who doesn't know you're having dinner with me?" Lucas' eyes narrowed, and at that, I realized how my abruptness could have been misinterpreted.

"None of the above. Matt is the guy who might have been the one but wasn't. We ended on reasonably good terms nearly two years ago."

He raised a skeptical eyebrow. "So, why the dramatic pause?"

"I didn't mean to bring him up. Bad first date etiquette and all."

Lucas' posture relaxed. "Is he still part of your life?"

"I guess so. We lived together for less than a year, but we dated long enough to have a shitload of mutual friends. I see him and we catch up, then he fades away until the next occasion."

"Very adultish breakup. All my exes probably have voodoo dolls of me with pins in them."

I laughed. "That's not very flattering. Are you trying to warn me you're like the Taylor Swift of gay men?"

"Something like that. I wouldn't say I'm a nightmare exactly, but I can get drunk on jealousy."

"Oh no." I snorted and the sip of beer I'd taken threatened to escape down my chin. "You can quote *Blank Space*. That's a red flag."

Lucas beamed at my response, and he found my thigh again. "Well, you recognized her song lyric, so you must be a closeted Swiftie too."

"Um, no. I'm not a closeted anything. The guys at work can't agree on a radio station, so I rotate between the major XM stations. Theoretically, it should be an even mix of rock, hip-hop, top 40 and country, but I swear that girl gets played on every channel some days."

"So, not a fan?"

"She's okay. I'd say I'm partial to the classic gay icon divas. You know... Cher, Madonna... But I can say I have grown to embrace the badassness that is Gaga and Beyoncé."

Lucas smiled and did a mock hair flip. "Now I know you did not praise Gaga and Beyoncé and leave out Miss Britney, bitch."

"Oh, man. No. Just *no*. Britney's voice annoys the shit out of me. And before you ask, I loathe Mariah, too. I don't care what her range is. Glass-breaking vocals is not an excuse to be such a fucking diva, and how many sequined, neck-plunging leotards can a single woman own? Edgy, sexy or classy is fine, and I'm totally cool with the curvy ladies showing off some skin, but she screams sad. Nothing worse than a washed-up pop princess who doesn't know her day has passed. Well, maybe a washed-up porn star, but honestly…"

Lucas flinched.

Reflexively, I shut my mouth and tried to recall my words. I swallowed hard. "You're not some die-hard Mariah fan, are you?"

"No…" Lucas said evenly, but his expression bordered on disappointment, and I studied his face, attempting to decipher what I'd said to cause such a reaction. "Finish your thought. What were you saying about washed-up porn stars?"

"Porn stars?" I racked my brain and shook my head until my last comment came back to me. "I don't know where I was going with that. It was a rant. I don't even watch porn. Well, much. I can't say I never watched porn because um… Well, the Internet and questioning teens are like peanut butter and chocolate. Am I right?"

"I know you don't watch much porn, Kyle." His expression upgraded to a bemused half-smile which, although still concerning, was a far sight better than a moment earlier.

I exhaled at the slight ease of tension between us. Maybe Lucas watched a lot of porn. It wouldn't have been the first time I'd come off judgmental without meaning to. "Well, yeah. I just told you. I wouldn't lie. I mean there's nothing wrong with watching porn. I don't have...like a moral objection to it. If you watch porn, it's totally fine with me, but it isn't my thing."

"I don't actually watch much porn either," Lucas said. He ground his jaw with the words.

"Yeah? Oh well, that's good." Back to rambling, I flailed for a lifeline. "I mean, it's fine. Porn seems like kind of fake, right? Like, I don't know about you, but the idea of having to fuck someone you just met —"

"Are you telling me the possibility of fucking in that study room didn't turn you on? It didn't excite you?"

"No. Oh God. Of course. I mean, of course not. That isn't what I meant. You totally did. Like, c'mon. Look at you. You know you're ridiculously hot. I could have pounded steel spikes into the ground I was so hard, but that's the thing, right? I was so into it until I realized that you... Well, I guess until I realized you weren't. I never asked you to explain that. Maybe I should have, but that's the thing about porn that doesn't work for me. Some of the men aren't even gay. It's like if I had to sleep with a girl for drug money or to feed my kids, which feels exploitive, and that is a major turn-off for me. But like I said, I don't care if you watch porn at all. Matt, my ex, watched it a lot. And I mean, a lot, a lot, because we had opposite schedules. And... Oh God. Never mind. It's fine with me."

"So, you don't like porn because you think the men who do it have to? What if they want a chance to show off their bodies, have sex in a safe environment and make some good money? Would it be okay with you then?"

"I guess. It's okay if you watch porn. I'm not trying to say it's bad."

"I don't watch porn," he said, not trying to hide his exasperation.

"Wow. Okay, then why are you so upset? Don't you think the whole gay-for-pay shit is wrong?"

He took a yoga-worthy deep, cleansing breath and paused long enough for my heart to enter my throat. "First, I think gay-for-pay is mostly an act. Many men enjoy the 'straight, masculine guy taking it up the ass' fantasy, and it does happen on occasion. But most studios won't hire genuinely straight men because it's hard enough to get a good scene from two guys who enjoy gay sex, so the so-called straight performers are usually heteroflexible, bisexual or, at the very least, bi-curious.

"I don't watch porn because I know what it's like behind the scenes, which ruins the final product for me. I also find it strangely amusing to see my friends having orgasms with each other, so it's kind of hard to jerk off to anymore. And I rarely, if ever, watch my own scenes any longer."

"You —" The words caught in my throat. I broke into a cold sweat as his revelation sank in.

"Yes, me. And I'm not a victim of terrible circumstances. I don't have a drug problem, and I'm sure as hell not gay-for-pay. I consider myself to be an exhibitionist. My parents know what I do. I'm not ashamed of it. It's a good job, and it lets me go to school full-time without borrowing money and having to work a ton of hours to support myself. I get cool, free stuff from fans, who, by the way, are mostly middle-aged women. My bosses are a loving, devoted couple who fucking inspire me. It does interfere with dating, and honestly, those exes I told you about are coworkers. I wasn't kidding about my jealous streak, and well, some people don't see the difference between on-camera and off-camera sex. When you didn't recognize me, I thought I'd try to date outside the business and see if that might be a better situation. I didn't plan to hide it from you, but I was hoping we could have gotten to know each other a little better before I explained what I do. But if you have issues with porn, you have issues with me, and I really like you, so I guess I need to know if this is something you can see yourself accepting, because I don't have plans to stop."

"So, you're asking me if I am willing to date you and not care if other guys fuck you?"

Lucas scoffed. "Um, well...I don't bottom on camera, but yes, I'd be having sex with other performers for work. If we ever decided to become exclusive, I'd continue to film, but I would be willing to go back to condom-only if that makes it better."

"Why?" I asked.

"Why condoms? I assumed you'd be concerned about safety, even though it's a low risk. Most guys—" His words ended abruptly. Panic flashed in his eyes like he'd suddenly realized how fucked up this conversation was for two guys who'd just met.

"Let me finish that for you. Most guys my age practice safe sex?" I said. What was with his generation's ridiculous refusal to use condoms? "Lucas, HIV was still a death sentence when I came out, so you'll forgive me if I don't stick my bare dick in every available hole."

Lucas narrowed his eyes and I could see him struggle to rein in his response to my overreaction. His confession had landed like a sucker punch right in the middle of a decent first date. And doing it without condoms? My anger clashed with concern for his well-being.

"Okay, wow. First, you're a top? Really?" Lucas said.

His response earned him a scathing stare. I wasn't sure who I thought I was fooling. I might be versatile, but we both knew I had been seconds away from bending over in that library and begging for it.

He went on, "And second, porn performers get tested regularly. I'd never be paired with a positive performer who had a detectable viral load, and like I said, I never bottom for my scenes. I am also on PrEP. The HIV risk is miniscule, probably less than getting fu—"

I opened my mouth to protest, but before I could speak, he rolled his eyes and corrected himself

"Or, rather, fucking some random guy, in, say…a library."

His accusation ignited some unearned, self-righteous rage in me. "I wouldn't have fucked you without a condom, Lucas," I shouted the bald-faced lie. I didn't carry condoms with me, and although Lucas hadn't indicated he'd planned to fuck me, if he had, I didn't know what I would have said. Despite my usually cautious nature, I couldn't say I'd gotten test results for every boyfriend before ditching condoms, nor had every guy I trusted proven to be worthy of my trust. There'd been a handful of doctor visits where waiting for the STI test results had given me more anxiety than a pop quiz.

There was the 'oh shit, what was I thinking' kind of slip-up, then there was plain, reckless stupidity, like signing up for a class of nothing but pop quizzes and being at Lucas' mercy to pass. I would have to be willing to trust him and untold numbers of porn stars enough to bet my health on it. I would never reach that level of faith, and that was merely a fraction of the problem I had with the situation. "I'm sorry, but I'm not interested in pursuing an open relationship, at least not without the possibility of something exclusive happening."

"It wouldn't be an open relationship. I could be exclusive except for work, if we got to that point. If you knew how porn was filmed, you'd realize there is such a difference between actual sex and sex on-camera. You said it yourself. It looks fake—and it is. It's not sexy. Sometimes there is zero chemistry, and even if there is an attraction, half the time it doesn't even feel that good. We stop in the middle for a light to get fixed or because a siren goes by outside the office. Three other people stand around watching us. I lose my hard-on because they want us in some crazy position and my scene partner needs a break because we've been filming for hours. I usually need to jerk it off-camera until I'm close enough to come. They turn the camera back on so they can get my cum shot. They edit it so that it seems continuous. It's frankly mechanical for me. It's different from sex with a boyfriend or a partner."

I stood, not swayed by his pleading argument. Sex was sex, and while I'd never had sex on camera, I had been cheated on and knew the sinking pit of heartache that came from knowing someone you loved had been intimate with someone else. Not anxious to relive that feeling anytime soon, I shook my head and conveyed my answer with a solemnly whispered apology.

Lucas nodded his acceptance, grabbed my glass and walked with it toward the kitchen. He began to clear our plates from the table, avoiding eye contact.

"Do you want some help?" I offered and prayed he'd say no. I needed to get away from that quivering lower lip of his. *Kryptonite. Pure kryptonite.*

"I got it. Let me walk you out." He placed the plates on the counter and stared for a beat. He was poised to speak, lips parted, probably to make another argument we both knew wouldn't change the reality of his job being a deal breaker for me.

We stood at the door. I didn't want to leave, and the way he regarded me let me know he didn't want me to either. He stroked my cheek and kissed me lightly. "So, that got kind of out of hand."

I nodded. "We seem to have that effect on each other."

He cracked a smile—a small one, but still enough to say he regretted the path our conversation had taken as much as I did. "If you change your mind…" he whispered across my cheek before pressing our lips together in the softest of kisses. "I was looking forward to getting to know you."

I made it all the way down the stairs and to my car before I realized my chest ached so much I'd forgotten that I'd injured my back. The dull twinge spread into my stomach and the taste of bile flooded my mouth. My whole body seemed to reject the idea of denying it Lucas. Except for my brain, all my other organs coalesced on it being the biggest mistake of my life.

Get over yourself, Kyle. It's one date. He's too young for you, anyway.

But deep down, it hurt, which, by itself, told me everything. Unfortunately, no one could accuse me of listening carefully to messages from my heart. So, like any rational man, I tried to forget about the entire evening and Lucas. The ubiquitous Taylor Swift sang from my radio about how the story of us started off good but now looked more like a tragedy. I turned it off because—damn that Taylor Swift—I did not need a reason to get emotional about bubblegum pop songs.

Chapter Three

The spring semester ended with little fanfare. I managed to squeak out As in both of my classes and work picked up to a point where I could only handle one summer class. I didn't see or hear from Lucas, which didn't surprise me since I was the one with the issue. Lucas was an almost-memory until the image of his naked body became inscribed into my brain.

To explain what happened, I'll need to introduce Kayla.

Everyone knows that cartoon image of the angel and the devil that sit on someone's shoulder and tell them what to do or not do. Well, that's my Kayla. Only she isn't the angel or the devil — she's both. She is the only person I know who can have a full knock-down, drag-out argument with herself. I never understood how she could analyze a situation and advocate some well-reasoned advice, only to support the opposite point of view once I'd conceded to her line of thinking. It's quite the skill, and trust me, it is as maddening as it sounds.

I met Kayla in high school when she smoked clove cigarettes, dressed like Winona Ryder and looked down on people who couldn't recognize the names of the obscure band T-shirts she wore. She's always been *that* friend for me. You could say she won me over with her snarky rebellion. She knows every secret I have. When my first boyfriend wanted to fuck me, she shoplifted an enema kit because I was too embarrassed. If I were ever in a horrible accident, she knew to remove all sex toys and lube from my bedroom before my mom found them.

After Matt and I had finally decided to split for the last time, I made Kayla promise to not let me get back with him. She hacked into my iTunes account and made me an 'I think I want Matt back' playlist. By the time I got to Beyoncé's *Single Ladies*, she'd cured me of my post-breakup amnesia and prepared me to carry on alone. She's the Grace to my Will. On the subject of me, she's basically a genius.

It all started with the selection of my summer course schedule. After having decided to take Mechanics and Materials, I surfed through the frustratingly slow website all Simmons' students had to use to register. After twenty-plus years of working in the construction industry, simple engineering structures were kind of my thing, and even at forty, I, just like every student, wanted an easy class for the summer. I clicked on the series of drop-down menus, navigated to the class number and sorted through the possible sections.

"Damn it."

Kayla lowered her phone and frowned. "Now what? Did it kick you off again? I told you being a first-year sucks. You don't get to register until everyone else has."

"No. Mechanics and Materials is only offered during the daytime, and it's once a week. My boss is flexible, but no way will he let me leave for three hours in the middle of the workday."

"Well, take something else." Kayla shrugged and went back to scrolling through her Twitter feed. You'd never know from her ambivalence that I'd gone to college because of her. She'd spent six years listening to me waver in my decision to seek a degree. She'd encouraged me to follow my dreams, then right as I got up the nerve to fill out an application, she'd asked me if I was sure I wanted to incur debt with virtually no payoff. A fair point... There was no mistaking that the degree was solely for me. Not having one hadn't held me back in my career and having one wouldn't change my income potential enough to justify the expense. I could sock the money into a retirement account or do something fun with it — buy a motorcycle, a boat or take some of those trips Matt and I had talked about. The construction industry was ninety-nine percent reputation, which I had in spades. No one gave a shit about a piece of paper.

Except me.

I had no idea why. No one in my family had ever been to college. My father had delivered mail his whole career. My mother was a secretary for a trucking company. But I remembered my envy when Kayla had left for university and when she had talked about her classes. The desire to get my degree had never left me.

"You should take another core class. If you take Mechanics and Materials, it won't count if you change your major."

"I'm not changing my major."

"Well, business is definitely more marketable. You could start your own company and use all your contacts to make way more money. Why go to college if you can't use it to improve your financial situation?"

Kayla's suggestion was one I'd heard before—from her, from Matt, from my parents—everyone who'd heard me talk about my job. My boss was an imposing brawler type from Pittsburgh named Rocco Salvatore. Raised in the housing projects of McKees Rocks, Rocco frequently spoke of people from his neighborhood like they were part of a large extended family. Besides construction, he knew Steelers football and not much else. He drove me crazy sometimes with his appalling lack of social graces and tendency to hire skilled laborers based on little but gut instincts, but we had an arrangement. I did the work and he earned the money.

Can I own my own business? It wouldn't be impossible, given my contacts, but the idea terrified me. I wasn't sure I'd ever possess the confidence necessary to strike out on my own, and even if I did, I wasn't sure I wanted to. I didn't mind most aspects of management, but getting that far away from the hands-on work? *Nah.* That wasn't for me. There was just something in me that needed to see concrete, tangible results at the end of the day—something I could point to and say, "That's where my effort went." In my current role, I was often at a job site, pitching in or double-checking my guys' work, but I was equally likely to work a twelve-hour day and have literally nothing to show for it.

I clicked links and reviewed the classes that worked for both business and engineering degrees. Kayla continued perusing her phone. She tilted her head to one side, flung her feet up onto my ottoman and smiled. "Of course, you have great instincts, so if engineering is where your heart is, you should follow your passion. You're so good with your hands, and your brain is wired to think spatially."

I ignored Kayla and continued my search. Unfortunately, the schedule made the decision for me. Most of the engineering classes I had the necessary prerequisites for were offered either during the day or were already full. "There are a ton of open evening business intro classes and let's see…" I clicked through the requirements, mentally eliminating those that sounded dreadfully boring. "There is an Introduction to Entrepreneurship. That sounds kind of interesting."

"Well, you should definitely explore classes that are of interest. You don't want to get to your last year and switch majors. The first year is the best time to confirm which program fits."

"So, you think I should take it?"

"I think you should, but taking classes outside of your major is like throwing money away. It might be better to take something basic, like English. It would work for any major. But like I always tell you, you are too risk-avoidant. This could be good for you. Step out of that comfort zone."

"Kayla, really? Can you not ever give me a straight answer?"

She smiled innocently. She put her phone down, relocated to stand behind me and rubbed my shoulders like she always did when we did that dance. "You asked my opinion. I'm your friend, and you work so hard. I don't want you to waste your money."

"Well, is it wasting money to take one business class I may not need or to take two years of engineering classes and change my major?"

"Give me your computer." She tugged my laptop off my lap and sat back in her chair. She clicked around while I grabbed a beer from the kitchen. "Okay. It's done. You're registered for the class."

"Which one?"

"That business class. You clearly wanted to take it."

"But I thought I was wasting my money?"

"You are. He might be in it, though."

"He who?"

"Kyle, you didn't look up the requirements for a business degree. You searched the requirements for a business marketing degree. That's Lucas' major, right?"

"So?"

"So," she mocked. "You don't give a shit about marketing. You want to see Surfer Boy again. Why didn't you say that? You could call him."

"I shouldn't."

"You should, and you should watch his porn so you can stop thinking about it."

"I most certainly don't want to see his porn."

"You do, and it will be good for you because you've built it up in your head as a horribly seedy thing, although it's quite tasteful and smoking hot."

"It would be too... Oh my God, did *you* watch it?"

"Of course. How could I tell you to watch it if I haven't seen it? I mean, if it were like incest porn, it would scar you. It's mostly standard jock-on-twink porn. He's aggressive for sure, but not any worse than David. Although, I gotta say, his thingy is quite impressive."

David, another ex, fucked me three times before I realized what I considered super intense S&M was his version of vanilla. Images of my brief time with David — my one toe-dip into kink layered on top of my memories from the library, Lucas' pelvis making a subtle thrust into mine. My cheeks heated, and I closed my eyes and imagined him holding me down against the table. With David, I always seemed to ruin the mood with uncontrollable nervous laughter. With Lucas...I wondered.

Kayla laughed, and I opened my eyes. "You're soooo adorable when you're crushing on a guy. I haven't seen you turn that shade of red since Matt gave you that Trophy Boy underwear and you opened them in front of your crew."

Lord! I relived the moment with a fresh wave of humiliation. Matt loved to give me sexy underwear and jock straps, but usually we exchanged those types of things in private. We'd planned to see each other before he left town to see his folks for Christmas, but a bout of bad weather had put an important project weeks behind, and I'd practically lived at the construction site to play catch-up. Matt had texted me that he'd left my Christmas present in my truck, and I made the mistake of following Kayla's orders to open it when she stopped by to bring me lunch. The entire crew practically pissed themselves laughing so hard.

"He should have told me to wait until I got home — and I am *not* crushing on Lucas."

"Oh, so you don't want to know what his dick looks like?"

I did. I *so* did. "I'm only human, but I'd like to find out like normal people, after a few dates, certainly not from my best friend…because eww, we've already had that moment. Need I remind you of Judd Fisher?"

Kayla sighed with nostalgia. "The only man we've ever shared." Her tone implied the memory was a fond one, which it most certainly was not. "He was a sweetheart. Too bad he was gay."

"My team does not claim men who sleep with men but have online profiles seeking women. We had a meeting."

"He could have been bi," she said defensively. "Don't be one of those gay people who think bisexuals are closeted gays. I think he was still figuring himself out.

Not everyone's sexuality fits into such a rigid little box, Kyle."

"I don't care what identity he claims—bi, pan... whatever. He's still a creep, and he wanted to have a threesome with us. That was... Just no."

"I would have done it."

Utterly horrified, I gawked at Kayla, and she burst into laughter. "Do my girl parts gross you out that much?"

"Girl parts don't gross me out. I could probably sleep with a woman if I had to, to like repopulate the earth or something, but you're like my sister. Are you telling me you could actually have sex with me?"

She giggled. "I could have sex with this..." She flipped my laptop around and there was Lucas in all his 'holy shit, he's gorgeous' glory.

"Give me that," I squeaked and yanked the computer onto my lap. "Where did you find this?"

The splash page of a porn site called *Goldenboys.com* featured Lucas' image by a pool, his skin glistening with drops of water that seemed to be cascading down his perfect torso. The picture kicked off a chant of 'I want, I want, I want' in my brain.

"Fuck." I trailed my finger over his picture. "I knew his stomach was the eighth wonder of the world." His abdominal muscles were every bit as sexy as I'd imagined them to be. Lucas' skin was a deep shade of bronze like he'd been kissed by the sun's rays. I choked on my saliva, trying to swallow. My audible gulp coincided with Kayla's supportive hand coming to rest on my shoulder. "Click on his picture," she said.

The screen brought up a profile of Tommy Bruiser and a full-frontal image of his body. "His... Oh my God." I pointed and mourned the loss of an opportunity.

Kayla sighed. "It's a goddamn work of art. It should be in a museum. Have you ever seen one that...?"

I shook my head and gestured, unable to find the word to do it justice. "You?"

"Long? Yes, but not in person. But thick? No. Sadly, I think he holds the record."

"It's perfect," I sighed. Lucas was perfect. My attraction was not only off the charts but the wall the charts were hung on. And we'd connected so well. I couldn't explain why. We just had. The hours we'd spent together that night had been nothing short of fantastic until I'd stumbled into the landmine of his career choice.

"I know, but could you? I mean they don't call him Tommy Bruiser for nothing. It seems like it would hurt."

The truth was that it probably would. I'd done my fair share of bottoming, but like everything in my life, I was cautious and methodical enough to not impale myself on a super-sized penis without a whole lot of preparation. The work-up to it, though... That thought had me forming an immodest amount of wood.

"So, are you gonna call him?"

I made a noncommittal sound and took another glimpse at the website. Lucas — or Tommy — wasn't the only image. There were three other men — all young, like Lucas, and gorgeous. I closed my eyes, shut the laptop and tried to picture myself with Lucas — him meeting my folks, me meeting his. They'd probably be close to my age. We couldn't hang in each other's social circles. His friends would wonder what Lucas was doing with me and mine might recognize — *Oh, God.*

The thought of my friends knowing what Lucas did for a living and having ready access to watch him have sex? They'd never let it go. No matter how badly I wanted him—and sex with Lucas would be incredible—it couldn't work. I'd been on plenty of dates, and I'd learned some things about myself over the years. When I brought up my dream house or my desire to get my degree, I was investing in the long term. It meant I cared enough to know if my two non-negotiable goals would be compatible with theirs. I'd told Lucas about both on our first date.

Even if I wanted, I couldn't go back. I didn't work that way.

Chapter Four

Introduction to Entrepreneurship began on a balmy Monday evening in June. I'd spent the day with a client and still had the remnants of a stress headache I'd developed after explaining why the kitchen in her plumbed and wired home couldn't be relocated without an impact on her budget.

Summer classes, especially those held in the evening, meant little traffic and easy parking, so I arrived with plenty of time to spare. I spent my found minutes indulging in an iced coffee from the campus Starbucks and people-watching in the quad. Lucas had been on my mind since my conversation with Kayla, and I couldn't deny every blond head caught my attention. When I thought about what it would be like to be with him, my entire body responded.

Class time approached, and I stood and stretched, noticing that I'd sweated through the semi-nice, button-up shirt I'd worn for my client meeting. Searching my bag for the faded T-shirt I'd stashed in anticipation of a late-night workout, I made a quick pit stop to change on my way to the Business Building.

I was on my way out of the empty restroom when I saw him. A fountain of perspiration erupted from every pore and I sucked in a breath. I sought the safety of the bathroom, splashed some water on my face and composed myself like the adult I fucking was.

Okay. So, that's a lie.

In all honesty, I gripped the sink and sucked in breaths like an asthmatic in a perfume factory. The water helped calm me enough that I could text nine-one-one to Kayla. My phone rang instantly.

"What?"

I regretted my text at the genuine sound of concern in Kayla's voice.

"I saw him. What do I do?"

"What?" I could hear the wind rushing past her phone and her breath while she walked, so I knew I'd caught her on her way out of work.

"*Him.* I saw Lucas."

"Oh yeah. Shit." Kayla's car beeped in the background, a door slammed and static filled the phone. "Hold on," she shouted. The car started, her seatbelt clicked and the radio blared briefly before falling silent. "Okay, talk. What did he say?"

"I don't know. I haven't gone to class yet."

"Where did you see him?"

"I was leaving the bathroom."

"Well, this is good. Go talk to him. Restart the conversation. But calm down first, Jesus. You're such a spaz."

"'Cause he's gorgeous."

"So? You're gorgeous, Kyle. Go be gorgeous together and have gorgeous babies."

"Not helpful. And I'm not 'Lucas gorgeous,' I'm like average-guy attractive, at best. Plus, I'm forty-year-old attractive, not twenty-whatever-year-old Lucas attractive. It's mildly offensive to put me in the same category. That's how wrong you are."

"Kyle. Honey. I hate to minimize this little panic attack you seem to be hell-bent on working yourself into, but calm your tits, okay? He's just a guy. He told you he likes you. If you like him back, then what is the problem? Go find him and ask him out. I have real problems."

"But he…. Wait. Real problems? What real problems?"

"Patrick's finally marrying the hoe and I know my mom is going to force me to be a bridesmaid."

"Would you please stop referring to Tracey as 'the hoe'. She's nice."

"My little brother wouldn't know nice if it slapped him in the face."

"You set them up. She was your college roommate, for God's sake."

"I know, but back then her life was fucked up like mine, and I thought Patrick would be, you know, a good influence. He was lonely and law school was stressing him out. They weren't supposed to fall in love. And Tracey wasn't supposed to get her act together and be the all-perfect trophy wife. My mother is literally obsessed with her. All I hear is 'Tracey loves to cook. You should ask her to teach you' and 'Tracey bought the cutest dress. You should have her take you shopping.' Yesterday, she told me I might want to follow the same diet plan as Tracey because I don't want to be the fat bridesmaid."

I laughed. Kayla's mother may have been hypercritical of Kayla's choices, but the woman was far too proper to insult someone's appearance. "Kayla, stop. Esther Anderson would never call *anyone* fat."

"Fine, but she was thinking it. Plus, Patrick wants them to marry at the same church where my parents got married. You know my mother will ambush me with a blind date every weekend until this wedding. God forbid her chubby, spinster daughter doesn't have a proper beau for her little brother's wedding."

"Aww. That's so cute."

"What is?"

"That you think I'm buying any of this."

"Did it work?"

"Yes. I am calmer now. Thank you."

"Why do you make me play these little distraction games, Kyle? You're forty. Grow up. I hate you."

"I love you too. Tell your parents, Patrick and Tracey that I said hello."

"You can tell them yourself. Patrick is proposing at brunch this Sunday. Bottomless mimosas... You'll come and be my designated driver. And don't tell me it's a family thing because, as my father put it, 'Invite Kyle. The gays love brunch.'"

I barked out a laugh. Kayla's father, Mitch, had been slow to warm when he thought Kayla and I might be an item. After he discovered how wrong he was, my being gay became almost a fascination to him, and Mitch liked to impress me with how down with my people he could be.

"So, talk to him?" I asked.

"Yes, simple. Just talk. It'll be fine."

"He might not be in my class."

"He is," she said confidently. *Too confidently.*

"How do you know?"

"I have my ways."

"Kayla Sue Anderson, you tell me immediately."

Her sigh served as confirmation. "Tommy Bruiser has a Twitter. He posted information about his class schedule."

"You follow him on Twitter?"

"Yes, and before you ask, I knew it when I signed you up. It's one class, Kyle. You needed a push. You haven't been that excited about a guy since Matt. You don't have to marry him. Have a fling. Get you some summer lovin'."

"I will never forgive you for this as long as I live."

"Oh, okay," she mocked, and I knew her eyes were rolling. Lifetime grudges lost a bit of oomph after more than fifty threats. "I think Lucas should donate the sperm. I mean, we're both hot as hell and blue-eyed, you'd be practically guaranteed the cutest kids on the planet. Talk it over. Let me know. I can get some eggs frozen next week. I'm not getting any younger, you know?"

"Kayla…" I whined.

"Go to class, Kyle. It will be fine. You should be more sex-positive. This is good for you."

"What in the hell is that supposed to mean? Are you calling me uptight?"

"Kyle. Sweetheart. Angel. I've met nuns more comfortable with sexual expression. If it feels good and no one is getting hurt, enjoy it. And I love you too."

I said goodbye to Kayla and took a deep breath. My little meltdown had eroded all my spare minutes, and my T-shirt had prominent pit stains and a small hole I hadn't noticed before. No way could I face Lucas dressed like a bum. I dug into my bag and freed my work shirt, applied deodorant, brushed my hair and ran the shirt under the hand dryer until it was dry and presentable. It wasn't the best I'd ever looked, but at least I didn't look like a homeless guy.

I rushed to the Business Building. Unfamiliar with the room layout, I took a few wrong turns before finding myself outside the correct door. Working to calm myself again, I took a deep breath, checked under my arms and wished I'd had some cologne or body spray. All I wanted was to open the door and slide quickly into a seat in the last row, undetected. I could hear the lecture clearly, so my chances that it was a big lecture hall were slim to nil.

I eased the door open and roughly fifteen heads turned to stare. My cheeks heated to molten lava and I apprised the intimate classroom, which was closer to the size found in a high school. Shifting my bag from my back to carry at my side, I muttered an apology to the professor and slid, wholly mortified, into the first available seat in the front row. I didn't have time to locate Lucas and lacked the courage to search beyond subtle side glances. Maybe Kayla was wrong. Or oh, God… What if I was in the wrong class?

A brief glance to my side and my neighbor's textbook set my mind at ease. My tardiness didn't appear to bother the professor, but he didn't offer me a spare copy of the syllabus he'd handed out, either. I listened and jotted down notes without enough context while he reviewed the papers for the rest of the class who'd arrived on time. For a summer class, the pace was intense. Our grade was comprised solely of projects and presentations that were due nearly every week. The instructor, whose name escaped me, sounded almost gleeful while he reiterated how much work we'd be doing. He gave a brief lecture on the meaning of entrepreneurship and types of business models from a sole proprietorship to LLCs. He finished on the topic of partnerships and introduced the first assignment.

"On the back, you will find your partner listed for the group project. Now, we did have one student drop already. Let's see… Mr. Cass, you are without a partner for the first project. So, please pair up with Group Three for now. If we have another student drop, we can match you with the other single. There is always a bit of shuffling after the first assignment."

The sound of Lucas' voice affirming the professor's instruction came from behind me. I turned in my seat to find Lucas, all perfect, biting his bottom lip. He smirked at me. Unlike mine, his face appeared relaxed, his expression somewhere between amused and mischievous, which I would later discover meant he was feeling playful—not tickle-war playful, more cat and mouse. It made me nervous. When I get nervous, I have to pee.

"How are you, Kyle?" he asked, all calm and sexy while I shifted in the hard seat. While other students were moving desks and greeting their partners, Lucas held my stare as if the rest of the world didn't exist.

"I'm good," I squeaked, to his obvious amusement. "How are you?"

"Oh, best night of the summer so far. When did you change majors?"

"I haven't." I cleared my throat. "Um, I'm exploring."

"Oh?" Lucas' eyebrow peaked. "Just checking out business marketing and decided to take the hardest intro class in the major with the hardest professor?"

"I didn't—" I cleared my throat again, and Lucas offered me his reusable water bottle. I took it and sipped it too fast. His smile grew when I choked a little. "I didn't realize it was so hard."

"Oh, it's hard all right." Lucas laughed with a purposeful glance down. "Well, I guess we should partner up now."

"Part—?" I stopped when a man tapped my shoulder.

"Are you Kyle?" he asked, clearly annoyed for some— *Oh, right, the class. Jesus, I will kill Kayla.*

I turned back to Lucas, but he'd already migrated to his own group.

"So?" the man asked again.

"Yeah. Kyle." I shook my head to clear thoughts of Lucas. "Yes, sorry. I'm Kyle."

"Good. I'm Steve. You want to talk about this first project or what, dude?"

"Sure, okay." Steve talked and I half-listened. Our first assignment was to pitch an idea to our partner. We were supposed to talk about why we were in the class, what our strengths were and convince the other person to buy into our concept. Each group would only present one plan. The originator of the proposal would introduce their idea, and their partner would offer a critique.

The instructor, who Steve called Dr. Mandell, reiterated that the activity was a participation exercise only, rather than a formal grade, which took some of the pressure off. I managed a weak argument about my years of experience in the construction industry but failed to articulate an actual business strategy or apply any concepts from the first reading, which I hadn't known to do. Steve, on the other hand, had grown up working in his parents' bakery, and he'd been thinking through his cupcake shop design for years. We put our presentation notes together rather quickly. Although, the raucous laughter from Lucas' group did not help my concentration.

Dr. Mandell assigned the group presentation orders. Steve and I were chosen to go first. While Steve waxed poetic about cupcakes, I stood in front of the class melting under Lucas' stare. I angled my body away from him and focused on Dr. Mandell, which helped. Then I managed to deliver my critique with an acceptable level of coherence. Polite applause and Dr. Mandell's nod of approval followed our presentation.

When I retook my seat, I noticed my desk had been moved. I twisted in the attached chair to confirm my position, and sure enough, Lucas' mischievous grin was substantially closer than it had been before. He leaned back and suddenly, Lucas' flip-flop clad feet were on the back of my seat and he wedged his toes under my ass and wiggled. Surprised, I shot forward, which caused the metal feet to scrape loudly across the floor. The presenters stopped and stared at me while Lucas choked back laughter.

When the presenters resumed speaking, I faced Lucas, intending to express my irritation, but one glimpse at his perfect white teeth biting on his lower lip and I caved. *Damn that smile of his.* I found myself smiling back before facing the front of the class.

During Lucas' group's turn, I wasn't surprised to learn Lucas had originated their concept. Lucas could probably have sold ice to Eskimos with his charisma.

"Good evening, all. My name is Lucas Cass, and I'm in the adult entertainment industry. Specifically, the gay adult entertainment industry. The porn industry is worth around ninety-seven billion dollars and each year produces more than thirteen thousand films netting over ten billion dollars in profit. Who among us has not indulged in porn at least one time in our lives?"

He paused, scrutinized the room and made direct eye contact with every red-faced person, including me, before he continued. "Pirating and the proliferation of social media and cam sites have impacted the industry's profitability while, at the same time, offering an individual performer more opportunity than ever to create a personal brand.

"I have nearly two hundred thousand followers on my social media platforms. This led me to obtain promotional deals with both adult toy companies and a popular underwear brand. I regularly receive fees for club appearances. Eventually, I am hoping to obtain my degree so that I can start a business where I help other performers create and promote their brands. I'd also like to start a company which would produce and market adult toys specifically for men. I'll let these hetero guys"—he pointed to his partners—"explain why this is a good idea. Basically, to sum up, if you've never had your prostate stimulated, y'all are missing out." The other men in Lucas' group cracked up and Lucas flashed a toothy smile at them and winked.

Dr. Mandell cleared his throat. I surveyed the room, expecting to see everyone shifting uncomfortably, but realized the only ones struggling with Lucas' business topic were me and Dr. Mandell. Everyone else wore expressions that ranged from entertained to intrigued. I suddenly felt very, very old.

Lucas' group finished their presentation, but I had stopped listening to frantically text Kayla.

I'm so old.

We're the same age, jerk.

No...like I act old. Is porn not taboo anymore?

What are you talking about?

Lucas told the entire class he does porn, and the only ones that seem remotely disturbed by this are me and the professor, who must be at least sixty.

Relax. You're overthinking this. You like him. Talk to him.

I don't think I can. He's too much for me.

Well, you won't know that until you try to put him in. Don't be a baby.

Ugh. I hate you. Seriously. What should I do?

Use lube. Lots of lube.

I hate you so much

No, you don't. Talk to him.

Maybe if I didn't answer, she would give up.

Kyle, talk to him.

Seriously, don't ignore me. Are you going to talk to Lucas?

What's happening? Why are you not responding?

She obviously wasn't giving up.

I'm in class. Stop.

Your class ended five minutes ago. Talk *to him.*

"Kyle." Lucas laughed. "You okay?"

Lucas stood over me in a nearly empty classroom.

I dropped my phone and he squatted to retrieve it, using my thigh to steady himself. He smirked as he handed me my phone. "Careful... You don't want to break this."

A text dinged, and he glanced at the screen in the split second it took for me to yelp, yank my phone out of his hand and shove it into my bag. "Th-thanks,"

"You're not going to check that?"

"No." I swept my other belongings into my bag. I got a nose full of Lucas as he rose to his feet, and I was struck by an intense desire to inhale him like fresh laundry. I needed air. Lucas-free air.

"Okay, but someone named Kayla wants to know if you talked to me."

"No," I repeated too harshly.

"You aren't going to talk to me?"

"I...uh... I need to go."

"Okay," Lucas stepped back and offered me his hand to stand. "I'll walk with you."

"You can't." I ignored his extended hand and stood.

He lifted an eyebrow. "I can't?" His stance and silence issued a challenge, but I didn't even dare a breath with Lucas so close. Finally, with a crooked smile, he stepped aside and gestured for me to walk ahead of him.

I bolted toward the door, his soft chuckle twisting my gut. Without turning around, I knew Lucas trailed behind me. My every sense became heightened by his proximity.

Halfway to the parking lot, I slowed then turned. "Why are you following me?"

Lucas smiled, and he placed his hands in the air. "Chill. I'm walking to my car."

"You're all…" I flailed my arms at him. He didn't try to hide his amusement at how flustered I was. "Stop being all stealthy."

"Not stealthy. Quiet. You said you didn't want to talk to me."

I closed my mouth and stared. Damn, that probably sounded way more asshole-ish than I'd intended. "It's not… I didn't mean…"

"Okay." Lucas smirked. "So, you want to get some coffee?"

"It's late."

A quick suck of his teeth and a shake of his head made it clear he'd lost patience. He pouted briefly then turned and walked away.

"Wait."

Lucas stopped but didn't turn around. He sighed and said, "Look, Kyle. I'm only gonna take so many swings at this ball." He turned to face me and his frown punched me right in the gut. I hated being responsible for that look.

"I meant that it's too late for coffee. I already had some before class. Any more and I won't sleep. I'm not twenty anymore."

Lucas tilted his head and stared guardedly.

Okay, then. I gathered he'd passed me the proverbial bat. "How 'bout a beer? The bar and grill down the street should still be open."

"That place with the red awning?" Optimism lifted the tone of his voice, and I instantly second-guessed my offer.

"Yeah." I breathed relief because his smile was back. "Would that be okay?

"Down, boy. You don't have to beg. I'll let you buy me a drink."

I chuckled. "Meet you there?"

"Yep." With a small hop, Lucas turned and rushed back toward the classroom.

"Wait! Where are you going?"

"Oh." Lucas laughed and turned to face me but kept walking backward. He gestured with a thumb over his shoulder. "Strangest thing. I just now, at this very moment, realized I'm parked in the other parking lot." He shrugged like his ruse to follow me hadn't been blown to bits.

Flattered, I couldn't help but laugh and shake my head. Why did he have to be so damn adorable?

"I'll see you there, Kyle," he yelled as he jogged away.

I did my very best not to freak out on my way to meet Lucas. *One drink*, I reminded myself while I navigated the back roads from campus to the main street. "Just don't be a weirdo," I delivered my pep-talk to the rearview mirror. "One drink. No big deal." *So what if his smile makes my heart skip?* I turned the wheel, taking a left into the parking lot.

Presuming I'd beat Lucas there, I parked and waited. I closed my eyes and took several deep breaths to stay calm. When I opened them, I yelped. On the other side of my window, Lucas' lips were nearly pressed against the glass. He pulled back, laughing.

I reached for the door handle but Lucas beat me to it and opened my door.

"You okay?" Lucas asked, his hand brushing across my lower back when I stepped away to close the door.

"Fine," I lied and walked toward the entrance, leaving Lucas behind.

He hurried to my side and looped his arm through mine. "It's okay if my beauty intimidates you." He batted his eyelashes to show me that he was kidding.

I huffed out a quick breath and nervously untangled our arms. "You're a modest one, aren't you?"

Lucas beamed at me and tugged on my shirttail to slow my pace. I turned to face him and a nearly empty parking lot. He cupped his palm over my cheek and forced me to make eye contact. "I'm a hopeful guy, Kyle. Now, are you going to let me get to know you?"

"I'm not—"

"I want to know you. That's all I'm asking for."

"Why?" I croaked.

"Because you're special."

"I'm not," I answered. "I'm just an average guy."

Lucas chuckled. He tugged me closer until my chest brushed his, clasped his hands behind my neck and held me there for a beat before bringing our foreheads together. We breathed the same air and that feeling of possibility flooded over me again. I couldn't pinpoint what about him spoke to me so strongly, but I could nevertheless sense it pumping in my blood and knew that I was in trouble. When he released me, he stepped back and traced a finger to my cheek. "I'm going to thoroughly enjoy changing your mind about that."

"Lucas, I haven't changed my mind."

He smiled and nodded his acknowledgment. "I'm going to thoroughly enjoy changing your mind about that, too."

"Lucas," I protested as he held me in his gaze. "I'm too old—"

Lucas moved his finger to my lips. "Buy me a drink, Kyle."

I nodded, and he grabbed my hand as we walked the rest of the way toward the door. He stepped in front of me to open it. "After you…" He guided me inside with a hand to my lower back. "Daddy," he added under his breath.

Mortified, I glared at him. He laughed, wrapped his arms around my body and squeezed. "Just trying it out," he whispered in my ear. My every hair stood at attention immediately upon feeling his warm breath across my neck.

"I-I-I'm n-not…." I stuttered. I didn't even know what I was trying to say.

Lucas shrugged. "That's okay. We'll work up to it."

I couldn't contain my laughter. Sitting in class, I'd felt sixty. Now, being the target of Lucas' unrelenting attention, I felt twenty again. Lucas waggled his eyebrows at me, but for a split second, I thought he might have been serious. "Wait. You're kidding, right?" I asked.

Lucas laughed off my question without an answer and approached the hostess stand.

The host offered us a choice between the bar and a booth. I chose the bar, thinking it would be less intimate, but as soon as we sat, Lucas proved me wrong. He rested his hand on my thigh and worked touches into our every interaction, as though determined to desensitize me.

He talked about his other summer classes and slowly his cocky veneer faded, revealing the same charming, self-effacing humor he'd shown during our first date.

"It was a disaster. There was literally sauce dripping from the wall. My mother got me all stressed over following her recipe to the letter, and it didn't say to turn the heat down or cover it. Apparently, she didn't think those steps needed to be explained. I scrubbed the wall bare but it's still stained. I'll probably need to repaint the whole apartment." He cracked up, and I nursed my beer, smiling.

"Why do you need to repaint? Just touch up that area."

"I want it to match. Forget *Fifty Shades of Grey*. There are fifty shades of white."

The reference conjured up memories. Kayla had taken great pleasure in reading the sexy parts of the entire sordid trilogy to me, complete with over-the-top narration. My face warmed, and I noticed Lucas was smirking. "What?"

"I knew it. You've read those books, haven't you? After the library...the way you responded. I know you have a kinky side. You know they have awesome erotica with two men, probably more up your alley."

Glancing around, I blushed. "I don't think... You should call your landlord. They probably have gallons of it lying around. I'm sure they will give you some, or at the very least give you the brand and color so you can pick up a small amount."

Lucas grinned, and I couldn't tell if he was amused by my embarrassment or grateful for the suggestion, but regardless, he let the topic of kink go. "Yeah, that's a good idea. Thanks, Kyle."

I shrugged. "No problem. If you need brushes or anything, I have plenty."

"Thanks." He took the bottle from my hand and tilted it. "You're empty. How about one more?"

I noted the time — almost eleven, and I had a crew to meet at six. Lucas downed his last swallow and flagged the bartender. "So, what's it going to be, Kyle?"

While he waited for my answer, he scraped his lip between his teeth. The intense way he watched me sent my pulse racing, and my internal dialogue had already abandoned the list of reasons I shouldn't kiss him to focus on the reasons I shouldn't go home with him. But God, did I want to. Lucas' sex appeal wasn't so much the confidence I'd seen in the library but the ease with which he was unabashedly himself. I somehow knew he was the type of guy to lay all his cards on the table and dare me to play. I had no clue how I was supposed to walk away.

"Sure. One more."

The bartender left to fill our order. Lucas took my hand and played his fingers over my palm. He brought my hand up to his face and, with his eyes laser-focused on mine, he slowly pressed his lips to the back of my hand. The energy of his kiss unleashed an overwhelming, and not entirely pleasurable, sensation, like a colony of ants crawling over my skin. I tugged my hand free and rubbed my arm to dull the tingles. *Jesus. What is this kid doing to me?*

Lucas camped in my personal space while we finished our third round. His right hand never left my body, and whenever I shifted, he moved with me. I became hyper-aware of where we were connected, and as soon as I'd become accustomed to his touch, he'd relocate, landing feather-like strokes over raw nerve endings.

We closed down the restaurant.

Slowly, Lucas walked with me to my car. My mind was on overdrive. I'd hadn't been so turned on in ages, and I'd pretty much told my better judgment to forget the list and take the night off.

"Thanks for the drinks, Kyle."

"You're welcome." I swallowed hard, and my lips itched to taste the sweetness of his breath.

"So…" We reached my truck and he paused to search me.

I fingered my key fob, knowing that once I pushed the unlock button, I'd have no choice but to leave. I shifted nervously, hovering my thumb over the button. "So," I mimicked, uncertain of what to say.

He cradled my chin and lifted my eyes to him. "I want to take you out next time. Friday?"

"You going to cook for me?"

Lucas laughed and ran his hand over my chest. I loved that he touched me so freely now. It was exquisitely slow foreplay. "I would love to cook for you, but don't you think we should stay in public for now? Until we figure some things out."

My willpower would snap like a twig in private. "Lucas, I know myself. I don't think I can handle your… Um…your —"

"My job?" Lucas offered.

"Yeah," I breathed out. "I'm not cut out for it. I'm sorry."

"A date, Kyle. Let's cross that bridge when we get to it."

"Lucas —" I protested.

"Baby," he whispered, tugging me to him. The endearment melted me. "Let me prove it to you. Work is work. This is different. I've never wanted anyone like I want you. When you walked into the classroom, I was so damn happy. I haven't stopped thinking about you since that day in the library. Stop fighting this. We can figure it out. Let me wife you up."

I choked out a laugh. "You want to *what* now?"

Lucas smiled. "It's an expression. Let me date you, call you mine, get all Facebook-official and post cute pictures of us on my Instagram. I want this so much."

"Your Instagram?"

"Yeah. My followers love when I'm in a relationship. They will ship us so hard."

I gulped. "Ship?"

"Root for us. Post comments on every video and picture about how cute we are. Do you have a Twitter? They'll want to know it."

I shifted uncomfortably and Lucas stilled me. "Or not. Oh shit. New plan. No Instagram. No Twitter. Just date and get to know each other. Privately. Please don't be scared off. I wanted to show you off, but I didn't think that through."

"Okay," I said, uncertain of my decision.

"Okay?"

"Yeah. Um, wife me up...or whatever. But no Instagram. No Tommy Bruiser, just Lucas Cass."

"Really?"

"I can't promise I'll be okay with it, but um... We can do what you said. Cross that bridge later or whatever."

"So, you're okay that I'll be working?"

I sighed. There was only one way to avoid losing my mind. "We date. For the summer. We're not exclusive. You're free to do...whatever you do. I'll be free to do the same. We can see what happens."

"Are you dating anyone else now?" Lucas appeared wounded by that possibility. I tossed my head back, closed my eyes and refused to acknowledge all the signs that our plan contained some glaring flaws.

"I think we should agree not to ask about what we do when we're not together."

"For the summer?"

"When our class is over, we can decide if things can be...different."

"Yeah?"

"Yeah."

"Okay." Lucas nodded. "The summer."

"I need to get home now. I have to be up at five."

Lucas grabbed my hips and shimmied them as he crowded into my body. He bit his lower lip and smiled seductively, broadcasting every filthy thought. "Come home with me?"

I laughed. "I need sleep."

"You can sleep," Lucas offered, but his smile gave him away. We both knew how unsuccessful we'd be at sleeping if I were in his bed.

"I think it might be best to limit the sleepovers until we figure out if it's going to work."

Lucas frowned, the panic evident. "For three months?"

"I meant the sleeping part."

Lucas sighed in obvious relief. I remembered when three months of abstinence felt akin to a cancer diagnosis. I'd weathered three-month dry spells, longer even — sometimes without even realizing. I doubted my forty-year-old libido could handle Lucas. How would I keep up? Then I remembered that I wouldn't be the only man charged with satisfying him. *Ugh, bad plan. Epically bad plan.*

"All right. No sleepovers." Lucas nodded and added, "For now."

He lifted one hand to my face and settled the other on my hip. I braced myself for his kiss. Ever since the library, when he'd wholly owned me, I'd dreamed about kissing him again. It was a chance to prove I wasn't as passive as he probably thought. He crashed his lips into mine, but I was ready. Confident. I opened for him and clasped my hand to the back of his neck. When he startled, I took control of the kiss and eased my tongue across the seam of his lips, pushing and moving us until my body pinned him to the door of my car. He dug his fingertips into my hips and moaned while I kissed the hell out of my cocky surfer boy.

When I'd kissed him long enough to prove my point, I stepped back. Swollen-lipped and breathless, Lucas leaned against my truck to keep himself upright. Pride surged through me. I might not be the only one to kiss him, but I could damn well be the best at it.

He reached for me, and I tugged him into my body and dropped a kiss on his forehead.

"Fuck. You do that again and I'm absolutely gonna call you daddy."

I chuckled and spanked his ass. "You got a daddy kink I should know about?"

He jumped and his eyes lit up. "Maybe." Lucas' face twisted with reservation.

I'd never had that sort of relationship before, but the idea of it didn't exactly turn me off. I stored that knowledge away, hooked a finger under his chin and tilted it to me. "You sure about that?"

His eyes dilated, and even with just the streetlight above, I could tell he was blushing. Arousal surged between us. *Oh, yeah. We're going to explore that someday.* I laughed softly. "Let's tuck that away for a rainy day."

Lucas exhaled and leaned into me. "I'm so hard right now."

I glanced down, and sure enough, his crotch had a prominent tent. I cascaded a hand between us and rubbed him. My eyes bugged out. "Damn, I convinced myself it was photoshopped."

He laughed. "Googled me, have you?"

"Um, only the homepage." I swallowed with the memory of Lucas' unreal body.

Lucas smiled smugly. "My tan and abs are touched up, but everything else is real."

"That's a shame." He peaked his eyebrow in question, so I clarified. "I love abs."

He took my hand and lifted his shirt, guiding my fingers over hard ripples. "Damn," I sighed again.

"Do me a favor?"

I nodded, breathless. *Anything*.

"Don't watch my scenes. I like that you don't know Tommy Bruiser."

"Really?"

"Yeah. I kind of lost my virginity on camera." His swagger dipped momentarily, as though his confession made him feel more vulnerable than he'd intended.

"Oh, wow. I can't imagine."

"I didn't look like this until a few years ago." The red in his cheeks deepened, but he brushed it off. "I was a really late bloomer."

I pictured an awkward pubescent Lucas and chuckled. "I won't. Truthfully, I don't want to."

"I know."

"You do?"

"Yeah. It's one of the reasons I like you so much. I know we said 'not exclusive', and I won't push if that's what you need, but know I won't be... Outside of work, it'll only be you." And with that simple confession, his cards were all face-up and laid before me.

I smiled and brushed the blond strands out of his eyes. "Thank you," I whispered.

"Good night, Kyle."

I kissed him briefly then climbed into my truck. "Good night, Lucas. I'll call you tomorrow."

Chapter Five

Brunch with Kayla's family was its usual hilarity. They seated our table for six in the back, window-filled room of the Dew Drop Inn, offering views of the expansive garden and the persistent aroma of their world-famous cinnamon roll French toast. I caught whiff after whiff as the tuxedo-clad servers carried plates from the kitchen to the outside patio.

Patrick's proposal had been planned to reenact his first meeting with Tracey. Although Kayla and Tracey had been roommates their senior years, she hadn't met Patrick, who'd gone to Boston for college, until a few years after they'd graduated. Patrick had been home for break, having finished his first semester of law school at UCLA. Meanwhile, Kayla had decided to bring Tracey to her family's regular weekend brunch. The sparks flew instantaneously. The rest, as they say, was history.

A reminder of how these things were supposed to look was precisely what I needed after my evening with Lucas the previous Friday. Leading up to our date, we'd texted or spoken every day and had had a great time at dinner — until he'd mentioned he had to work the following day. The mood took a nosedive, and though we'd parted with some kissing, he hadn't insinuated we continue the evening and neither had I. I'd spent my Saturday trying desperately to not think about Lucas and what he was doing.

"Patrick did good," I whispered to Kayla. She poured mimosas from the pitcher into our glasses.

"Kyle, my good man" — Mitch sat next to me and patted me on the back — "what's new with you?"

I took a sip of my drink. "Not much, work and school — the usual these days."

"How are your folks, dear? Are they enjoying their condo?" Esther asked.

"Good. Yes, they love being in the warm weather. They're planning to take a cruise for their anniversary. Forty-five years next month."

"Oh, goodness. What fun. We should do something like that, Mitch. Have you been cruising before, Kyle?"

Kayla choked back a laugh, and I avoided her eyes. "No. It looks like a good time," I answered with as close to a straight face as I could manage. Thankfully, neither Mitch nor Esther knew Kayla was the one who'd gotten me shitfaced, stuck a sailor hat on my head and shoved me into my first gay bar on the night of my twenty-first birthday with orders to cruise the go-go boys. It was the last time I ever let her watch *Queer as Folk* with me.

"You should take one of those gay cruises. I saw something the other day — a whole show about places that cater to men who love men, a 'gaycation' they called it. Wild."

I chuckled, and Kayla groaned. "Dad...stop."

"Well. The show called it a 'gaycation', Kayla, not me. Have you heard of that, Kyle—a 'gaycation'?"

"Dad. I beg you to stop saying 'gaycation'."

I laughed and Mitch shrugged but continued muttering to me under his breath while Kayla spoke to her mother. "It sounds like something a young man like you would enjoy. Men in nut huggers grinded all up on each other. That's what *they* called it, not me. I'm just the messenger. Don't take Kayla. I don't think this is an event where you take your fag hag."

I barked out laughter, spewing mimosa all over the table and my shirt.

"Did you call me a 'fag hag'? Dad, honestly." I shared a look with Kayla that let her know exactly how often I would use the conversation against her, just as Patrick and Tracey arrived.

"Sorry we're late," Patrick announced and explained that they'd gotten stuck behind an accident on their way to the restaurant. Tracey, with her ebony hair and smooth, dark skin, was, like always, lovely and stylish and the exact opposite of her fair-skinned, green-eyed boyfriend, who appeared even more red-faced than usual. I suspected the hand Patrick had jammed in his pocket, likely fingering the ring, explained his somewhat frazzled appearance. Despite Kayla's reservations, they did make a striking couple, and I was honored to witness such a pivotal moment in their relationship.

"Mitch, don't call your daughter a hag," Esther chastised, having missed the context. "Kayla, honey, you will meet a nice boy someday. Look at her bone structure—like my mother's. She's beautiful, and you don't look forty, sweetheart. I'm sure there are still some nice men out there. Tracey, do you know someone who might be a match for our Kayla?"

Tracey ignored Kayla's death glare and took the bait. I pressed my hand to Kayla's leg to prevent her from launching herself over the table while Tracey and Esther discussed potentials. I refilled her mimosa one-handed. "Drink," I commanded.

She downed her glass in two gulps and slouched deeper into her chair. Unlike me, Kayla had no desire to find a husband. When she did date, she kept it intentionally casual with men just as consumed by their careers. I'd stopped analyzing her motives. She didn't fear being a wife and mother. She just didn't want that life. The few times she had tried something more, she ended it before it had become a 'distraction'. Her job, freedom and independence were more important to her, and I'd long ago accepted the explanation wasn't any more complicated than that.

Near the end of the meal, Patrick exchanged a look with his parents and I knew the moment had arrived. He picked up his glass and clanked it gently with the dull edge of his knife. The table grew quiet, and Tracey froze in mid-sentence. Patrick pushed back from the table, gushed about how his life had changed at the very table where we sat, espoused Tracey's beauty and dropped to his knee.

We held our collective breaths while Tracey, apparently stunned speechless, tearfully nodded her head and watched Patrick slip an impressive princess-cut diamond ring on her finger. The entire restaurant erupted in applause as the happy couple embraced — and I cried like a baby. For the first time since Matt and I had ended, I ached for my own such moment — or at least the possibility of one.

Kayla handed me a clean napkin and patted my thigh. Leaning over, she whispered, "It'll happen."

I glowered at her and shook my head. I knew that in choosing Lucas, I'd started from a place where that future didn't seem possible. Doubt clouded my brain. *What kind of idiot am I?* No matter how scenic the ride, our relationship would inevitably hit a dead end. I wanted it all—marriage, maybe some kids, a dog and my house on a lake. At my pace, I'd need a cane to get down the aisle. There were seventeen years between us. What had I known about life at his age? *Nothing.* Certainly not enough to plan a future.

Kayla wrapped her arm around my waist and gathered me into her side, I dropped my head to her shoulder. She kissed my scalp and patted me. "None of that. It'll happen. Trust me," she repeated.

After leaving the restaurant, Kayla wasted no time in pumping me for information. "But you said the date went fine?"

"I don't know. It did. Dinner was good. The conversation was perfect. He's funny and adorable. He asked me thoughtful questions, and he's just ridiculously attractive. But there is just no way it is going to work."

"Okay. Why is that exactly?"

"Because he gets paid to be naked and I'm...me."

"Oh, Kyle. Can you just once not get in your own way? Why does it have to be all or nothing? Either he is the man of your dreams or completely untouchable?"

"Because he's... I like him...a lot. And there's no way I will just magically be okay with the fact that he fucks for a living."

Kayla did not seem surprised. "I know. But it's not like you usually expect guys you just started dating to be exclusive."

"True."

"I mean, typically, you would just avoid asking until it mattered, right?"

"I guess."

"So, you know with Lucas that isn't where things are heading. You skip over the whole 'define the relationship' awkwardness, enjoy each other and have some fun, maybe learn some sex tips from an expert for the next guy."

Deciding I lacked the mental strength to go another round with Kayla on the merits of casual relationships, I shut my mouth and, as she often did, Kayla took my silence for agreement and changed her entire position.

I dropped Kayla off and drove toward home, still reeling from the entire morning. A phone call arrived just as I pulled into my driveway but I ignored it, still deep into my own neurotic analysis as I headed toward my garage to find something to clear my head. It came in the form of an old wine cabinet I'd bought at a garage sale months ago that I had plans to refinish.

Sweat dripped down my back while I rubbed sandpaper over the cabinet door. The rhythmic scrape focused my mind, and I permitted myself to acknowledge that buried in all her double talk, Kayla might have had a small point. Every time I met someone, I instantly ran them against an unwritten soulmate checklist of sorts. Except for Matt, no one else had ever checked all the boxes. And even then... "*How long did you try to force it to work because you were convinced it was supposed to?*" Sometimes it wasn't good to let Kayla's words marinate too long, because now I doubted my doubts. I stopped working to grab a beer from the kitchen.

I'd purchased my house ten years earlier and methodically remodeled it room by room. Initially built in the 1960s, the place was small—barely twelve hundred square feet—but the inside had been gutted and the once-walled-in rooms were now open and airy, giving the impression of much more space. I'd since added a utility room, closet and sunroom to the back and a covered porch to the front. The walls of the main area were a light neutral gray, and the floors were a rich maple hardwood that I'd saved for a year to afford. Every appliance, cabinet, countertop and fixture had been placed with my own two hands. I loved it and my mood always improved when I walked in the door.

I showered, changed my clothes and checked my phone. Lucas had called three times. I paused a minute before texting.

Hey.

I know, I know. So lame. But Lucas responded immediately, which filled me with a weird, happy, excited energy that just… *Ugh*. Despite all my internal angst, I couldn't deny I wanted to see him again.

Hey, yourself. What are you up to today?

I would probably spend the day wallowing in self-doubt and sanding that cabinet until my arm fell off, but that didn't seem like a good answer. I needed a less pathetic alternative.

Studying.

What? We're in the same class. No assignments due this week.

I have reading to catch up on.

Can I take you to dinner tonight?

I didn't reply.

You know you want to say yes.

Yeah. Dinner's good. My turn to pay, though. What are you up to?

I think I'm gonna see about that paint job. The wall being messed up is pissing me off. The office gave me the color.

The next text made me smile.

What's the difference between eggshell and satin?

I sighed. Lucas needed a paint finish that would withstand a good scrub, and a satin or eggshell would fit that bill. However, his apartment certainly had jacked-up walls that would show defects if he used too much sheen.

Get a semi-gloss.

What's that?

Do you want me to go with you?

Oh, God. Yes, please. I'm seriously intimidated by home improvement stores.

Fine. Be ready. I'll pick you up in about thirty minutes.

Let me come get you. You're doing me a favor. I can drive.

I texted him my address, and by the time I'd showered and changed, Lucas was knocking at my door.

I opened it and drew in a breath. *Damn*. Lucas was gorgeous, and the sparks that flew between us were every bit as bright as the ones I'd seen between Patrick and Tracey. Maybe, just maybe, the issue was my checklist and my stubborn vision of a future that I could no longer remember dreaming up.

"Hi." He leaned in and kissed my cheek. Looking around, he added, "Your place is beautiful."

Pride swelled in me. "Thanks. Want the tour before we go?"

He nodded enthusiastically. "This is the family room," I said, stating the obvious. "The kitchen and dining" — I pointed to the custom cabinet-lined half-wall, which, in addition to extending the countertops with a peninsula, also separated the kitchen from the dining room — "I built that last year."

Lucas moved to the wall and took it in from every angle like he was appraising a work of art. He entered the kitchen, and my heart skipped a beat when his focus zeroed in on the single custom piece in the room. Running his hand over the classy glass-etched pantry doors, he gaped at me with admiration. When I'd bought the house, it had been missing a pantry. I'd converted it from a tiny laundry closet. I opened the door and showed him the shelving system I'd designed, which pulled out and rotated, so you could see items in the back. The slick feature more than doubled my storage space.

"That's so cool." He laughed while playing with it. "My mom hates her pantry. She'd love this. Where did you get it?"

"I built it," I said.

"Get out." He shoved me gently.

"I'm happy with the way it turned out."

"You should be. It's genius." His enthusiasm activated my brag button, and I walked him through ten years' worth of projects around my house, enjoying his rapt attention. He asked questions. He stroked my ego. When he asked about the stone wall that featured a fireplace, I happily recounted the story of the eccentric millionaire who'd ordered a shitload of rocks from some European importer without consulting anyone.

"An actual rock-climbing wall? Get out."

"Yeah. She ordered all this beautiful stone and thought I could build her a rock-climbing wall in her backyard. I tried to give her alternative uses for the stone, but when the neighborhood association refused her wall, she ordered me to get rid of it." I ran my hand down the stone. "Even after having masons break it up for me, I got it for a deal."

"It's stunning." He marveled at it, touching it the way I always did.

"Oh, yeah." "Thanks."

Our eyes met, and he pushed his hair out of his face and grew serious. "Kyle." He swallowed.

"Yes?"

"Show me your bedroom."

I gulped. "You sure?"

I'd considered saying no for as long as it took the blood to rush into my dick, causing it to throb. Clearly, I had no self-control when it came to Lucas. Not only had he erased a lousy morning by his mere appearance on my doorstep, but he'd also spent the last thirty minutes making me feel so damn good about myself. I took him by the hand and guided him down the hall to my bedroom.

I expected a frenzy of heat to take over, but instead, Lucas gave me slow, purposeful caresses. We kissed, stopping only long enough for him to tug my shirt off me. He stared at me, his eyelids heavy with lust. I didn't fully understand what he saw in me, but I found myself believing him anyway.

I closed my eyes, picturing my own body, imagining his perspective. Silver stands dusted my chest, mixed in with the same mousy brown hair that covered my head. My job was physical, so my pecs, arm and leg muscles were taut, even if they paled in comparison to Lucas'. Although my belly was flat, it was soft. I flexed anyway, as though pure willpower could summon muscles to the surface.

I reached for his shirt but he stopped me. He shook his head. "Sit. Let me see you."

I obeyed, and with a hand on my chest, he nudged me back. I shifted up the bed and he removed my shoes, then bent to take off his own while I scooted toward the middle of my mattress.

Straddling my waist and resting back on my thighs, he dragged his hands over my chest, lightly at first.

I squirmed. "Tickles," I explained.

He resumed his massage, pressing more firmly, kneading me.

When he lowered to kiss me, his cock pressed against my belly. I snaked a hand under his shirt and lifted it so I could touch his abs. Lucas shifted his pelvis and aligned our cocks. I grabbed his ass, moaned with the contact and rolled my hips to get more.

He slipped his lips off mine and hissed with pleasure. "Fuck," he moaned. He lifted his upper body and gazed at me. With his arms locked beside me, he shifted again, sliding his dick over mine. He closed his eyes while he grinded against me.

As good as that felt, I missed his lips. I tugged at him until his arms collapsed. Chest-to-chest, I held him tightly and kissed him hard, wanting to be more for him — sexier somehow, younger, more adventurous... anything. Recalling how he'd reacted to that playful spank in the parking lot, I forced myself to stop exploring his perfect, firm body long enough to lift my hand into the air and slam it down on his ass.

He cried out and lust-filled eyes met mine. *Oh, yeah. He likes that.* I did it again, then a third time, eliciting a low growl from Lucas' throat. The need to flip our dynamic surged through me. I rolled him off me and roughly yanked at his shorts.

A foreign, brazen voice escaped my lips. "I need to see this thing for myself." Usually, I was the man who tipped his ass in the air like a cat in heat and waited for pleasure, but at that moment, I became obsessed with making Lucas moan again. An exhilarating, unexpected desire spurred me into action.

With my help, Lucas shimmied his shorts down, and I stripped them off, catching his foot awkwardly in the fabric. He yelped, and for a moment, my confidence faltered. "Sorry," I murmured and turned his head so I could suck on his neck.

"'Isokay," he breathed. "Fuck me." He writhed under me. My hand found his cock and stroked. "Oh, God," he cried.

Without stopping to look, I knew his cock would be the biggest I'd ever seen up close. Wrapped around his girth, my fingers barely overlapped, and the weight of him was noticeably more substantial than my own. The second I slid down the shaft and realized his length could have easily accommodated a second hand beside mine, I lost my mind with desire. I ripped my mouth away from his neck, turned my head and watched myself stroke him. He moaned and arched into my touch. I licked my lips. His cock was long and thick, with prominent veins along the shaft and a helmet-shaped head. My own cock drooled at the sight of him pulsing into my hand.

"Jesus," I cried. I gawked at him and the same overconfident smirk he'd worn outside the library. "The pictures don't do it justice."

He quirked his lip knowingly and rolled his eyes. Okay, apparently not the first time he'd heard those words. Anxiety crept into my thoughts, but I tamped it down. I had no intention of letting anything as silly as reality spoil the moment.

"Take this off." I tugged at his shirt. His upper body curled, and he yanked at the neck of his T-shirt, exposing his flexed abdominals. *Hot damn.* Eight perfectly sculpted ripples laid out in four symmetrical pairs covered the full length of his torso. A longer, equally solid muscle ran the narrow width of his pelvis below his navel, framed on both ends by flawlessly cut obliques. I reached for him, splayed my hand over his stomach and, before he even had his shirt pulled clear, scouted a path for my tongue to explore.

I positioned myself at my starting line—his nipples. My previous experience with nipples had been mixed. Some of my lovers had enjoyed theirs tugged and played with, while others had bluntly told me to move along. I didn't consider mine to be a particularly sensitive erogenous zone, but Lucas'—

I licked my lips and rolled the soft bud in my mouth. I nibbled, scraping my teeth along the now-firm peak and assessed his sensitivity. He gasped, and I smiled against him, running my hands ahead of me while I weaved and licked my way over his torso. When he struggled to reach his cock, I removed his hand and pinned it to the mattress.

I tightened my hold on his wrist, and he moaned so beautifully that I nearly gave up my resolve to go slow before I ravaged him.

I tasted every inch of his torso, lavished every divot between every muscle and kissed my way from his belly button down toward his groin. All the while, he watched me.

I clasped the back of his thighs and guided his knees to his chest, exposing him fully. I buried my face between his legs and kissed along the fleshy part of his inner thighs toward the jewel in the center. His smell drove me wild. I breathed him in before taking a slow, experimental lick down his shaft and over his balls.

Lucas cried out, encouraging me with his breathy pants and a hand clutched to the top of my head. I licked from crown to base and sucked on the head, then moved lower to taste his entrance. Enjoying the tremble in his thighs against my hands, I held him in position and teased his opening.

"Fuck," Lucas exhaled in a rhythmic chant. His thighs quaked against my palms as I slowly lowered his legs.

He curled up and grasped the back of my head when I took his cock into my mouth, I kept his eye contact while he stretched my mouth and pulsed his hips up. The firm press of his palm turned to gentle caresses through my hair until Lucas' body fell back to the bed and he whimpered noises of blissed-out pleasure. I stroked over his belly and massaged his muscles. He clasped his hand over mine and squeezed.

"Fuck me, Kyle."

I loved the sound of his gravelly, ragged plea more than I should have. I doubled down on his cock and pressed a palm against my own. A moan escaped from deep in my throat, and he yanked on my hair and gasped, "Fuck, Daddy."

I glanced up between his legs, my mouth thoroughly stretched, and melted under an intense, eager stare. He needed me to play along. I could sense how badly he wanted to be manhandled and devoured. His desire to surrender rolled off him.

With a tight grip on his hip, I rocked back and drew up to my knees. Yanking his left leg over his right, I turned him until he lay flat on his stomach. He wedged his hand underneath his body and adjusted himself. Soon, his swollen cock appeared between his thighs, so wantonly beautiful and laid out for me. I couldn't help but take another lick.

"Move your hands," I demanded and tugged his arm so that his hands were again visible. "Grab my headboard and don't move them until I tell you." He peered back at me, a sliver of doubt in his expression, but I didn't blink. Might as well go full balls-to-the-wall committed to his fantasy. I doubled down. "Do it." I smacked his ass.

He murmured something that sounded like a curse as I landed another hard spank on his exposed backside. A pink outline of my handprint remained visible when I pulled away. One glimpse of his ass bouncing after each thwack had me biting my lip to keep my arousal under control.

"I'm going to make this so good for you." I licked his reddened flesh and pulled his thighs farther apart. Taking my time, I rubbed the thick, slippery, mushroom-shaped cockhead, sucked his balls and pressed a thumb to his taint. I dipped down, feasting on his entrance until my fingers slid easily in and out of him.

I rimmed and fingered him until he became incoherent with pleas for more, all the while dreaming up lines that would play into his fantasy while I fucked him. He wanted a daddy, but being unfamiliar with the scenario, I wasn't sure if he liked the older-man-in-charge dynamic or if he wanted to feel like a good boy, someone who pleased me.

Unzipping my jeans, I used an undignified dance to lower them far enough so I could kick them off. Lucas chuckled softly into the pillow until I smacked his ass with my free hand, reached for a condom and tore open the wrapper with my teeth. His breath hitched with anticipation and his shoulders and back tensed. I pushed a finger inside him and decided to take the second pause necessary to grab my lube.

He moaned the loss of my finger. As soon as I uncapped and drizzled the liquid on his pucker, I pushed my finger back inside. He lifted his hips. "That's it, honey. Ride back on my hand. Show off for Daddy."

He jerked his hips, impaling himself fully. He moved seductively and layered in plenty of moaning and cursing for good measure.

"Good boy. You gonna do that with my cock, baby? You gonna work that ass for me?"

Lucas eyed me, panting softly as he lifted his hips to take three fingers like he was born to be fucked. "Yes, Daddy. I want your cock so bad. Give it to me. *Please.*"

My cock throbbed with the slight whine in his voice. He sure played up his strengths — batting his eyes like a goddamn virgin and begging to be fucked. Only then did I fully join Lucas in our little role play. *Damn.* It blew my mind I could learn something new about myself at my age. I rolled on the condom and watched his body welcome me home. I roared with pleasure as he clenched around me. "Fuck, Lucas. You're so tight, baby."

Despite my weight, Lucas managed to rock up to meet my thrusts, tilting his ass up for me. That arch would have killed my back, but Lucas' spine flexed like a Slinky. I pressed up until my form resembled the start of a push-up and I angled my cock. I connected with his spot on the first pass. Lucas cursed. "Right there. Right. Fucking. *There.* Please, Kyle."

Emboldened by his response, I locked my arms and pistoned my hips, up and down, again and again. With each thrust, Lucas fell apart a little more. My filter fritzed out and I said every filthy thought that entered my head in between our endless chorus of pants, grunts and curse-filled moans.

During a particularly hard set of deep thrusts, Lucas' hand left the headboard and reached back to still my thigh. "Slow down, Daddy."

I slowed immediately, but his body language didn't match his request. His body still took me easily and his hips vibrated under me. His hand sought out mine and squeezed, a silent encouragement to keep up the play.

"Didn't I tell you not to let go of the headboard?"

He managed a strangled cry and shifted his hands to grip the slats again. I dropped my knees to the mattress, balanced with one arm and wrapped a hand around his neck. His pulse raced under my fingers. "Who's in charge of making you feel good?"

"You are," he cried. His voice dripped with need.

"And who owns this ass?"

"It's yours, Daddy. All yours."

I buried myself inside him, and he hissed. "Oh, fuck, Kyle, you fuck me so good."

In a single motion, I shifted my weight to my knees and tugged his hips up until he was on all fours. He immediately rocked backward on my dick, which throbbed inside his passage. I clasped his waist, and he rose to my challenge.

"Fuck, babe. I want to come," he cried out. I realized too late he was asking permission. He roared, "Oh *shit.* Kyle, I'm coming."

His muscles clenched like a vise around my cock, and he impaled himself with a primal cry. I could do nothing to stop the orgasm spiraling through me. I surged forward, collapsed on his back and emptied everything I had into him. Consumed with lust, I bit his shoulder and shuddered as the last shockwave rocketed through me.

The fog of endorphins cleared, and my leg and back muscles seized from exertion. I couldn't find the wherewithal to care about the soreness which would undoubtedly get worse before it got better. Lucas shook under me, and I rolled off him, panting in time to his labored breaths.

I said the only thing I could manage. "Goddamn."

Lucas turned toward me, his chest heaving and skin flushed a brilliant red. He choked out a laugh and tossed his arm over my body. "That was" — he sighed and dropped a kiss on my cheek, before moving to my lips — "perfect."

"Yeah?"

He rolled his eyes and thumped my cheek, as though he found my question disingenuous. Perhaps it was. I'd known hot sex before, but we'd lit the sheets on fire.

Lucas fell back to the mattress and laughed in exhausted delight. I raised an eyebrow in question. "I liked you too much when I thought you were a bottom. This was more than I hoped for."

I laughed, took a few deep sighs of utter satisfaction and waited for my heart and respiration rate to normalize before removing the condom. "You inspired me. All that daddy talk does something for me after all."

He curled up next to me and craned his neck to kiss me. "I loved it."

"Yeah, I could tell. It's a bedroom thing, though, right?"

With a gleeful noise, he said, "Yeah, I wouldn't try telling me what to do outside of bed. It might not end nearly as well."

"So, is that the best way for you to get off?"

He shook his head, suddenly shy. He wanted to say something more. Words of encouragement formed on my lips, until I realized it might be unsafe territory and stopped myself.

He cuddled into me and stroked me absentmindedly before answering, "I don't need it. You know?"

I pushed the hair out of his eyes so I could see him clearly. "I'm versatile," he muttered. "I like to switch, but I don't get it as often as I like. It's been... It's been difficult to find someone who didn't expect me to be a certain way in bed. Don't get me wrong, I know my dick is practically a novelty dildo and I'm happy to indulge my partner, but it's rare for me to get past that stage and get to have the kind of sex I want. Before you, I can't think of a single guy who took the time to pleasure other parts of me. I know we aren't supposed to talk about it, but you need to know that this was amazing, Kyle, and it was amazing because of *you*."

I rolled to my side and propped my head up with my palm. "I'm glad you told me. I still don't get why you'd want anything to do with me."

"Because you're sweet and thoughtful—and fearless."

"Hardly," I huffed.

"When we met, I thought you'd followed me because you had a chance to fuck Tommy Bruiser."

"So not how that would have gone down," I confessed, "but continue."

Lucas smiled knowingly. "You couldn't form a complete sentence. I knew you had never done anything like that before. I loved that you were willing to follow me anyway."

"Most men would follow you, Lucas."

"Few do things that they're afraid of, and most men wouldn't have left for the reasons you did. I'm in awe of you, Kyle. You're like that unicorn they talk about."

I laughed. "Unicorn?"

"Yeah. A sexy man who doesn't know he's hot. You've got your shit together—a good job, a house which you basically built on your own and you're driven, like me. You're talented and creative, in addition to being a genuinely nice guy — total unicorn. To top it off, you're great in bed. I'm all in. What else can I say?"

"You're quite the charmer, aren't you?"

"It's all true."

My face warmed and I kissed his forehead. "I have a feeling I'm not going to be great at following our rules."

Lucas beamed his brilliant smile. "Does that mean I can sleep over tonight?"

I rolled on my back and checked the clock. "It's barely three. Let's shower and get your paint job done. We'll see what happens."

Chapter Six

It became abundantly clear that Lucas did not belong in a home improvement store. He'd been clingy since we'd left my bed, and while I appreciated the affection, I was all business the second we stepped through the sliding double doors. Lucas paused to grab a cart but I proceeded straight to the paint counter, picked up a quart of semi-gloss paint and handed over the color. While I waited for the attendant to mix it, Lucas navigated through the crowded aisles and explored the myriad of brushes and supplies in the painting section with the enthusiasm of a kid in a candy store.

He picked up a fourth item — a bag of roller pads — and I shook my head with an amused smile. "I've got all the supplies we need," I explained. Frowning, he put them down.

After receiving his paint, we traversed the aisles. I held my tongue as he picked up random objects, patiently reassuring him that I had whatever it was on hand.

"Do you have this?"

I turned to see Lucas scoop up an industrial-size paint sprayer from a floor display and rest it on the cart. I couldn't hold back my laughter. "No. That I don't have."

His eyes lit up. "It says it spreads the paint more evenly. We need one." He heaved it over the edge of the cart with a broad smile. His chest puffed out and he strolled along in front of me.

I bit my lip to keep from saying anything. The oversized box made the cart awkward to push, and when Lucas glanced over his shoulder, he quickly returned to help. We moved along. I pushed the cart and he walked next to me, looking satisfied with his selection. We wandered into the patio and garden section, an area of the store where Lucas was clearly more comfortable. He pointed out flowers and decorative items he liked and asked my opinion as though we were making a joint purchase for a shared home. Part of me wondered how close we'd get to the checkout before he stopped playing around, but I wasn't about to do anything to ruin his fun. Shopping with him was strangely domestic, and I enjoyed being with Lucas, even if we were both pretending to be more to each other than we were.

We approached the checkout, and I motioned him ahead of the cart. "You sure you want this?"

"You think I'm stupid for buying it?"

I couldn't figure out why, of all things, he wanted that sprayer, but he had eyed it so longingly that I couldn't flat out answer him honestly either. "Not stupid. Just don't understand why you'd need that when you live in an apartment."

"I don't have any tools," he sulked. "You have everything. It's very emasculating."

"Well buy something practical, like a drill set. Or better yet, get a hammer. They're under ten dollars."

"How much is that thing?"

I inspected it and estimated the price based on the brand and features. "Like three hundred, give or take."

His eyes bugged out.

"Yeah." I laughed. "So, let's use my stuff, and you can work on getting your own set of tools when you buy your first place."

He sighed heavily. "Fine. I'll put it back." He lifted the bulky box from the cart.

"Take the cart," I offered.

"I got it," Lucas insisted and, clearly struggling, returned it to the aisle where we'd found it while I checked out.

On his return, he caught my eye, strutted and flexed his bicep, then promptly tripped over a display, drawing a surprised laugh from me. I willed my face to relax the over-the-top smile Lucas had inspired. "Smooth," I teased as he neared me. "Here. Hold your paint, show off."

We exited the store, and he tucked his arm around my waist. I squeezed him gently before lacing my fingers with his. It'd been a long time since I enjoyed something as simple as holding hands with someone.

Lucas drove a yellow Mustang, and to be honest, the flashiness made me cringe a little. It was such a 'look-at-me' kind of car which, combined with its lack of power, left me struggling to see its appeal. And I couldn't quite reconcile it with the same guy who moments before had tripped over a store display and owned it like a fucking boss rather than shirk away. Lucas' authentic brand of confidence didn't need showiness. *Ugh, it's just a car. Overthink much, Kyle?*

"I can see smoke coming out of your ears. What's going on in that pretty little head of yours?" Lucas laughed and opened the trunk using his key fob. He placed the paint next to the supplies I'd stashed from my garage.

"Nothing. Just thinking," I said.

Lucas' bemused expression suggested he had read my thoughts and invited me to elaborate, but he didn't push. "Well, don't hurt yourself." He laughed.

We drove to his apartment, and Lucas advanced through a handful of hardcore rap songs and listened to less than a full verse of some classic rock song I didn't recognize. He studied my face then navigated to a Beatles station on his Spotify and scrutinized me again. It struck me that he was searching for something someone my age might enjoy, which was sweet but brutal for the ego.

"Listen to whatever you want." I smiled and patted his leg.

"But what do you like best?"

"My taste varies. Honestly, whatever you want is fine."

At a stoplight, he searched his phone and added a few songs to the queue. When the light turned green, I was treated to ten minutes of Lucas singing Taylor Swift songs at full volume until, thankfully, we arrived at his apartment and unloaded our supplies.

Lucas tried to help, but his version of helping involved a submerged paintbrush handle and a screw to the outlet cover dropped behind the refrigerator. I suggested he let me handle it, and in short order, I had Lucas' kitchen wall prepped and painted, but Lucas was nowhere to be found.

"Babe," I called for him, loving how naturally the endearment fell from my lips. When he didn't respond, I searched his small apartment. I found him in his bedroom, lying on his bed, reading. "Hey, you okay?"

"Yep," he answered without looking up. I knew that tone. That was the universal tone for 'you've fucked up'.

"I'm sorry, Lucas."

He dropped his book. "I wanted your help today, not for you to order me out of the kitchen like I'm some sort of incompetent child. I told you I'm only into the daddy thing in the bedroom.

"I know. I do it all the time, babe. It was nothing."

"That's not the point," he said in a low whine. His sexy pout stirred up something inside me. I moved toward him, suddenly awash with memories of the sex we'd had and was newly turned on. I kneeled on the bed and knee-walked up the mattress and straddled his hips. "No whining or I'll have to punish you."

His pout morphed into a smile he tried gallantly to conceal. "Oh no. You can't be all sexy daddy now. It's not the time. Besides, I think you've got it backward. I should punish *you*."

I sat back on his thighs, relocated his book to the nightstand and kissed him gently. "I'm sorry. I don't mix work and play well."

"You're good with your hands." He cupped my palms and kissed the rough calluses. "I know it was nothing for you, but I want to learn."

"Next time, I'll teach you instead of taking over. I promise. And I'll tell you what. I've wanted to finish my garage this summer after the semester ends. You want to help?"

"Yeah." Lucas nodded and hauled me down for a kiss. "But I want to learn how to use real tools, not a hammer. And I want to feel like I'm learning from my boyfriend and not my dad."

"Boyfriend?"

Without answering my implied question, his expression asked if I was okay with the label. Since I'd already pissed him off about the painting thing, I didn't feel the need to respond. Despite my 'free to do whatever' rule, I was never the type of guy who bed hopped, and if Lucas wasn't either... *Where is the harm?*

I laughed and shifted out of his lap so I could lie next to him. "It's fine," I said. "How do a table saw and drywall tools work for you? I'll even let you wear my tool belt."

"Perfect," he answered.

"At the risk of seriously ruining this daddy deal, why exactly did your own father not teach you how to work with tools? I'm getting the impression he's not a blue-collar man."

Lucas barked out a laugh. "Ah...no. My father is an accountant. Or was. He's retired now."

"Really? My dad recently retired. Wait... How old are your parents?"

"You don't want to know."

"No. Probably not, but tell me anyway."

"My father is sixty-seven." I sighed relief before he added, "And my mother is forty-two."

"Forty-two?" I choked.

"She'll be forty-two next month."

"Forty-one!" I sat up and hyperventilated. "Lucas, holy shit. I'm the same age as your mom."

"Calm down."

"I can't breathe."

"Oh, for fuck's sake. Calm down. It's not the end of the world. Also, I'm adopted."

"What?"

"My parents adopted me when I was five, okay? So, technically, my mom would have been pretty young if she'd given birth to me. And clearly, they won't be scandalized by our age gap, since they have us beat by eight years."

"I didn't know you were adopted."

"It hasn't come up. It's not a huge family secret or anything. My mom had to have a hysterectomy shortly after my parents got married, so they decided to adopt. My birth mother died and, supposedly, she didn't have any family. I was in the foster care system for about a year, but honestly, I don't remember much before my parents took me home.

"I've been loved my entire life and my dad is great, but he's more of a 'help with homework' kind of dad. He taught me how to play chess, and we go to movies and stuff like that."

He paused, and I lifted my palm to rest against his cheek. "He sounds like my dad."

"Tell me."

"My folks are great, too. My parents are happily married. They retired to San Diego. Our family was...average, I guess."

"Average—you like that word."

"It's usually accurate when describing most things about me."

Lucas shook his head. "Kyle, you're so much more than you give yourself credit for."

"I'm glad you think so."

"I know so. I'm also getting hungry. You ready for dinner?"

My stomach growled right on cue. Lucas rubbed my belly and leaned over to kiss my cheek. The gesture sent my heart into my throat. He was…ugh…too damn sweet. We kissed again, and I'd tugged him until he rested on top of me. Another growl erupted from my stomach. With a soft chuckle, Lucas said, "Enough of that. Let's get you fed."

At that moment, I knew all the rules I'd set to make our crazy fling remotely compatible with my feelings about relationships… Yeah, those were entirely fucking worthless.

Chapter Seven

It turned out that Lucas' lips were, in fact, impossible to say no to.

At first, the weekdays became a black hole of time neither of us acknowledged. I spent mine working, meeting Steve to finish an overwhelming amount of complicated case studies for class and trying not to obsess about Lucas. On the weekends, we spent time together, mostly hanging out and talking about all the things we wanted to do but rarely leaving my bedroom. I loved how smoothly our energy flowed from silly to serious to sexy and back again. It was as though some emotional USB connection kept synchronizing our moods.

Some weeks into our summer class, I gave up trying to limit our time to the weekends. We'd meet for dinner after class, and unless one of us had some unescapable commitment, we were together.

We were enjoying a lazy afternoon, taking advantage of a rare homework-free weekend. Lucas was on my couch, his feet stretched over my lap while I watched television. A quick glance at the iPad propped up on a couch pillow over his chest told me he was on Twitter, happily tapping away. I respected that he liked to engage with his followers, but it was an unwelcomed reminder of what I was working so hard to ignore.

"You okay?" he asked.

I never did hide my emotions very well. I nodded and diverted my attention to the television.

"I don't have to do this right now," he offered.

"It's fine," I answered unconvincingly. I fixated on the commercial, knowing if I looked at him even once, he'd know where my head was at. Neither of us had reopened the conversation about what would happen at the end of the summer. "I should probably go for a run or something. We've been couch potatoes all day."

Lucas sat up, tapped his screen to open the weather app and frowned. "It's too hot now. Let's wait till the sun goes down."

"I'm kind of restless. Need to do something."

Whatever annoyance Lucas felt about my suggestion evaporated with a few more clicks of his iPad. "Perfect," he declared, stood and grabbed his shoes.

"For?"

"Just grab your running shoes and trust me."

The instructions sent a chill up my spine. The truth was, I was a planner. I never went to the grocery store without a list, never made a big purchase without consulting consumer reviews and never set out for a run without a route in mind. But one peek at Lucas—his head cocked to the side, a grin splitting his face, the excitement in his voice—and it was so painfully obvious Lucas didn't see me like I saw myself. There were moments when I wanted to be the guy he thought I was so much that I let myself believe it—a guy that, without asking a single question, grabbed his shoes and followed him to the car.

Three and a half hours later, not even Lucas' shirtless body in running shorts could compete with the beauty of the Pacific Ocean as we finished the four-and-a-half-mile perimeter loop at Point Lobos in Carmel. Sweaty and winded from our run, we made our way back to his car.

"See? Now wasn't that better than running around the neighborhood in the middle of the afternoon? I told you it'd be worth it."

Wiping my forehead with my shirt, I smiled my agreement. By any standard, running in ocean breezes on the beach trumped a suburban loop. "You realize we drove over two hours to run less than five miles, right?"

He laughed nervously, opened his mouth to speak then closed it. Lucas took his time getting situated in the car. He started the engine but kept the car in Park, even after our seat belts were buckled. His gaze swung to his navigation screen like he expected it to tell him our destination. I wished I could see his eyes because I didn't know how to interpret his sudden shyness.

"Actually, I sort of had something in mind."

"What?"

"I thought it'd be nice to watch the sunset. I mean…with you. I wanted to go to the beach."

"That's —"

"Sorry. It was dumb. Let's just get dinner and go home."

"Don't apologize, baby. I was going to say that's amazing. I would love to do that."

"Really?" He met my eyes. "You don't think —"

I knew what he was going to say. Lucas had a black belt in dirty talk and shameless flirting, but with romance, he hesitated. There was nothing about sunsets on the beach that said 'casual relationship,' but the suggestion had sent my pulse racing. "I think it's perfect. Let's go."

We drove south toward another trailhead, parked along the road and hiked a short distance toward the beach. Lucas brought the blanket he'd stashed in his trunk and spread it out on the sand. I kicked off my socks and shoes and flopped down. The sun had already started its descent, but there was plenty of time left to enjoy. "Come here, Lucas."

"I didn't plan this out well. I'm all sweaty." He twitched, glancing nervously at the four ladies setting up a bonfire closer to the shore about fifty yards down the beach.

"Did you plan it at all? We could have gone for a swim if we'd brought towels and a change of clothes," I noted. I chuckled at the face Lucas made. "It's fine. I like you sweaty. Now come here." I yanked his hand until he was on the ground. He smiled at me and his resistance melted away. I opened my legs for him to settle between, and he eased back into my arms.

Lucas watched the water, periodically glancing up at a flock of birds swirling over the cliffs to the north and to the women who had started dancing at the water's edge. We didn't talk, but when he twisted to gaze directly into my eyes and smiled, I could see his vulnerability.

I braced my arms behind me, leaned back and Lucas' back settled against my chest. His blond hair, still damp, clung to my skin while the sunset cast a dazzling array of colors, bathing the sky in pink and orange as it dipped into the water. I thought about what an unlikely set of circumstances had led us to that moment, how nervous he'd made me at first. Now here we were, sharing a moment that felt like it'd been written for us all along.

The last sliver of sun dipped behind the Pacific Ocean. "Kyle," Lucas whispered.

"Yeah?" I asked.

"Thanks," he said.

"This was all you, baby. I just wanted to go for a run."

* * * *

There was a notable shift in our dynamic after that day at the beach. We didn't discuss it but things were more settled, and our time together took a turn from dating to being in a relationship. After working all day and spending hours with our respective groups finishing classwork, we'd still found time to be together.

After the end of a long week, I was looking forward to staying home for a night with Lucas and offered to grill some burgers for dinner, but Lucas had other plans.

I was in the garage working on my wine cabinet. Lucas appeared in my driveway with four grocery bags and a smile so big they could have seen it from the space station.

"That doesn't look like burgers."

"I'd really like to make you dinner," he said shyly. "I've been practicing. Here. Take this. There are two more bottles of wine in the car."

I kissed his cheek and accepted the offered grocery bags. His jog back to his car to grab the wine removed all my concerns. He was so adorably exuberant about cooking. He followed me into the house and immediately started unpacking the bags.

Fresh herbs, chicken stock, butter, bacon, chicken, garlic, mushrooms, peas, onions, noodles…and still more wine. "Lucas, this seems" — *complicated and expensive* — "like a lot of work."

"I got it." Lucas searched around, sizing up the best countertop for prep. "I just need you to point me in the direction of your cutting board, knives and cookware then feel free to go back to your project."

I moved around the kitchen to retrieve the supplies he'd asked for while he washed the produce. I finagled a saucepan and some larger pots from the drawer and offered him a choice. He grabbed the pan and the Dutch oven, placed them on the stovetop and his confidence faltered.

"It's electric," I clarified. "You just turn the nob. There's no igniter."

Lucas blushed. "I got this, Kyle. You can go finish your cabinet."

I nodded, opened the refrigerator to reach for a beer and paused. It struck me that in all the meals we'd eaten together, we had never cooked anything. "I really need to clean this out." I gestured to the numerous takeout containers and pizza we'd gotten over the last week.

Lucas flashed a grin over his shoulder and went to work peeling the garlic. "Man cannot live by pizza and Chinese food alone. I've gained like ten pounds this month."

In the months I'd lived with Matt, never once had he seemed as at home in my kitchen as Lucas did. He hummed to himself while he chopped and sliced ingredients. Matt and I had taken turns preparing meals, but it was a chore that we did alone. The more I thought of it, all domestic tasks had been divided between us — grocery shopping, cleaning, cooking, even running errands. Every dollar spent was tracked, every job negotiated and assigned. Lucas was so different. Memories of strolling through the garden section of the home store brought a smile to my face.

I followed my gut and shut the fridge. "Can I open this?" I gestured to the wine bottle.

Lucas glanced up and smiled. "Yeah. I bought one to cook with, but the others are to drink. I figured if you have the cabinet, might as well stock it."

"What do I owe you for the groceries?"

Lucas frowned, so I let it go and uncorked the wine. I rinsed the thin layer of dust off two wine glasses before pouring one for myself and one for Lucas. I washed my hands and handed him his glass. "What are we making and how can I help?"

Lucas handed me the recipe card. Coq au Vin appeared in bold letters above an intimidating list of steps. "What the hell is 'blanched' bacon?" I laughed, but Lucas was undeterred.

"You can slice the mushrooms and dice an onion." Lucas handed me the knife and slid the cutting board my direction. He grabbed the saucepan from the stovetop and filled it with water. "Julia Child says you have to blanch the bacon to remove the saltiness. It just means you boil it first, then put it in cold water."

I held the mushroom and sliced carefully. "I know how to fry bacon. Also, the recipe says to serve with buttered noodles. That doesn't sound any healthier than eating out."

Lucas hip-checked me out of his way as he grabbed his wine glass. "We can work it off later."

After finishing the prep work, I attempted to help, but once several recipe steps converged and timers started going off, Lucas got frazzled. After a while, I gave up and followed him from counter to counter, cleaning up behind him and randomly groping him to try to keep him from getting too anxious. By the time the meal was ready, I was far more horny than hungry.

I sliced into the chicken to ensure it was done and could barely contain my hysterics. "Is Coq au Vin French for purple chicken?" We were nearly two bottles into a good Pinot Noir, so it's possible that wasn't nearly as funny as I thought.

The sheer disappointment on Lucas' face tempered my reaction. I picked a piece of the chicken off the bone with my fingers. "It still tastes good, babe," I said, eliciting only a weak smile from Lucas.

We moved to the table, but Lucas was distracted, busily tapping on his phone, trying to figure out what had gone wrong. "I should have used a burgundy. My recipe didn't say that, but Alton Brown is saying if you use a good burgundy, it won't stain."

"The chicken is delicious," I reassured him, taking another healthy bite.

"It should be a rooster," Lucas said, shrugging.

"What?"

"Coq. It's French for rooster."

"Like cock?" My laughter returned, escaping with an inadvertent snort that sent me into further hysterics. "You made me cock?"

Lucas shook his head as he laughed, more at me than my joke. "How drunk are you?"

I shrugged and took another sip of my wine but did a quick inventory. I was lightheaded and my lips were slightly numb. Neither were good signs, but there was one dead giveaway that I'd passed tipsy. "Have I been laughing inappropriately?"

"A little." Lucas chuckled.

"Then very. Kayla informed me my wine drunk is highly entertaining. Am I entertaining you?"

"Yes, immensely."

"I love this purple cock, baby." I took a bite and moaned around it.

Lucas nearly spit out his wine. "Holy shit. I'm buying you wine every day."

"Then I will swallow your purple cock every day, too."

"Kyle, take it easy. I have plans for you later."

I inspected my lap and rubbed myself. I had a semi, and no doubt Lucas could inspire me with even a modicum of attention, but there was something else being wine drunk brought out in me. "Not tonight," I said, taking another swallow of wine.

Lucas scraped the noodles off his plate and chewed his last bite with care. He swallowed, and I fought to keep my eyes focused on him to gauge his reaction. Or non-reaction, it would seem. "Lucas?"

"It's fine," he said. "I don't expect sex every night, babe."

A loud guffaw exited my mouth that must have amused Lucas because he sat back and grinned. "Oh, we are definitely having sex tonight. It just doesn't matter if *I* get hard enough to fuck *you*."

Lucas' eyebrow disappeared into his hair. "You serious? You've had a lot to drink."

"Haven't ever tried a cock as big as yours. It's good to be a little relaxed."

Lucas frowned. "I don't want you to have to get drunk to be with me."

I shook my head, cackling like a hyena at Lucas' assertion but powerless to control the volume or cadence of my laughter. I really shouldn't drink wine. "Don't have to be drunk. Just need to get fucked." I stood, stumbling a bit, and grabbed his hand. "Now, Lucas. C'mon."

I led Lucas to my bedroom. I could see the hesitation, so I did my best to fight through my haze and find enough sobriety to show him that how much I wanted him had very little to do with the alcohol I'd consumed. The truth was that since that day in the library, I thought about it all the time. Dreamed about it. I loved to bottom, always had, and since Matt was the last guy who'd fucked me, it had been a long freaking time since I'd done so. The alcohol had merely given me the courage to ask for it. "I need you. Please."

The words I had held back from Lucas flowed too freely. "I want you to fuck me. I want to feel you inside me." I threw myself at him, my naked desire consuming his resistance and burning it to ashes.

I swayed as my eyes closed, my brain swimming in a 'we-are-so-gonna-get-fucked' pool of anticipation when Lucas sank his teeth into the flesh of my shoulder. I moaned.

"Come on now, drunky." Lucas guided me to the bed and yanked off my pants. My erection sprang free.

"See? Not too drunk," I slurred. "I made a purple cock for you too, baby."

Lucas half-smirked, "Kyle, shut up."

"No." I shook my head. "Make me. Like I do you. I want it like that."

Lucas shifted up on the bed and straddled me. "You want me to hold you down, Kyle?" He pinned my wrists to the mattress, and I struggled just because it was hot.

I nodded. "Yeah." He squeezed tighter, and I moaned. "Want that. Touch me, babe."

Lucas laughed. "Now that I know wine is your truth serum, we're going to play a little game of what does Kyle really think."

"No," I moaned. "Suck my cock."

Lucas thrust his pelvis against me, laughing at the happy noises I couldn't contain. "Which is it, Kyle? Am I pinning you down and fucking you, stroking you or sucking your cock?"

"Yes, please." I closed my eyes while Lucas' manipulated his hold and slid his cock up and down my shaft.

"Do you like being my daddy in bed?"

My eyes flew open. "What?"

"Told you. This is truth time. I ask you a question, you answer it then I get you off."

I moaned as Lucas let go and reached for the bedside table. He freed a plug I hadn't realized he even knew was there. "Answer me."

"Yes, I like it."

"Good." Smiling, Lucas opened the lube and rubbed it over the silicone. He motioned for me to lift my ass, slid a pillow under my hips and nudged my legs farther apart.

He lowered his head to my crotch and blew air along my twitching cock. He peeked out his tongue and flicked it lightly under my cockhead then stopped. "But you sometimes want me to take control?"

"Yes." I rolled my eyes. What had I just been saying? "Want you to stop teasing and fuck me *now*."

Lucas laughed and took his time kissing along my shaft.

"Don't stop," I begged when it became clear he was stopping.

"Not what I asked, baby. Do you want me to tie you up? Blindfold you? Gag you? Would you like it if I made it hurt a little? Not a lot, just enough so that you'd be totally focused on my cock sliding into your tight hole and filling you up. Would you like that, baby? Would you let me make you helpless and fuck you?"

"Fuck, Lucas," I murmured.

He slid his tongue up my shaft and the head of the plug teased my opening.

"Mm, baby… You're so eager for this. Let me hear you," Lucas said, then slid the plug into my ass and my cock down his throat.

I made a strangled cry as he thrust the toy in and out of me. "Fuck, baby. You're so hot like this," Lucas said. "So fucking hot."

"Fuck me," I begged.

"Not yet. I want this ass nice and open for me."

"Yes," I moaned again and took my cock in hand, desperate for more pressure.

"No, baby. You come when I give you this big dick and not one second before."

"Want that big cock in me. Need to be fucked."

"Oh, baby. I'm gonna do you so good. You'll feel me all week, Kyle."

"Want it. Turn around. Fuck my mouth."

Lucas didn't hesitate to reverse his position. He knelt at my head and fed me his cock while he fucked me with the plug, frantically working my hole open. I tried to deep-throat him and quickly gagged. He retreated, but my mouth chased him.

"Fuck, baby. You want to be slutty tonight? Let go and tell me what goes on in that head of yours," Lucas said.

"Want to go back to the library. Want it over the table, hard and fast. Wanted you so much that day."

"Yeah? You want me to strip you naked and hold my hand over your mouth, so no one hears you scream? Hold you down and make you take this cock with just spit for lube? The things I wanted to do to you that day, Kyle. I went back to that study room the next day, baby, and I jerked off on the table just thinking about you bent over for me." He thrust his hips and moaned loudly while my throat squeezed around him.

"On your side, baby. I need to feel that ass."

I was vaguely aware of Lucas placing a condom before a wet slick of lubed fingers massaged the nerves around my hole. Lucas moved my top leg forward and guided the head of his cock into place. I pushed back, chasing more of the sensation. Lucas stilled me, and he kissed my ear and the back of my neck, setting off a cascade of chills down my spine. "I've been driving this dick for a long time, baby. Let me do this."

He lifted my knee higher to my chest and pushed in. The sensation was overwhelming, the stretch eye-wateringly intense. I quickly sobered as the hot length of Lucas' cock slid farther inside. The needy sound that left my throat was unrecognizable.

"That's it, Kyle. Hold still and relax."

"I need —"

"I got you, babe. Let me give this to you."

He worked himself inside me slowly until I swore I could feel him in my stomach. "Wait. Don't move," I begged, afraid one stroke would either split me in two or make me come.

He froze, giving me a few seconds to adjust before taking a long stroke. "Not so drunk now, are you?" He kissed along my neck, reassuring me with endearments far more tender than I expected.

"Yeah. Fuck, Lucas. Your cock is... I've never..."

"I got you, baby. You feel amazing too. I love it when you talk to me. Don't stop, okay? Tell me what you want."

When I couldn't find the words, Lucas took over, biting me, kissing me and talking me through all the naughty things he wanted to do to me. "Tell me I can have you like that, Kyle. Tell me you want it."

"Want everything with you. Do anything...fuck. Shit. Oh, fuck." The tide of my orgasm started deep in my ass. The powerful spasm stole my breath, and I gasped with the convulsion. Suddenly, my cock jerked and shot rope after thick rope of semen onto my thigh. Instinctively, I brought a hand down to stroke myself, but Lucas groaned and pushed into me with so much force that I could do nothing but brace myself against his punishing thrusts.

"Fuck, baby." Lucas released a guttural cry and shook violently against me. He bit into my shoulder at the height of his release.

He held me tight to his chest, his hot breaths a rhythmic cadence, lulling me asleep with his cock still inside me. I shook awake when he carefully slid free from my body. I touched myself where he'd been, marveling at how my body had accommodated him. Lucas rolled on his back, his hand still on my side. I lay there, sated and embarrassed, recalling all he'd coaxed out of me, and I waited for Lucas to speak.

Finally, a deep sigh of satisfaction escaped his lips. "C'mere," Lucas murmured. I rolled toward him, tucking myself alongside him, and splayed my hand over his abs. He tilted my chin toward him and kissed me. "You okay?" he asked. "Sore?"

I nodded.

"In my defense, this was all your idea," Lucas said smugly.

I chuckled, buried my face into his armpit and inhaled his musk. "It was good," I mumbled.

"Good enough to do it sober?" Lucas asked.

I nodded.

"Good enough to try what we talked about?"

"Lucas, I—"

"Don't hide from me." Lucas coaxed me to meet his eyes. "You just need to be honest. Do you want to or do you just like fantasizing about it?"

I knew there were countless guys—some he worked with, others just randoms from social media—who would give their left testicle to fulfill every one of Lucas' sexual whims. I'd be an idiot to refuse when Lucas could have his pick. "Maybe if I get really drunk."

"No," Lucas said emphatically. "I don't want it if you have to be drunk to give it to me. It's just a question. There's no wrong answer here."

I sighed, because any possibility of what we'd talked about doing would require more than one kind of lubrication on my part. It wasn't that I didn't get turned on by it. I did. But what Lucas was suggesting? I closed my eyes and tried to find something sexy or flirty to say to reassure Lucas I could be who he wanted.

Maybe there was no wrong answer but there was clearly a right one. Lucas and I were a summer fling, and I'd been fooling myself that we'd ever be compatible for the long term. I shook my head. "Nah," I said, "it's just a fantasy."

Chapter Eight

I showered alone and took inventory of my worse-than-usual aches and pains resulting from that weekend's rigorous activities. A bite mark adorned my lower neck and a mysterious bruise explained the tender spot on my hip. I felt slightly debauched and had to admit that I loved it. Ever since I'd discovered Lucas' ability to turn me inside out with his sex-drenched voice whispering amazingly creative filth into my ear two weeks earlier, I'd been asking him to top me. Hell, that weekend, I hadn't even had to ask. Oh, we still took turns. Lucas loved the daddy-boy dynamic far too much to give it up. He read me like a book and adjusted accordingly, and I seemed to do the same for him. I had never enjoyed a more gratifying sex life.

I stepped out of my shower to find Lucas naked at my vanity, his back to the mirror. He held his cell phone, frozen in his preferred selfie angle.

"What are you doing?" I asked.

He lowered his phone and frowned. His neck and chest were somehow even hotter covered in the marks I'd given him. "If you're taking a picture for me, I'd prefer your front. Love those abs, baby."

His frown neutralized, and he at least tried to smile for me. "I have to tell you something, but I don't want to break our rules."

I laughed. "Oh? Like the rule about no sleepovers? That worked out well." I hip-bumped him out of the way to grab my toothpaste and brushed while he stewed.

"Kyle..." He exhaled my name like a prayer.

I spat and rinsed my mouth. "Say it. Rules aside, I'll deal."

He turned and showed me his back. "Damn," I murmured. Deep purple fingerprint-size spots dotted his hips, and there were several clear bite and scratch marks on his neck, back and shoulders. I didn't realize I'd gotten so carried away. "I'm sorry." I turned so he could see the damage he'd caused. "I'll have to wear a collared shirt today. Again."

Lucas cleared his throat and chewed his lip. "But I don't wear a shirt to work," he mumbled. "And makeup will cover the bruises, but the bite marks? I'm not allowed to film with these. I should have said something earlier."

"Oh," I said.

I should've elaborated but couldn't find the words. Reality had invaded our little bubble, and all my concentration focused on holding in my resentment. "So, can you... Is there a way to reschedule?"

"The other model was flown in for the shoot. I'll call the director and see what they want to do. They may let me shoot anyway — or they could recast me."

Lucas' noise of disapproval ejected my smile. "Kyle, you have to understand that, either way, this impacts my reputation."

"I'm sorry," I said and managed to feel some remorse for any damage caused to his career. "I won't do it again."

Lucas' eyes widened. "You will absolutely do it again, but maybe not right before I film." He glowered at me and seemed to realize what that meant. He'd have to tell me when he filmed. Another rule to toss in the trash heap. It'd fit right next to the one about no sleepovers.

I tossed my head back and pinched the bridge of my nose. "Fine. I guess let me know if I need to be careful." I toweled myself off and channeled my anger into progressing through my morning as quickly and mechanically as possible. Lucas tried to smooth things over with affection, but I found for the first time that I could resist his charms. The entire conversation needed to be zapped from my memory, and I couldn't pretend otherwise.

Work was…not good. I'd accidentally emailed the wrong blueprints to my electrician, sent pictures of drywall defects to the client rather than my contractor and lost my shit at some kid who'd delivered a twenty-five-thousand-dollar custom, hand-blown glass chandelier to the wrong house—all before noon.

I was absolutely no use to anyone, and I took my frustrations out on the staff, vendors and random office equipment.

Lucas hadn't texted me the outcome of his conversation with his boss, so my imagination vacillated between images of Lucas fucking some other guy and crying over the loss of his job—both of which left me slightly nauseated. We'd said goodbye that morning with a passionless kiss. He'd said he would see me in class, which sort of suggested he planned to leave me alone. As much as space seemed like a good thing, it bothered me that he was giving it to me. I'd fallen for Lucas too hard, too quickly, and my rational self hated the man who'd spent the last two months being unbelievably freaking happy.

The thought of Lucas keeping such a big part of his life — which his work clearly was — segregated from me inexplicably made me angry. It wasn't only the porn. Since the day of our beach trip, Lucas had stopped accessing his social media accounts from my house. Intellectually, I knew he maintained Tommy Bruiser online, but out of sight, out of mind.

Waves of emotions rolled through me too fast to process. One minute I was sure I had to end things and the next I had keys in hand, determined to make up. I hated knowing Lucas had sex with other men. I knew I would. It was why I had walked away from him on our first date. But, the alternative had become equally unbearable. Tommy Bruiser was a stranger. Unless I got to know him, I wouldn't know things about Lucas. Things, it had occurred to me, that his fans probably knew — and that his fans wouldn't know about me. Like we were dating while still in the closet and it didn't feel right anymore, not with how strongly I felt about him.

I sat at my desk and stared absentmindedly out of the window. Part of me wanted to call Kayla, but as much as I loved her, I knew she would tell me to end it. Lucas was supposed to be a fling, and for Kayla, flings came and went all too easily. I wasn't built that way. It was the same reason I never fostered a puppy, leased a car or rented my tools. When I liked something, I got attached. And when I considered it mine, I didn't give it up without a fight.

The fact that I hadn't sought her advice was a damn good indicator of where my heart landed on the matter. Lucas was mine.

Intellectually, I'd always thought Matt's need to keep things separate had led to our breakup. We might have lived together, but we never overtly committed to being together forever. Even though he'd slept in my bed, he'd still paid rent on his fully-furnished apartment. During the holidays, he visited his folks, and I visited mine. He had his own bank accounts and credit cards. He had his goals and dreams — and I had mine.

I didn't want that in a partner, and without even asking, I knew Lucas didn't either. He was an all-in kind of guy, just like me, which might have been the very thing that made him perfect for me.

I palmed my phone, scrolled through the messages exchanged with Lucas and reminded myself why I liked him so much.

"Well, you're smiling, so it can't be that bad." I peered up to see Rocco standing in the doorway. "Bob called me, said I needed to send you the fuck home before you killed someone."

I rolled my eyes. Bob was a project manager who'd happened to witness the chandelier debacle. "I wasn't that bad."

Rocco shrugged. "Still... I can't remember having any complaints about you. This morning I've had two."

"Who else?"

"The Smithfields' real estate agent wanted to make sure the drywall redoes would be comped since, as you so eloquently worded it, 'they screwed the pooch.'"

I groaned. "Sorry, Rocco. It's been a morning."

"You need to leave?"

"No, I need to work."

"Can you do that without losing me any more money?"

Rocco had never been one to mince words. "I'll get it together."

"See that you do," he said and walked away.

Alone again, I picked up my phone and decided to rid myself of the burden of guilt until I could figure things out.

Hey, sorry about this morning. I was an ass. Hope you're having a good day.

Lucas didn't respond, but that wasn't the point. I considered following up with a text that told him I loved him but thought the better of it. I'd been in love before. My head may not have been entirely there, but my heart surely was. Regardless of how much I wanted to erase our rough morning, I needed to see his face the first time I said it, and I needed to be sure my head was in on the decision. We'd both been close to saying it. I could just tell sometimes by the way he looked at me. Yet neither of us had, and if I had to guess, the same thing that held me back held him back too—fear that we wouldn't find our way around our obstacle. And the knowledge that at some point, sooner rather than later, we'd be forced to acknowledge that fact.

A flooring defect discovered on a final walk-through consumed my afternoon. I pulled into the university parking lot with mere moments to spare before class and ducked into the classroom. Dr. Mandell had already begun his lecture on growth planning.

After nearly an hour, he transitioned to explaining the details of the next assignment.

"This assignment will span the remaining weeks of the semester and make up a substantial portion of your grade. You will work in your pairs to develop an analysis based on the idea established during week one. Using the readings to assist you, you will study the operational management of your chosen field and submit a single growth analysis and marketing plan for your business. This analysis must include an executive summary, a SWOT analysis, financing considerations and, most importantly, a target demographic and marketing plan. You'll want to view the industry from all perspectives — owner, consumer and regulatory agencies."

Dr. Mandell opened the conversation to questions, and I took the time to glance in Lucas' direction. His head hung low, and I got the distinct impression he was avoiding me. When the question and answer portion of the lecture ended, Dr. Mandell gave us the remaining time for group work.

"Mr. McMillan and Mr. Cass, a word please."

Lucas' frown asked if I had a clue, and he stood to approach the podium. I trailed him and braved a brush against his fingers as we stood side by side. "Gentlemen, it seems Steve Reynolds decided to withdrawal from my class."

"The drop deadline was weeks ago," I protested.

Dr. Mandell nodded. "Yes, it's unfortunate and very late in the game, but there's not much I can do since he also withdrew from the school. I understand he had to return home — an illness in the family. I've shuffled the teams, and since Mr. Cass was in a group of three and you two seem to have gotten friendly, I thought pairing you would be the least disruptive solution. Now then, I've spoken to your other team members, Mr. Cass, and they've decided to use the adult toy line aspect of your research. Therefore, you're free to continue with the website or video production business line. It was ambitious to try to do both, and either on their own would make for a reasonable scope. I've done some research on your industry. While unconventional, it certainly makes for an interesting case study. Of course, you could also pursue Mr. McMillan's original topic."

Lucas' brows furrowed, and he glanced away. I could feel his disappointment, and I spoke without considering my words. "We can use Lucas' topic."

Lucas turned back to me, his eyes owl-wide before he dropped his gaze to the floor.

"Very well. I look forward to seeing your work." He dismissed us without a second thought, but Lucas waited a full two minutes to look at me again. I knew because I counted every single second.

"You didn't have—" Lucas began.

"I texted you."

"I know," he whispered. "I shouldn't have blamed you for the marks. I never gave you any reason to think it wasn't okay with me."

"Lucas—" I said at the same moment he'd started talking.

"Send me what you and Steve came up with."

"No. Neither of us cares about that topic. You were really excited about your project."

"I'll read up on the bakery market."

"No, you won't."

"We can't even…" He sighed heavily and shook his head. "Kyle, how is that supposed to work?" Lucas' voice rose in exasperation. A student in the first row cleared his throat and flashed an annoyed scowl. Lucas smiled apologetically and kept his gaze lowered when he sighed. "I'm not going to do this here. I'm going home. We can talk later."

"I'll come with you. Or better yet, come home with me."

Lucas' eyes darkened like an approaching storm but he nodded slowly.

I led him out of the classroom and drove home with an eye focused on his car in my rearview mirror. We parked in my driveway and, silently, Lucas followed me into my home and took a seat on the couch.

For our relationship to work, I couldn't be afraid to ask why he looked so drained. Part of me prayed someone else was responsible. I ripped the Band-Aid off my emotionally hairy brain.

"Did you film today?"

His head lifted, and I frowned at the doubt in his eyes. "I thought we don't talk about it?"

I didn't want to know, but I needed to. "Tell me."

"Yes, I filmed today."

"Are you tired?"

He fought a smile and failed. "Actually, yes. I had to pull off some pretty strenuous positions because they couldn't film my back." I could hear the playfulness teed up in his voice, kicking the tires on the topic.

"Are you hungry?"

He nodded, and I ventured into the kitchen and plucked out cartons of leftover Chinese food. Minutes later, he joined me. "Do you want the beef and broccoli or the pork lo mein?"

"I'll take the pork," Lucas answered, opened the cabinets and extracted plates. He took over warming the food while I set the table.

We ate in uncomfortable silence across from each other until I couldn't stand it any longer. "I think we need new rules."

Lucas sat back in his chair and searched me. He bit his lip, and his smile approached a wattage that illuminated the new darkness we'd stumbled into. "I think we need to stop making rules."

I considered that. "No, we definitely need rules, just not the old ones."

"Okay. What are the rules then, Daddy?"

I rolled my eyes. It was *so* not the time. "I think I should stop pretending you didn't have sex with someone else today and you should stop pretending that having sex for money is like any other day at the office."

He mulled that over for a beat. "Are you saying that you want to keep dating?"

"Yes. I don't want to end things. I want to figure this out. I'm not sure how."

"Do I get to add rules?"

"Sure."

"You have to open your mind."

"I'm trying," I confessed. "I spent the better part of this morning thinking about Matt."

Lucas recoiled, and I explained. "Why we broke up, rather. One of the reasons he wasn't the one is because we didn't truly merge." I explained the issues Matt and I'd had and added, "I want to know about your life, Lucas. I want to know how you spent your day, even if it's hard to hear."

Lucas stood and hauled me up to my feet. He placed his hands on either side of my face and held me in his gaze. "Kyle, I love you."

My heart skipped a beat when he kissed me. He slipped his tongue over mine, and I lost myself in the pleasure of his touch. We parted, and I decided to give my brain a break. It had a terrible track record of reliability anyway. I said aloud what my heart had decided weeks ago. "I love you too."

After we cleaned up dinner, Lucas led me to my bedroom with his laptop by his side. I wasn't sure what to expect. Lucas' smile had grown dirtier as the reality of our decision settled in.

"We have homework," Lucas connected his laptop so that it displayed on my television screen. "We need to review the industry from all perspectives, including the consumer."

"Yes," I agreed. "Lucas, I'm not ready to watch your porn."

"Not mine," he blurted, "but I think we should sample the industry. I thought it might be helpful for us to watch high-quality porn, like the stuff my company does, and compare to sites like *Pornhub* and *Chaturbate*. *Onlyfans* might be relevant too."

"So, basically, we're gonna watch a lot of porn."

"Well, tonight we will start with something from my studio. I want you to watch a full Goldenboy's scene. I think it's important that you understand the different aspects of the market. Some sites have amateur videos and make money by ad revenue. Studios sell memberships and products. There is no shortage of free and pirated porn, so their marketing strategy needs to hit on why people should pay for their memberships. Quality is one of those factors. Exclusive talent, like me, cultivating their fan base is another."

"Then?"

"Then we'll talk about it."

"Okay."

"Do you have any preferences?"

"Besides not seeing you?"

"Yeah. My company has other guys like me, but we also have some that fall more into the twink category and others who have a lot of ink or piercings. There are a wide variety of themes too—orgies, domination, spanking, toys, threesomes, slings... If you want to see something in particular, we might have it."

"Just pick. I trust you."

Lucas thought for a minute. He searched the site by model name for a guy named Sebastian Hill. A list of his scenes came up with thumbnails. He resembled Lucas—same age and build, lacking in body hair and tattoos. He wasn't nearly as well-endowed as Lucas but he was still well above average. He was hot, no question.

"I chose Sebastian because I've never worked with him."

I relaxed, although the word 'work' to describe what Lucas did made my skin crawl. "Would you?"

"I don't pick my scene partners, but the chances are low. I don't bottom on camera, and he saves that for his boyfriend, but if he ever did decide to bottom, there's a high chance we would be paired."

"Why?"

"Because we probably have the largest fan base at GB, and they love to pair first on-camera bottoms with me."

I laughed. "That's mean. No one should take your dick for their first time. Don't they have starter tops?"

He grinned, clearly enjoying the fact that he could talk to me about his porn and I hadn't lost my shit. "It sells."

"Sex usually does."

Sebastian and his scene partner, Cody, a rail-thin boy with a rainbow flag tattoo on his right shoulder blade were first shown having a picnic, almost romantic. The scene progressed to sex on a couch but remained on the tame side. The sex seemed real enough to me. The men kept eye contact in between exaggerated moaning and cursing. Their positions changed a few times, from face to face then chest to back, and finally, Sebastian pounded into Cody bent over the side of the couch. The end of the scene captured my attention. Sebastian and Cody kissed in the missionary position, panting and whispering like they were the only two people in the world. As I watched, Lucas unbuttoned my pants, freed my cock and took me into his mouth.

The sudden heat and wetness accelerated my arousal, and I ran my fingers through his hair and spread my legs to make more room for him.

Lucas licked my shaft and smiled at me. "Watch the video," he reminded me before he closed his lips around me and stroked his hand around the base. I turned my attention back to the television. The cadence of Cody's breathless curses matched Lucas' mind-bending rhythm. I closed my eyes and concentrated on the wet frenzied sounds of Cody jacking himself and Sebastian's balls slapping against his skin.

Suddenly, Cody released a deep, guttural moan, and I erupted in one powerful convulsion. I opened my eyes to Lucas, still on his knees, licking me clean.

Lucas observed me while I recovered my breath. I gathered my thoughts and searched for reassuring words. I didn't want to feel the way I did. I tried to think of sex like eating, a biological necessity to be filled indiscriminately. And I didn't want Lucas to feel judged.

But the joy of my orgasm faded way too quickly and left me only with crushing disappointment.

The men I'd watched had been connected. That attraction couldn't be faked. Their bodies had been used for shared pleasure — real pleasure. So, maybe it wasn't love but I didn't want to share Lucas with anyone like that. I didn't want to think about it. And under no circumstances did I want to see it. I hung my head, and I heard Lucas expel a breath full of frustration.

"I'm sorry," I whispered. Lucas whimpered, joined me on my bed and gathered me into his arms.

"Baby, don't be sorry." He stroked my hair and sighed. Although the first battle ended in a loss, we drifted off with his arms tight around me, refusing to concede.

Chapter Nine

"So, this is the boyfriend." Case Everwood greeted us outside the entrance to Goldenboys studios with chaste kisses on both cheeks. Exactly as Lucas had described, Case resembled a gayer, younger version of Tom Brady. I wondered if he had spent much time in front of the camera. Lucas' boss and his husband, Robert, co-owned the company. Lucas had explained that Case managed the creative aspects and directed the scenes while Robert handled the business side, including hiring models and dealing with the website. While I stood by awkwardly, Case examined me and smiled approvingly at Lucas. "He's as delicious as you described."

Blushing, I entered the studio and followed Case around for an impromptu tour. The large warehouse had unfinished ceilings and lacked any of the polish you'd expect from the headquarters of a successful business. In the front of the space were a reception desk and several offices with four walls and no ceilings. Case led us to a large room with a pool table, big-screen television, shelves of video games and consoles, a popcorn machine and a refrigerator. Snacks filled the counter that ran along the back of the room. Except for the video games and the current lone occupant, it bore a striking resemblance to the common room of Kayla's sorority.

A man with stunning, big brown eyes and a body that belonged in an advertisement for Gold's Gym lounged on the leather couch, holding a PlayStation controller. "What's up, Tommy?"

Lucas' eyes flicked briefly to me before he answered. "Hey, Evan. Not much. This is my boyfriend, Kyle." He looped his arm through mine and squeezed me in a side hug.

"Hey." Evan waved with his free hand without lifting his eyes from the game.

"This is where the models hang out," Case said. "Evan, let me finish this tour, and we'll get started. Have you seen Sam?"

Evan's turn toward Case moved his robe just enough to expose his lap. I sucked in a breath and averted my eyes from Evan's uncircumcised penis to Lucas. Heat spread like lava through my body.

"Yeah. He's douching," Evan said. "Hey, Tommy, is your new boy gonna film?"

I whipped my head back to Evan and his exposed junk. Lucas placed a hand on my shoulder and squeezed. His touch grounded me. The corners of Lucas' eyes crinkled. "No, he's just taking a tour," he said with a nervous laugh.

An explosion followed by machine-gun fire distracted Evan from Lucas' answer. "Fuck. Die, asshole," he shouted at the television and pounded buttons on the controller. "Case, put me down for a scene request with him."

Case and Lucas shared a knowing glance. "Ignore him," Case said.

Lucas patted my shoulder and led me out of the lounge. "I'm sorry about that."

I swallowed. "Have you…?" I cleared my throat. "Um… Have you worked with him?"

To his credit, Lucas didn't bat an eye. "Yes. Evan and I have filmed a few times together and in group scenes."

Case chuckled and rapped his knuckles on a door. "Sam, you about ready? Do I need to shave your hole?"

The door swung open, and Sam, a tall, lanky boy with sharp facial features and bloodshot eyes, appeared, wearing a robe and carrying a bong. "Robert already did. My ass looks good enough to eat." He wagged his eyebrows at Lucas. "Just got to brush my teeth. You know Evan. Boy will eat the booty like groceries, but God forbid your breath isn't minty fresh."

Case laughed. "Add some Visine, would ya? We're setting up the lights now. Why don't you grab Evan and get comfortable on set?" Case turned toward Lucas. "Can you finish the tour? I need to grab my camera. Robert's in his office, and he can answer your school questions. Kyle, it was good to meet you. We have Taco Tuesday tonight. Come meet more of the guys."

Case scurried off and left Lucas and I standing at a door. A large sign with bold lettering warned people that they were entering the set and issued an ominous threat not to enter when the red light was illuminated. Lucas opened the door and ushered me inside.

"This is where we film. Only Case, Robert, the sound guy and the models are allowed in here during a shoot." I followed Lucas while he pointed out aspects of the set and clamped my teeth down on my tongue to keep myself from saying anything stupid. Sam and Evan entered the set behind us and flopped on the bed. They shared a quick peck on the lips, and Evan set up his phone with music. Sam, unbothered by Evan's focus on his phone, pushed Evan's robe aside and licked Evan's dick.

My heart rate sped up as I whipped my head toward Lucas for an explanation. He cringed and explained. "They're getting ready for pictures. Let's go see Robert."

"Lucas, can we?" I nodded toward an exit sign. "I need some air."

"Yeah. Sure." Lucas led me to a fenced patio with lawn chairs behind the warehouse. "Sit. Relax for a second." After I calmed, Lucas squatted in front of me and held my hand. "Do you have questions?"

I nodded.

"Fire away. I want you to get comfortable with my job, Kyle. Ask me anything."

"So, Evan and Sam…"

Lucas nodded as though he'd anticipated the issue. I almost believed Lucas about on-camera sex—the audience, interruptions and the technical aspects would minimize intimacy, but he hadn't mentioned any 'warm-up' activity. I couldn't help but wonder about the line. What about the night before? Or hell, the week before? Did he flirt with his colleagues online? Did he send them pictures of his hole and cock and text what he wanted them to do to him like he had me? I took a deep breath and shook my head to remove the images.

"Sam's been in the business about three years, but he's not an exclusive. He works with other studios. I've never filmed with him before, so there's a chance he tries that with all his scene partners. Based on their Twitters, I think the two of them have a friends-with-benefits thing going on. No one would touch me like that before a scene. We all respect each other's boundaries here, particularly with guys who are in relationships. And we all know the signs if someone wants to stop for any reason during the sex. Robert is furiously protective of us. Anyone who crossed a line would be shown the door, no hesitation. I'm fortunate to work here, because not all studios are as professional."

Okay, that made me feel a tiny bit better. "So, you do pictures together first?"

"It depends. We usually film some B-roll. That's the scene set up and pictures on the same day then film the sex the next day. Some scenes don't have much B-roll. It's just the sex. I'm guessing that's what's happening today. So, they are probably gonna do pictures before sex."

"You plan the positions ahead of time?"

"Yeah. Case talks through the scene with us. We have some input into positions. At the end of the day, Case wants good sex to film, so if we don't like certain things or if some positions will make us come too fast, he listens to us, but he has a vision for how he wants the scene to progress. I'd say about half is scripted and the rest is letting the models do their thing. Sometimes Case asks us to try out positions. Like, when Evan and

I filmed, Case wanted me to pick him up and bounce him on my dick, but it didn't look good on camera."

Lucas lifted his hand to massage the back of my neck. His Adam's apple bobbed, and I knew we were both feasting on the same memory. Arousal set off tingles under my skin. A shiver traveled down my spine with thoughts of Lucas lifting me off the bed, holding my back against the wall and thrusting hard against my prostate.

God. The experience had not only opened my eyes to Lucas' unexpected strength but also my own ability to cling helplessly to him while he'd brought me to perhaps the most intense orgasm of my life. *'Hold on to me,'* Lucas had whispered, and I had. I didn't remember being self-conscious or nervous. I'd just obeyed without hesitation, trusting him to make me feel things I'd never felt before. I swallowed hard, and Lucas leaned forward until his forehead touched mine and breathed with me.

"Baby," he sighed before he released me. The same intense gaze I'd followed outside the library the day we met greeted me. Lucas scanned me like he planned to take me right there in the courtyard. Sometimes the feeling of being that desired overwhelmed me, enough that I wasn't sure I could trust it. After all, I wasn't a porn star. I didn't have a tenth of the sex appeal as the men who worked with Lucas. But as much as I didn't understand it, I couldn't walk away from it — from him — either. Not again.

For the first time I'd wondered what would have happened if I hadn't left that day in the library? If I'd just let him fuck me? Would he even remember me now? Hell, would I remember him as more than a semi-anonymous sexual encounter I told my friends after too much wine? A story they weren't likely to even believe. Such a random series of events had brought Lucas into my life, and now, after what amounted to a blip of time, really, I couldn't imagine how I'd feel if I lost him.

Those sobering thoughts reminded me where I was. I cleared my throat and focused on my surroundings and Lucas, whose face showed more concern than arousal.

"You okay?" he asked.

"What do you mean it didn't look good on camera?"

Lucas danced his fingers over my scalp while he waited for me to say what was really on my mind, but I let the silence linger on. Eventually, he stood and stretched, letting the moment we shared go without commentary. "The pictures are technical, so we worry about lighting and shit. When we film, less so, because you can only do so much while you're moving. Case and Robert both have cameras, so they shift to get better angles if they need them. But when I tried the standing position with Evan, he was nervous about being dropped, and you could tell. I couldn't keep him high enough. His body blocked the view. Basically, it didn't work for Case, so we scrapped it. My point is that it doesn't matter what feels good. It's all about making a good product. All decisions are about that. That's why it's so different from real sex. When I'm inside you, I don't have to think about how it looks…just how it feels. How I make you feel."

Lucas ran his fingers through my scalp again, and I pushed against them to feel the pressure, reminding myself what his touch did to me and that nothing that went on in the warehouse behind me could be anything close. He focused intently on me, and I met his gaze. When I opened my mouth, Lucas shook his head. We didn't need to say it. He knew where my mind had gone. Not knowing what else to do, I nodded. *Message received.*

The door opened and Lucas turned to greet Robert with a hug. While Case could easily have been on the other side of the camera at GB, Robert Everwood was a total bear, complete with dark, thick body hair, a protruding gut and abundant ink. "Hey, Tommy. Case said you had some business questions for me."

Robert introduced himself and Lucas got down to business. I listened while Lucas fired our prepared questions at Robert. In addition to his financials, we learned his take on the industry. His thoughtful answers pleasantly surprised me. I didn't know what I expected, but Robert wasn't it. He had all the data we needed — industry trends, market share, profit and loss. They spent a ton on marketing, and he walked us through what had and hadn't worked in their past campaigns. "The goal is to sell memberships. That's how we make most of our money. Models sell memberships, not ad campaigns. One of our most successful ideas was to give each model a subscription referral link. They promote our site with their referral link, and if someone signs up, they get a cut. If a model has a few super fans, those fans will also promote that link. Basically, our job is to find models who don't only perform well but also see it as a business. Take your club opening last month… We had a surge in sales right after that event."

"Why?" I asked.

Lucas' face brightened, "That was my idea. I opened that new gay club on the Westside. I autographed my dildo and took pictures with anyone who bought one or could show me the membership confirmation. It was insane."

I gawked at him. "How did I not know you had your own dildo?"

Lucas' frown answered my question. *Oh, yeah.* I'd shut that topic down.

"Tommy hasn't shown you his toy collection? It's amazing. One of the most popular lines at Playland in years. You should hook your boy up, Tommy."

Lucas patted my thigh. "Don't worry. You get the real thing whenever you want it."

Robert smiled, and I tried to return the sentiment, but my stomach flipped-flopped and my anxiety over the situation started to give me a headache. "Is that all you needed, Tommy?"

Lucas nodded and stared at me for a beat. "Thanks so much for your time, Robert. I'm gonna go. Sounds like Case will need you soon anyway."

"Sorry about that. I know you asked to bring Kyle in on a day we weren't filming, but Sam lives in Missouri. His flight got delayed by that big storm that blew through the Midwest yesterday."

"No worries. Hey, do you know if Sam and Evan…"

"Who knows. I can't keep up, but they were all over each other last night at dinner, so I'd say they're fucking."

Lucas laughed, "Thought so. Thanks again, Robert."

Lucas ground his teeth on our way back to his apartment. The music played low enough to tune it out, and I avoided my thoughts by filling in the details of the notes I'd managed to take during our discussion.

I startled when Lucas finally broke the silence. "Did we get everything we need?"

"Yeah." I nodded. "I think you're right about the marketing plan. It should be model-focused, not site-focused."

"Yeah, Robert gave us some great stats to use in our project. What are the chances we finish early?"

"What's the hurry? The deadline is weeks out."

"I know. I thought we could get done early. Nothing wrong with that, right?"

I shrugged. "I work full-time," I reminded Lucas. He sent a pained expression my way and that's when it dawned on me that he worked too. "What's the real reason?

"I'm committed to a full-length project this August. It's six parts, and they'll start filming before the end of the semester. Sebastian decided to retire, and Case wants me to film his part, which is more extensive than the one he originally cast me in."

My stomach cramped, but I forced a smile. "That's good, right? The part, I mean."

Lucas nodded. "Yeah, it's a lot more money and I get to travel."

"Travel…" I gulped. "Where?"

"We're filming B-roll, and the first three parts are in Vegas," he replied. "I'll miss the last week of class. If Dr. Mandell will let us turn it in early, I thought you might want to come with me. I'll be there for a week, but I only work two of those days."

"Okay, well I guess we'll get it done early then."

"Kyle, are you mad?"

"No," I answered, and to my surprise, I wasn't.

"Do you want to go?"

I glanced at him. I did like the idea of taking a trip with him. I'd been to Vegas with Matt. Beyond the debauchery and drunken assholes, Vegas had a romantic side. It'd be too hot at Red Rock but hiking in Mt. Charleston could be lovely. Plus, the Bellagio fountains, maybe a spa day… I loved the spa at the

Palazzo. But the trip wasn't a romantic getaway, it was a business trip. And Lucas' business involved sticking his dick in other men, which would upend all romantic notions. "Next time," I said. His face fell, so I added, "We can plan a long weekend when you don't have to work."

He smiled, but his eyes didn't leave the road again until he'd parked his car.

The project was a beast. It was twenty to thirty pages long, including five years of projected income for our business and five years for our competitor, which was what we'd needed the Goldenboys' data for and an eight-part marketing strategy. Since we'd electively shaved off days at the end of our timeline, Lucas and I didn't have time to talk about anything other than marketing porn. We tried to work together, but things between Lucas and me felt off, and it wasn't possible to ignore the change when the cause of it was the focus of our evening. Ultimately, we agreed we needed a divide and conquer approach anyway. We decided to do our respective parts alone. Since Lucas was a million times more passionate about the plan than I was, he assigned me to most of the data-gathering and took on the creative pieces himself. We drafted our plan via the computer, speaking about it only when necessary.

My heart was heavy every time he'd send me a draft. His work spoke volumes. He loved the industry, practically idolized his bosses' success and his plan read like a love letter to the sexual revolution. I spent nights on my couch, staring at my laptop, missing him and alternating between berating myself for my hang-ups and rationalizing my feelings. What was my problem? Was it jealousy? Was it insecurity? Or did I have a real issue with gay sex? I never thought of myself as having any internalized homophobia. The first time I'd had sex, I had wanted to bottom. There had been nerves for sure, but no shame. It was the same with my friends. I'd never had an issue with effeminate gays, drag or anything queer. I just liked monogamy. I wanted someone to myself and there was nothing wrong with that.

Was there?

Chapter Ten

The night Lucas departed for his business trip, I had dinner with Kayla, who made no secret of her thoughts about my constant phone checking. I ignored her heavy sigh and glanced at Lucas' latest text, confirming he'd submitted our final project.

"Thank God that class is over," I muttered. Although, technically, there was one more class left, I had no intention of going now that the project had been turned in. "The only thing I learned was that I absolutely do *not* want to take another business marketing class as long as I live. If it weren't for Lucas caring about his grade and needing the class for his major, I would have procrastinated the shit out of it and done the literal bare minimum."

"So, what you're saying is you put a ton of effort into a project you care nothing about."

"Exactly."

"Because you're in love with a porn star."

I peered up from my carbonara and met her blue eyes. Damn, she knew me too well. "Exactly."

She shook her head in mock disapproval. "I should have known you'd fuck up a summer fling."

I started to object, but she stopped me, filled up our wine glasses and sighed. "Tell me all about it."

So, I did. I laid my soul bare, and after two bottles of wine, confessed my reservations, which she shot down one by one. Even I started to wonder why we couldn't make it work. "I'm not kinky enough in bed for him. He'll get bored with me."

She laughed so hard that she snorted wine through her nose, and the results made me smile, despite my humiliation. Kayla composed herself and did her best to take me seriously. "Kyle, I'm sure you're not bad at sex. Just a little conservative on the adventurous scale."

"But why? Why am I not adventurous?"

"Because you care what people think too much. It's hard to let go when you're worried about being embarrassed," Kayla answered frankly, then paused as though selecting her next words carefully. "Kyle, can I tell you something? It might hurt your feelings, but I think you need to hear this."

I took a sip of my wine and nodded my permission. I needed to hear the truth like only Kayla could say it.

"Judd Fisher didn't want the threesome. I did."

"What?" I gasped.

She twisted her face in regret. "I don't anymore, but after you and Judd dated, he and I went out that one time and he was outstanding in bed. I mean, I came like four times. Then we put two and two together and figured out he'd gone out with you too. When I confronted him, he sort of insinuated that he liked you, but you weren't sexually compatible and he didn't plan to keep seeing you. At first, I suggested it to prove him wrong, but the way you reacted to the suggestion? I kind of got his point. You have every right to say girls aren't your thing or that it'd have been too weird cause it was me, but it was almost like you were afraid to try something new. I don't know… Maybe Lucas is just too different from you. Maybe you need someone more your speed."

"He's literally everything I want in a partner. He's thoughtful and funny. I want to try new things, but then I get all in my head and worry I'll look like an idiot or worse, that Lucas will figure out I'm too boring or vanilla or whatever. He won't even let me get too drunk. I swear Lucas knows like every position in the *Kama Sutra*. And it's not just sex. Last week we ate at Tony's. I ordered the daily special — some risotto dish because he insisted I would love it — but the whole time, I kept thinking I should have been safe and ordered the rigatoni. Why would I do that? Why am I like this?"

Kayla gasped. "You didn't go to Tony's and not get the rigatoni? Fifteen years and you've never ordered anything else. I don't believe it."

I fished the receipt out of my wallet and thrust it at her. "I did. Lucas encourages me to have an open mind about everything and everyone. We rearranged the bedroom. Now my bed is angled in the corner so he can watch me take a shower in the morning. He helped me create a Pinterest board so I could start planning for my lake house. I research ideas for island-based cooktops with splash guards for an hour because you have no idea how much he loves to cook, even though he makes a huge mess. I want to be able to try everything he wants — even a threesome with a woman, although I can't imagine him asking for that."

She reviewed my receipt and her jaw slacked. "Kyle —" she began with cheerless caution.

"I want him, Kayla. Like down to my toes, I want him. But every time I think about his Vegas trip, I want to throw up."

She frowned. "Have you asked Lucas to stop?"

"I can't."

"Why?"

"Because he loves it. I don't think it's the sex so much, but the adoration. He's an expert at social media. His fans shower him with attention. The other day he accidentally tweeted just 'The' and got over three hundred comments and likes. He talked on and on about his fans being the best in the industry. I can't ask him to give that up for me. Even if I did…" I sighed and took a sip of my wine for courage but couldn't quite find the words. I didn't think he'd pick me. *Why would Lucas settle for a guy like me when he can have anyone he wants?*

"It sounds like you know what you need to do, but you just don't want to do it. Unless you think he'd offer to stop."

"That would be my dream scenario, but he won't — at least not anytime soon. The project we did? The entire thing revolved around how he wants to stay in the business after he's done filming. He isn't doing porn for a side job. It's what he wants to do for his career. Trust me. He's all in. I think it's bigger than sex for him. I'm not sure why."

"Okay, so you need to get out, Kyle, before you fall deeper. It's only been a few months."

"I can't. I've tried. After our visit to the studio, I thought up a million conversations, but I couldn't bring myself to initiate any of them. I spent years with Matt and never felt anything close to the way I feel toward Lucas."

"It's so early, Kyle. Has he even met your family? Or anyone you're close to? Have you met his friends? You've been in a bubble. Anyone can have titanium-strength rose-colored glasses with a good sex haze. You need to see if Lucas' shine holds up when you're living the life you've lived for forty years. If not one thing changed about him, would he still be the perfect guy? Because, if not, then you're setting yourself up for failure. I must tell you that I've always pictured you with an older man—someone distinguished, reserved. I'm having trouble picturing Lucas as the forever guy. I'm sure dating a young, hot guy is exhilarating and awesome for the ego—"

"You make it sound like I'm having a midlife crisis."

"Well, I wouldn't say that, but at Patrick's engagement brunch, you were pretty sad. I'm just suggesting that before you decide, you should see Lucas in your real life. Maybe the decision will be clearer. But you're right. If porn is Lucas' ambition, then you have a decision to make. Either you accept it or you cut your losses."

"Should I ask him to go to San Diego to meet my parents? They're back from their cruise around the time Lucas gets home from Vegas. Or, I know, let's have a party."

Kayla cringed. "Oh, sure. You could—"

"An engagement party for Tracey and Patrick." The idea was kind of perfect. Tracey and Kayla were college roommates, and Patrick had introduced me to Matt. As a new couple, my friends frequently hung out with Matt, Patrick and their friends, and our circles sort of merged. There were surprisingly very few close friends of mine who wouldn't be invited to such a party. Unfortunately, it also meant I'd need to invite Matt.

"Will you help plan it? I'll host and cover the expenses."

"Um. Are you sure you —?"

"It's perfect."

Kayla sighed. "Okay, let me talk to them and nail down a good date."

* * * *

Perfect is the enemy of good.

Kayla may have talked in circles when it came to my relationship with Lucas, but those were the words that had become my mantra. No doubt what Lucas and I had was good. I'd even go so far as to say great. I missed him like crazy, and he occupied nearly my every thought from the moment I woke up to the minute I went to sleep. Lucas and I needed to stop segregating our relationship from our real lives. I either loved and accepted Lucas as he was or I needed to let him go. Based on how much of a mopey bastard I'd been without him that week, the latter wasn't going to happen.

I decided to pick Lucas up from the airport and move forward with a real relationship test drive. No more denial. I couldn't just pick the parts of Lucas I loved and ignore the rest. I needed to see everything, without filters, rules and a highly controlled environment. With a deep sigh, I stashed my rose-colored glasses on the bedside table and created a Twitter account.

Tommy Bruiser's Twitter feed was more like Lucas than I expected — a lot of funny videos, memes and random pictures of him, some I remembered seeing, others I didn't. I paused at a video of him jacking off and recognized his Vegas hotel room. Knowing he shared something publicly when I thought he made it for me felt — well, not great. Renewed doubts surfaced...a lot of renewed doubts, not about Lucas, but about my ability to deal with his job. I thought the video proved he'd been thinking of me. It was one of the few things that I'd held on to during his trip that kept me sane. But maybe he just needed to get off? Maybe he hadn't been thinking of me at all?

With a sigh, I scrolled through our text exchange from his trip. The video had come with a message. *I miss you so much.* I closed my eyes and played it again with the volume turned all the way up. I focused on his labored breaths, his slight gasp while he fingered himself, the rough squelch of his lube-covered fingers. When he came, I smiled. He mumbled it, but there — on his final breath before he released — my name was on his lips.

Reassured, I persisted in my exploration. Next came Tommy's Instagram account and YouTube channel. I tried to check out something called Snapchat, but that shit confused the hell out of me. I might have accidentally sent twenty pictures of my thumb to who knows where.

By the time I needed to leave for the airport, I'd managed a thorough submersion into the world of Tommy Bruiser. Call it an animalistic instinct or deep insecurity, but the drive to mark my territory overwhelmed me. If I had to share a piece of Lucas with over two hundred thousand thirsty horndogs, then I at least wanted those horndogs to know Tommy Bruiser belonged to me.

A dozen perfect red roses in hand, I arrived at the airport. I paced in a small area outside the security checkpoint, itching to feel him in my arms. Big public displays weren't typically part of my repertoire. I smiled awkwardly as a strange woman demanded to know all about the 'lucky girl' I waited for. A year ago, I'd have fled to the parking lot, but something about Lucas made me wish I'd thought to make a sign, too. I wanted him to know I was all in, that I could do it — that I *would* do it, for him. I would let go of my inhibitions and all my insecurities and just be happy. Because, even a week apart had felt like I'd been missing something as vital to my existence as an organ.

I heard his voice, and my heart played hop-scotch in my chest. The crowd parted, and there he was. My Lucas. His head was tossed back mid-laugh, his blond hair tucked under a backward-facing hat. He wore skin-tight jeans with rips up the legs, a half tucked-in faded tank top and rainbow Vans. My mouth watered. *God, he's beautiful.*

Case, Robert and a third man I didn't recognize were with him. Case noticed me first, and he nudged Lucas, who glanced up and bestowed on me the brightest grin I'd ever seen him give. Pride surged through me. I'd put that smile on his face. No one else. Me. I felt like a goddamn superhero.

He screamed my name and came at me in a full sprint. I dropped the flowers to brace for his arrival and swept him into my arms, nearly losing my balance when he launched himself onto me. He wrapped his legs around my hips and molded his mouth to mine. A few people laughed and whooped, but I didn't care. I held on for dear life and kissed him until he'd had his fill and he slid to the ground.

"What are you doing here?" Another kiss and he playfully scraped his teeth along my jawline.

"I wanted to pick you up." I dipped to pick up his roses, brushed a few damaged petals out of the way and handed them to him. "Here. These are for you."

He brought them to his nose and inhaled. "Thank you. They're beautiful. You didn't have to pick me up. Case was gonna drop me off."

"Oh," I breathed and struggled to keep the disappointment off my face. Maybe I should have waited for him to call me?

"But I'm so thrilled you did. God, I missed you," Lucas said with too much alacrity.

"We texted every day."

Confusion clouded his face, and guilt twisted my gut. I'd been careful to respond to every message, but I couldn't deny I'd been succinct. I wasn't trying to be distant, but when I thought about what he was doing, it'd hurt.

"It wasn't the same."

"I know. I'm sorry, but I did miss you."

He nodded, read me and touched my cheek like he needed proof to confirm my presence. Goosebumps peppered my skin. God, I wanted him so much. I shored up my resolve. I would get over my issues.

Case, Robert and the other man waited a respectable distance, watching us. Case took my glance up as permission to approach. Robert followed while the third man lingered behind.

"Well, well. Looks like someone is ecstatic to be home. I trust you no longer need our ride services, Tommy?" Robert asked.

"No. Kyle came to pick me up. Wasn't that so sweet?"

The third man approached and cleared his throat. "Tommy, would you introduce me to your handsome beau?"

I reached my hand out to introduce myself but Lucas knocked it down. "No way, Ken. Not a word of this on the blog."

Ken huffed. "Oh, you do know how to ruin my fun. Think of the click bait — Tommy Bruiser has a bona fide sugar daddy."

All sorts of protective warnings flared in my body. "Now wait a goddamn minute —"

Lucas placed a hand on my shoulder and squeezed. "It's fine, babe. Ken is kidding. He's a porn blogger, and we have a mutually beneficial self-promoting relationship. He wouldn't dare aggravate me by publishing personal information without permission, not when I'm so generous to him and grant him exclusive access."

"An exclusive interview?" Ken's tone made me think that wasn't something Lucas — or Tommy, rather — did much. But his perfectly arched eyebrow didn't budge and neither did his forehead, so I couldn't be sure.

Man, Botox is some crazy shit.

"Yes, exclusive. But this and him" — Lucas pointed to me — "are off limits."

"You can mention me," I said quietly.

Lucas' eyes bugged out. "What? No, he can't."

"Yes. He can. Your fans should know about me — about us. Tell them if you want. I don't mind."

Lucas squirmed. "Are you sure?"

"Yeah, I'm sure. But no pictures — at least not of my face. I don't think any of my coworkers read porn blogs, but that's still a no...for now."

Ken regarded us like he'd smile if his face weren't frozen. "Well then...an interview. A couple interview, perhaps?"

"No," Lucas answered sharply. "An interview. I mention my boyfriend. No last names and Kyle doesn't participate."

I glanced at him, grateful that he understood the limits of my concession. We said our goodbyes and walked together to the car.

"You don't have to—" Lucas began.

"I know. I want to. If we're going to be together, I want to share it with the people in our lives. My friends, your friends, our families—even your fans. I don't want them thinking of you as single and available."

"For the record, I don't tell them I'm single or available."

"Yeah, but you post videos of yourself jerking off."

Lucas' jaw fell open, and I grimaced. "That came out harsher than I intended. I joined Twitter. I follow you now."

"Wait. Are you Bruce R Lover?" Lucas laughed, tucked his bag into the bed of the truck and climbed into the passenger seat.

"Yeah, how'd you know?"

"You liked a shitload of old pictures and videos on all my platforms, but none of the X-rated stuff. I checked out your profile on the plane and saw you only followed me. I thought I had a stalker. Damn, I owe Robert twenty bucks now. He said it was you, but I told him it couldn't be because my boyfriend doesn't want to know any details about my porn life."

I used the exit gate pay station as an excuse to devise any plausible justification for my one-eighty. No good could come of Lucas knowing the truth about my doubts, not once I'd made up my mind that I would find a way to deal with his job. "I'll pay off your debt."

"No way. That's the best bet I've ever lost. I love that you follow me. I love your screen name even more. Do you think I could post a video of us, one without your face?"

"Which video doesn't show my face?"

"The one I recorded before I left of you face-fucking me. I watched it a million times in Vegas — used it to get hard. You can see your dick, but there is nothing that would identify you. It's crazy hot."

"No," I answered sharply then softened my tone. "Those are personal. Speaking of personal, can you not send me videos you take for Tommy? Let's not blur the lines. When we have sex, that's for us. When you send me a video or pictures, it's important that it's for me. You can take videos for Tommy if you need to, but those aren't the ones I want."

Lucas smiled. "Sure thing, baby. My fans are going to flip. I can't wait to tweet about us. I want to share how fucking happy you make me every damn day."

I attempted to smile through my heartburn. Why did Lucas care so much what total strangers thought? "Well, let me see if I can one-up myself?"

"What?"

"I'm having a party for Kayla's brother, and I want you to meet my friends. I want to introduce you to everyone."

"What if they ask what I do?"

"Tell them whatever you'd like. I can't say I'm comfortable with it entirely, but I won't ask you to lie for me. This is what you do. It's something that I should get used to, and lying about it or asking you to lie about it isn't fair. I'm proud to be with you. Your job doesn't change that."

"Oh my God, who are you right now?"

"I'm trying, Lucas. I want this to work. I love you, and I know I've been a little off since we finished the project. I had some things to figure out. Be patient with me."

"I forgive you, but can you try to talk to me instead of shutting me out? I love you so much. What day is the party?"

"Next Saturday."

"Oh. In the evening, right?"

"Yeah. Starts around seven."

"Well, do you think you'd have time to go to lunch with me that day?"

"Sure. Kayla will set up for the party."

"Good. It's my dad's birthday. I'd like to introduce you to them, too — if you're okay with that."

I took a deep breath and threaded my fingers with his on his lap. Touching him comforted me instantly. "I'd love to, baby."

"Well, now that that is settled, take me to bed, lover. I've got a week's worth of fantasies stored up for you."

"Oh really?" I laughed. "Care to give me a preview of coming attractions?"

The excruciatingly slow trip made even slower by Lucas' filthy imagination tormented me with details of what Lucas had planned to do to me in that library.

Chapter Eleven

Lucas' father did not match the stodgy old former accountant that I'd pictured. On the contrary, he resembled Christopher Lloyd from *Back to the Future*. He looked nothing like Lucas, which I should have expected since Lucas was adopted, but nevertheless, surprised me. Looking at my own father was always like holding up a mirror set twenty-some years into my future.

Mr. Cass, or Greg, as he'd insisted I call him, greeted me warmly and made excuses for his wife, who apparently ran behind schedule more often than Lucas. We were ushered to the family room, featuring a large, worn leather sectional, a matching well-loved recliner and an expansive fireplace. The tables were full of knick-knacks and pictures of Lucas. Above the mantel, a painted portrait of a three- or four-year-old Lucas in a sailor outfit made me want to 'aww' aloud. Instead, I exchanged a look with Lucas to acknowledge how adorable I found it. Lucas blushed, plopped onto the sofa and flipped the footrest lever in a single movement I imagined he'd done a million times before.

Greg smiled broadly as though he'd caught our exchange and took a seat in the recliner across from Lucas. He followed my gaze to the mantel. "We had that painted from one of the pictures the adoption agency had of Lucas when we brought him home. Sit," Greg prompted me. I took a seat next to Lucas and didn't resist when he grabbed my hand and dragged it onto his lap.

"So, Lucas, how was Vegas? Mom said you had quite the time."

Lucas squeezed my hand before he answered. *Did he feel me tense?* "It was great, Dad. The part is fun, and I've got pages of scripted lines in this one. It's an *Ocean's Eleven* parody. We took a bunch of footage running through a casino, and Evan tripped and fell into a fountain. It was hysterical. I'm trying to talk Case into letting me put a blooper reel on YouTube. My fans will die."

"Well, it's good that you and Evan are getting along again."

"Yeah, we're cool now." Lucas shot me a pained face.

"The same Evan who I met at the studio? Why weren't you getting along?" I asked, uncertain I wanted the answer.

"Yeah. We used to date for a minute and a half like a year ago. We're fine now."

I tensed again and forced myself to exhale. Lucas shot his dad a panicked look anyone could have interpreted as a warning to change the subject immediately. I squeezed his hand. "It's fine, Lucas. We both have exes. You're probably going to meet Matt tonight."

Greg let out a hearty chuckle. "Oh boy, Kyle. Now you've stepped in it. Lucas has a possessive streak—always has. It's why we never added any more children to our family, Lucas would have put them in a box and sent them back to the orphanage. He couldn't bear it if he weren't the sole center of our world. I don't see him accepting any less from a boyfriend."

"That's not true," Lucas objected.

"What's not true?" A woman, as beautiful as Lucas but in the completely opposite way, appeared. She was sylphlike, with flowing jet-black hair and beige skin. Asian facial features were easily appreciated, but I couldn't pinpoint her ancestry. "Hi, darling. Sorry I'm running behind. This must be Kyle. I'm Joann, Lucas' mom." Joann approached and I stood then crouched my six-foot frame so she could embrace me.

"Well, aren't you lovely?" She smiled her approval and patted my chest. "So nice to meet you finally. Lucas hasn't stopped singing your praises since your first date."

"Thank you, ma'am. It's nice to meet you, too."

"Oh, Joann is fine. Greg, Lucas honey— Did you not offer Kyle a drink?"

"I'll get it." Lucas jumped up. "Beer, babe?"

I didn't usually drink so early in the day, but I accepted. A little alcohol to lubricate the conversation couldn't hurt, and Greg held a tumbler I suspected contained whiskey. "So"—Joann sat on the arm of her husband's chair—"tell us about yourself, Kyle."

I always hated that question. I usually froze, unable to think of a single interesting thing to share and ended up recounting how average I was. Since I wanted Joann to like me, I aimed for a more Lucas-approved answer. "Well, let's see. Born and raised in California. I work for a custom home builder and go to school part-time at Simmons. I'm spending most of my time now getting to know your son and planning my lake house."

"A lake house?" Joann's eyes widened. "That sounds interesting. Do you already have the land?"

Damn, now I sounded lame. "Just planning right now. I haven't been ready to pull the trigger. I have rough sketches, and I'm researching ideas for custom features that really make it a showcase of my work. I want each room to have something I designed and built myself. Right now, I have so many ideas that it's hard to stay focused."

Lucas returned with two beers and handed me one. He beamed at me, which I took as his approval. "Kyle is going to teach me how to work with my hands, so I can help." He leaned into me and positioned my free arm over his shoulder.

"I offered to teach you to take a proper measurement and use a table saw without losing a finger," I clarified.

"And cut drywall. For the garage."

"True," I said. "Lucas offered to help me finish my garage. It'd be nice to work out there all year-round without space heaters. They make me a little nervous."

Lucas' parents smiled their approval, but I worried about the optics. I wasn't crazy about Greg and Joann getting the impression I wanted to parent Lucas, because, I mean, who would be okay with that? Our age difference already made me self-conscious enough. Lucas' parents thinking of me as a perverted old man who jerked off to their son's porn before entrapping him in a relationship was my worst nightmare.

"Well, I'm glad you'll be learning from an expert. Do you camp, Kyle? Lucas begged us to join the Boy Scouts as a child but I was never comfortable with their

Christian slant. Plus, I suspected they wouldn't welcome Lucas. Even at five or six, he didn't march to the beat of anyone's drum but his own. I feared they might try to change him."

"I camped with my dad and uncles a few times. We're not big on roughing it, but I like to be outdoors. My dad is a retired mail carrier. I think he liked to spend his leisure time off his feet and out of the elements."

Greg laughed. "Well I sat at a desk all day, and I would agree."

We chatted for nearly an hour before Joann served lunch. We shared a pleasant meal full of stories of Lucas' youth. I genuinely liked Greg and Joann, and we bonded over my shared affection for their son.

Greg wasn't that different from my own dad — laid-back and a bit on the lazy side, content to let his wife do most of the entertaining. Although Joann and I were virtually the same age, it didn't seem that way. Perhaps I held an old-fashioned view, but I associated her grace and manner of speech and the way she doted on her husband and Lucas with women of my mother's generation, rather than my own. The age difference between Greg and Joann really was a non-issue, and their relationship gave me a better understanding of why Lucas remained unconcerned about ours.

After our meal, Lucas showed me around his old neighborhood, including a walk up to his elementary school.

"Swing with me." Lucas chuckled, then plopped down and pumped his legs.

I sized up the playset and the worn metal chains that secured the plastic seat to the fasteners. "My ass is too big for that."

"Is not," he said and stuck his tongue out to express his displeasure.

"Brat." I sat gingerly on the swing next to him and swayed back and forth without letting my feet leave the ground.

"Maybe I want you to spank me, Daddy," he teased and pumped his legs even higher, swinging like a pendulum.

"Save it for the bedroom, Lucas. This setting is…" I regarded our surroundings and shivered. "You'll make me feel like a perv."

"So, I can't talk you into fucking me on this playground. It'd be fun."

"Pretty sure I'm not getting turned on here."

"How about my old room?"

"Nope. Not if your parents are home."

"But I'm horny."

I huffed. "You're always horny."

"Seeing you at my parent's house, having lunch with them… They loved you. They wanted me to find someone to take care of me, and they know you will."

"I'm not trying to adopt you, Lucas."

"I know. That's not what I meant. Did I tell you my mom's half-Vietnamese?" He swung past me again, facing dead ahead.

"No. I don't think you mentioned it, but I thought she might have some Asian roots. Are you close to that side of your family?"

Lucas shook his head. "My grandparents were white. She's adopted too."

"Oh, wow. It's cool you have that in common."

"Three years ago, she found her biological family and she wants to spend some time over there. They plan to go—her and my dad."

A small change in Lucas' voice set the hairs on the back of my neck on end. "That's nice. Why'd she wait?"

"I didn't want her to go. In fact, I begged her not to."

"Why?" He swung by another few times, and I finally stood to get a better peek at his face. His cheeks were red from the wind, but he didn't look right. "Lucas, stop." I reached out to grab the chain and the swing jerked to a stop.

Lucas put his feet down and focused on the ground while digging a circle into the dirt with his shoe. I put a hand on his back to comfort him. He trembled under my touch. "It's hard to explain."

"Try me."

Finally, he met my eyes. "You don't know what it's like to not know a single soul you are biologically related to. My mom told me her hysterectomy was traumatic because it meant she'd never have biological children either. When I came out, she worried I'd give up on having kids someday. My mom and I used to talk about that a lot."

"So, if she meets her family—"

"Then I'll be the only one who doesn't have a biological relative."

"Oh, Lucas. I wish I could do something to take that feeling away from you. I can promise it won't change how they feel about you and tell you I'm here for you. Besides, who's to say you won't have your own kids someday?"

He gazed at me and smiled—a weak attempt at one anyway. "Someday is a long way off and it's not the same. My mom always said we had a special bond because we knew what it felt like to not know where you came from."

"Did you ever try to find your biological family?"

"My parents are enough for me. Besides, they'd never be as cool as my parents are. I'd just be disappointed." Lucas' brilliant eyes were red and blotchy, as though straining to hold back tears. A part of Lucas fell into place, a big part. The porn career, his fans... Maybe they all filled some missing piece for him. And I began to hope that, with time, perhaps I could fill it instead. Three years? The timing of his mother's discovery coincided with his time at Goldenboys. That couldn't be a coincidence. I wondered if it had started as a rebellion or a way to punish them. Or perhaps something less dramatic — a test to make sure they'd love him no matter what he did.

"Just because your mom wants to meet her family doesn't mean you're not enough for her."

"I know that."

"So, what is it then? Tell me."

"What if she moves there?"

"You think they would pick up and move to Vietnam? I just met them, but I don't see that happening. Even if they did stay for a while, you're an adult. You live on your own, take care of yourself now. It's not like you wouldn't see them again."

"You don't understand. What if she loves them?"

I interpreted his question to mean what if she loved them more than him. "I do, Lucas, more than you think. They were all you have, and I'm sure it's normal to be a little threatened by this, but your parents clearly adore you."

"I hate the thought of her meeting them. Literally, hate it. I'm a horrible person."

"Of course, you're not. What if you went with them?"

"No way," Lucas declared, and I knew without asking his parents had already made that suggestion, probably more than once.

"Come here." I tugged his sleeve until he stood, wrapped him in my arms and ran my fingers through his sweaty hair. "Love you." I kissed his forehead. He smiled at me, a little brighter than before. "You won't be alone, babe. I promise."

Lucas ran his hands under my shirt and tucked them into the waistband of my shorts. My heartbeat sped up with his warm touch. "Kyle, I need you. If not here, can we find someplace to get naked?"

I pulled back to search his face. His lower lip was tucked between his teeth, and he no longer appeared sad at all. Had Lucas always used sex to avoid his feelings? Was that part of his exhibitionism? A way to prove to people he wasn't unwanted? I wasn't sure, but I was more concerned about what was going on in his head than in his pants. "We should get home soon. The party is in a few hours, and we both need to change."

"We have time."

I checked my watch. "Probably, but are you sure…?" I peered around, and he grabbed my arm. He led me to a corner of the building and pushed my back against the wall. "What are you—?"

The words were cut off by his tongue shoved down my throat. He moved his mouth strong and aggressive over mine, and the brick wall scraped against my back. Before I knew it, his hand was massaging over my cock, attempting to coax it to life.

"Lucas…" I whined.

"I'm going to suck your cock right here," Lucas whispered in my ear. He rocked back, his face issuing a challenge. I glanced around at the empty playground.

A flood of 'what ifs' successfully dulled my enjoyment of his ministrations.

Lucas flashed his arousal, but undeterred, winked and sank to his knees. "C'mon, please."

Everything in me screamed that it was wrong. It was the wrong place, the wrong time. We'd just been talking about his mother. He was in a weird headspace. It all seemed so damn inappropriate. But I wanted him. I wanted his mouth on me and I just once wanted to be the guy who hadn't left the library cubical, who didn't worry beyond the moment. He flicked his crystal-blue eyes, filled with desire, up to me and lifted his hand to rest over mine, which had tightened over my belt buckle. It was there, through his blond lashes, that I found permission to let go.

Chapter Twelve

Lucas was quiet on the drive back. Too quiet. And he'd made it clear he didn't want to talk about it. The lack of knowing was eating at me.

While Lucas dressed for the party, I wore a path between the couch and the kitchen. Lucas was an exposed nerve, and I was about to douse him with ice cold water in the form of all my friends and an ex-boyfriend. The engagement party was going to be a minefield, but any suggestion that he sit it out would have been taken wrongly. Before I could decide how to approach the situation, Lucas appeared and short-circuited my brain again.

He'd styled his natural messy blond hair with product that tamed his waves into purposeful golden curls. He wore charcoal fitted slacks and a light pink button-down shirt and a black bowtie. His extensive collection of Vans had been replaced with a pair of classic black leather dress shoes. He'd accessorized with a pink-faced silver watch, square silver cufflinks and a matching tie tack. Despite being twenty-three,

Lucas could pass for a teenager in his standard attire. Tonight, he could have walked off the cover of *GQ*. I was in awe of him. "You look incredible, babe."

"Yeah, I clean up pretty good, don't I?" He did a little turn for me.

"You do." I eyed the shorts and T-shirt I'd worn to his parents'. "Guess we'd better get home so I can change too."

* * * *

As expected, Kayla had already finished setting up and gone home to change. I left Lucas watching television alone and re-emerged to appreciative whistles from both Kayla and Lucas. I didn't have time to fret about the first meeting of my best friend and boyfriend. As much as I talked about them to each other, neither should've needed an introduction.

Less than twenty minutes later, my house overflowed with people.

When Matt arrived, I sipped my bourbon and Coke and continued speaking to Patrick as though I hadn't noticed. Even though I had no residual feelings toward the man, his presence put me on edge. Kayla would accuse me of being angry about the way things had ended, but that wasn't it. Although Matt could have waited for the bedsheets to cool a little before dating again, he did at least wait until we'd agreed to end things. It gave me a smidge of satisfaction to know rebound-man hadn't lasted longer than a few weeks.

"Hey, Matt." Patrick stood and hugged my ex warmly. "Good to see you, man. Thanks for coming."

"Anything for you. Congrats on the engagement." Matt scanned the room like he was prone to do. His gaze paused momentarily at Lucas, who was across the room refreshing his drink, before swinging back toward me. "Hey, Kyle. Good to see you."

I offered my hand, which he used to tug me into a friendly hug. I didn't think anything of it—Matt had always been a hugger—but Lucas appeared out of nowhere and cleared his throat, prompting Matt to make room for him.

"Hey, baby," I greeted him with a kiss on his cheek and smiled at Matt slightly more smug than I ought to. "Babe, this is Matt. Matt and Patrick used to work together. Matt, this is my boyfriend, Lucas Cass."

Lucas offered his hand, which even though he was clearly befuddled, Matt shook. Lucas slipped his hand away from Matt's grasp and, smiling, used it to stir his drink before taking a slow sip.

I didn't know if people expected a scene, but our little group doubled in size following the introduction. Matt was more reserved than usual, but he stayed put and engaged with Lucas and me occasionally as part of the group, like I had with many dates he'd brought to group functions. I took a seat on the arm of the sofa, and Lucas seized the opportunity to lean against my lap. The conversation continued, and I joked with my friends while Lucas touched me at will. All that desensitization training must have paid off because I barely noticed his slow caress of my knee and thigh until my pants grew tighter. I alone seemed to notice Matt's agitation. He had a good poker face, but I knew his tells.

Patrick and Tracey excused themselves to circulate, and the group dispersed. Kayla did an admirable job of keeping the crowd mingling and refilling glasses, while I mostly kept an eye on Lucas, who had relocated to his own seat when a spot opened. The remaining group drank and ate, and the conversation remained lively. Lucas sought stories about me from my friends and charmed them with stories of his own. He was affectionate and attentive as usual, and no one in the room would have doubted we were a happy couple. I hadn't remembered how much that feeling meant to me.

"Are you Kyle?" a voice asked from behind me. I turned and greeted a guest, a somewhat effeminate black man I didn't recognize.

"I am. Nice to meet you, um…"

"I'm Simon, Tracey's cousin. Kayla pointed you out. I just wanted to say I love your house. I'm an interior designer, and you have a great eye."

"Hi, Simon. I'm Lucas, Kyle's boyfriend." Lucas thrust out his hand. I choked on my bourbon. Apparently, I wasn't the only one who needed to mark my territory.

Simon smiled at us, equally as amused, and took a small step back to give Lucas room to attach himself to my side. I laughed at Lucas and shook my head. He had no reason to worry. Lucas relaxed, and I could appreciate the moment he realized he'd needed to chill out. "Simon, did you notice the floating mantel on the fireplace? Kyle installed the steel supports himself because the stone is extremely heavy. Isn't it gorgeous? Let me show you around. Kyle needs to relieve Kayla of her hostess duties anyway."

"Oh, I'd love a tour. Thank you." Lucas ushered Simon off, and I could hear him tell the story of the eccentric woman who'd sold me the stone.

I watched Lucas until he disappeared into the other room. When I glanced up, Matt stood in front of me. "What gives, Kyle?"

"Huh?"

"That kid. Are you seriously dating him?"

"Don't be rude. Yes, Lucas and I are dating. Did you miss the part where I introduced you to him?"

"Where did you meet him? Grindr?"

I rolled my eyes. "When have I ever hooked up with an app, Matt? C'mon. We met at school."

"You're lying. I know who he is, Kyle. Half the men here know who he is and the other half are straight."

I should have been prepared for it, but I wasn't. *How famous is Tommy, anyway?* "I told you his name, so I imagine you should know who he is."

"Don't be cute, Kyle. Is this some sort of financial arrangement? Are you trying to make me jealous? Do you know what people are saying about you right now?"

I couldn't believe it. Matt diminishing Lucas as a Grindr hookup was terrible enough, but to suggest Lucas was an escort rose my blood pressure enough that I swore I could feel it pump through my body and hear it whoosh between my ears. *Good God, was he always so full of himself?*

I clenched my fist around his biceps, dragged him to the extra bedroom and shut the door. "He's not a hooker, Matt. He's my boyfriend. Are you trying to ruin our perfect record of civility in public? 'Cause, if so, by all means, keep it up."

He kept it up.

The whole story makes me sound like a total Neanderthal, so I'll summarize and say he absolutely shoved me first.

My right fist connected with bone seconds before Kayla grabbed my shoulder and yanked me backward, causing my left fist to meet dead air. "What the hell are you doing? Matt, go see if Tracey and Patrick need anything," Kayla barked, her nails buried deeply into my skin.

Still shaken and holding his jaw, Matt obeyed. He knew Kayla well enough not to argue. Before I knew it, I was in my backyard being publicly scolded.

"What the ever-loving fuck, Kyle? Who are you?" Kayla seethed. "I don't know what is happening with you, but clearly this thing with Lucas has to end."

"But, Matt—" I objected.

"Matt what? He hit you first? He started the same crap he always does. So what? You hit someone, Kyle. This. Is. Not. You. Do you hear me? I know you think you love that kid, but he's a *kid*, Kyle. You're not. You're a forty-year-old man, and I'm worried about you.

"You spent the entire evening babysitting Lucas when you should have been helping me. Sure, he's hot, but c'mon. You can't tell me it didn't embarrass you to have him sit on your lap and paw at you like he's a puppy in front of your friends. Then to top it off, you start a fight at my brother's engagement party? I know Lucas' dick probably rocked your world, but my God, you see my point, right? This is why I threw the party with you, so you would see Lucas doesn't belong, so you would know it's time to end it. I can't deal with you like this anymore. Just cut it off already. This insanity has to end."

My mind spun from Kayla's verbal assault, and my chest clenched painfully as I searched for the words to defend myself. I loved Kayla, but she was…just wrong.

Or jealous or something. We'd had plenty of disagreements before. I'd even stopped speaking to her for a day or two, but in all our years of friendship, she'd never intentionally hurt me.

I never thought in a million years when I found 'the one' she'd make me choose between him and our friendship, and I never thought it'd be such an obvious decision. I closed my eyes to blink back tears. Flashes of our friendship ran through my head. Surely she would see how impossible she was being. I opened my eyes to tell her that it didn't matter if Lucas fit in with our friends, he fit with me, and she needed to back off, but when I opened my mouth to speak, the screen door slammed shut and a blond ran in the opposite direction.

"Lucas," I cried and took off after him, my heart threatening to pound through my chest. A crowd formed at the back door, so I detoured to the side gate instead to save time.

"Kyle, just let him go."

Kayla's voice didn't slow me down. If I couldn't make it right with Lucas, I would never forgive her. And, for once, I meant it.

I met up with Lucas on the front porch. His face was wet. Instinctively, I reached for him.

"Don't," he said, jerking his arm away and taking my heart along with it. He wiped his face with the back of his sleeve and sniffled. "I forgot I don't have my car. Go inside so I can wait for my Uber alone. I think we've made enough of a scene for one night."

"Lucas," I pleaded, "let me explain."

"Explain? Explain what, Kyle? You and Matt weren't exactly quiet. I heard everything. *Everybody* heard everything. Your friends think I'm a rentboy. So what?

You think I haven't been offered money by fans? That people don't see a stripper or a porn star and think all sex work is the same? It happens all the time. And I couldn't care less, but can you honestly tell me that it doesn't matter to you? That the party wasn't some big test in your mind to see if I'm worth lowering your high standards?"

"Matt's an asshole."

"Oh, and that is why you hit him?"

I recoiled. The last comment Matt had sent me into a blind rage and my juvenile response... "Lucas..." I pleaded for mercy.

Lucas rolled his eyes. "He threatened to tell everyone my dirty little secret. You didn't really answer Matt's question, though. How excited will you be to finally spend the holidays with your boyfriend? I mean, with your *whore*? Guess you're really slumming it with me, huh?"

"Lucas, stop. Matt knows how to push my buttons. We had an ongoing feud over the holidays. It has nothing to do with you."

"Oh, so you're cool with your parents and everyone in there knowing that you're dating a guy who fucks on camera for money?"

His volume was loud enough that I was pretty sure my neighbors three streets over knew. I couldn't help but shush him.

Lucas sneered. "You're ashamed of that, aren't you? And therefore, you're ashamed of me. And that's why you hit him. The thing that kills me, Kyle, is that I never asked you to do this. I would have dodged any questions, but someone asked if I was Tommy and you told me it didn't matter to you. Why not say you weren't ready? I was fine with that plan. I'd much rather have lied about my job than have everyone in your life know you're embarrassed by me."

"It does bother me, Lucas. I told you from the beginning it bothered me. I also told you I'm working on it. I just don't want anyone thinking I'm not enough for you. I didn't think."

Lucas wiped his eyes again to hide his tears. I would have set myself on fire if I could have taken away the pain I'd caused. I tried again to touch him, but he ripped his arm away. "Everything you said about being proud to be with me... Why didn't you tell me Matt was some fancy lawyer? I bet you were never embarrassed to bring him home to meet your parents."

"God! Lucas, please stop. Matt doesn't mean anything to me. I love you. And I'm sorry I reacted poorly to Matt's threat. I couldn't listen to him say horrible things about you."

"That's my point, Kyle. He wasn't saying horrible things about me. He said I was a sex worker. Maybe he was wrong about the details, but I am a sex worker. I have sex for money. It doesn't make me a horrible person."

"Lucas, tell me how to fix us."

"You don't, Kyle. You can only change you and your attitude about my work. There is nothing wrong with me, and we're pretty perfect together. But even if I quit porn today, I would still be an ex-porn star, and you would still have to come to terms with that. I can't be with someone who makes me feel ashamed for being myself." He glanced up as a car turned onto my street. "That's my Uber."

"Lucas, please don't leave. I'm sorry.

"I know, baby. I need some space, and I think you should deal with your friends in there alone."

"Let me take you home at least."

"You can't leave the party you're hosting. Kayla's right. We did let her do most of the work. Give my best to Patrick and Tracey. Call me after everyone's gone, and we'll talk some more." A horn honked, and for a split second, I didn't want to wave the driver away. Was I ashamed to be with him? I looked at him and found my answer.

"I'm coming over tonight. We can finish talking. I am proud to be with you, Lucas. I don't care what Kayla or Matt or anyone else thinks."

Lucas half-smiled with doubt etched all over his face. "But *I* care what *you* think. I'll be home. If it gets late, I'll leave a key under the mat for you. Just wake me up."

"Okay. I'm sorry…about everything. I love you."

"I love you too. We'll talk later."

Even though Kayla had clearly done damage control, the crowd granted me a wide berth as I made my way toward my bedroom. Kayla was in the dining room, where we'd set up the bar, mixing a drink. She watched me, her face still readily communicating her anger. I couldn't deal with her judgment.

My room was a vibrating coffin. The music had been turned up, probably to drown out Lucas' and my argument. I threw myself on my bed, yanked a pillow over my head and screamed.

The door clicked open and a wave of Taylor Swift's *Look What You Made Me Do* flooded in. I wondered who I needed to murder.

"The bed looks ridiculous there."

"Ugh. Matt, give it a rest," I said into my pillow.

"Kyle, sit up. I brought you a bourbon."

I lowered the pillow and gave him the dirtiest look I could manage that would still end with me holding that drink.

"Why did you move it? You never changed anything in all the time we were together," Matt asked.

Thoughts of Lucas made me smile—stupidly, I'm sure. "You sure you want to know?" I tossed back the bourbon and let the burn subside.

Matt followed my gaze behind him and the clear line of sight the new bed position shared with the shower.

He groaned, "Never mind," sat on the bed and leaned against the footboard.

He stared at me for several minutes with a too-familiar stony expression. I used to call it his lawyer face because he claimed to use it with clients he knew had held back meaningful information.

"Stop it," I said, instantly pissed that I'd broken first.

He smirked.

Bastard.

"I'm sorry I ran my mouth," he said.

"I'm not sorry I hit you."

He rolled his eyes, stretched his legs on the bed and kicked my shin. "Yes, you are."

"You deserved it."

"I know. So, Tommy Bruiser, huh? In a million years, I never saw this coming."

"His name is Lucas."

"Okay, fine...Lucas, then. You want to walk me through how you fell in love with a teenaged, cocky-ass power-top?"

I snickered at power-top and part of me wanted to tell Matt precisely what Lucas looked like when he called me daddy, but that wouldn't be any different than

Lucas posting our private videos to Twitter. Still, I smiled with the thought.

"What?"

"He's twenty-three."

"So."

"You said teenaged, but he's twenty-three."

"Kyle, you're forty."

"So?"

"Cut the shit. Would you talk to me, please? Kayla is going to be no help here. She'll just pull her double-speak. I know you arguably as well, and I want to help. Explain it to me. I know it's not his dick. You've never been a size queen."

I raised my eyebrow, smirked and waited for Matt to acknowledge the glaring opportunity he'd set up for me to crack a small-dick joke at his expense. His eye roll and a playful 'fuck you' sufficed.

"I don't know what you want me to say? It all sounds horribly cliché. The sex is amazing. He makes me feel good about myself. He gets me to try new things. I miss him when he's not around. He laughs at my jokes. He makes me laugh. He's smart and ambitious and curious. He likes for me to teach him shit. I just love him."

"You had me at the 'sex is amazing'," Matt cracked.

"Why do I bother?"

"Kyle, lighten up. You've always been too uptight about sex."

"I don't remember sex being a problem between us."

Matt huffed in disagreement, and I wanted to punch him again.

"What the fuck does that mean?" I asked.

"It means exactly what it sounds like. I'm not surprised you think there were no problems in our sex life because you never asked."

"Well, I'm sorry you were so unhappy with our sex life. Maybe you ought to have said something."

"Kyle, you weren't trying to hear about my issues. The truth is we're both nice guys, so it worked until we tried to make it more. But when you hit me tonight... I think that is the first time I felt any real passion coming from you."

"We fought all the time."

"No, we argued about appearances. How it would look if we spent the holidays apart or if I didn't get rid of my place. We never argued because our schedules were crazy or you missed me. We didn't argue because it'd been weeks since we'd had sex. We cared about each other, but I think we both knew something was missing. We didn't have a tenth of the passion you showed toward Lucas."

I stared at him blankly. "That's not..." *Fuck, I can't deny he's right.* "I'm sorry."

"I know. Me too. And I did love you, Kyle. And I know you loved me too. I wish I'd had the balls to speak up sooner. You don't know how often I think about the first time you broke up with me. You were so right. I resisted living together because I knew I didn't want the same things as you did. Maybe if we'd just ended it then, we could have stayed friends."

"Then why did you push so hard to get back together? Why move in here?"

"I don't know. Honestly, you were the first guy I'd dated who'd broken up with me. We mostly got along, and like I said, you're such a good guy. I felt like I was the one with the problem, and you know I hate admitting I'm not good at something. I just thought eventually if I stuck with it and we lived together like you wanted to, it'd finally click for me and we'd be on the same page. But you kept upping your expectations, and we'd break up then I felt like a failure again. It was a vicious cycle, and for what it's worth, I'm sorry.

"Anyway, this isn't about us. I didn't mean to mess things up for you with Lucas. I was surprised and hurt. I think I'd convinced myself you weren't capable of more. You were too level-headed to make out in public or be irrationally jealous. Even when I'd bring new guys around, you were always so polite — like it didn't bother you to see me with someone new even though we'd broken up literally days before. Seeing you with Lucas, it dawned on me you were fully capable all along. You just didn't feel it toward me. You have to admit, I wasn't the only one pretending."

"And I didn't think I could feel worse."

"Forget it. I've forgiven you, and Lucas isn't even mad. He's hurt. I'm sure it's not anything you can't fix with a leather whip and a sling."

I growled. "What the fuck?"

"Why are you mad? I'm the one who has to find a new favorite porn star. Do you know how many times I've jerked off to him? In this very bed? I have to buy new sex toys. It's very upsetting. But seriously, did you put a sling in the house? I have to know."

"I don't know what you're talking about."

Matt stared incredulously at me. "Holy shit. You've never seen his porn, have you?"

"I don't have to watch him. I get the real thing, which is not anything like his porn, I'm sure. And it's none of your business."

"See what I mean? Uptight. Well, since I'm clearly in the running for the ex-boyfriend of the year, can I give you some unsolicited advice?"

"Could I stop you?"

Matt rolled his eyes and kicked my shin again. "First, put Kayla in her place. I know you love each other, but your relationship is getting a tad codependent. Second, don't tell Lucas what he wants to hear. Trust him to handle the truth about how you feel. It's the only way you're going to get past it. Think about it. The day I moved out for good, you told me you'd wasted your thirties on me. I know what you're after in life, Kyle. Don't waste another decade with the wrong guy."

"I don't know if I can get past the porn. I hate knowing he's with other men."

"Then trust him enough to tell him that. You're probably analyzing everything he says and does, instead of just talking to him about it."

A knock on the door preceded Kayla's entrance. "Hi," she said meekly. "The party broke up. Patrick's waiting by his car to say goodbye, Matt. He said he would call Kyle later. Can I come in?"

Matt flashed a sympathetic smile and patted my leg. "Don't worry about what I said earlier. Nobody was saying shit about you and Lucas except me. The truth is that we are all jealous as fuck."

He paused to hug Kayla on his way out. "It was good to see you, Kayla. You did a great job tonight. Sorry we ruined your party."

She smiled and nodded. I had never seen her so unsure of herself. After Matt closed the door behind him, she waited until the front door closed too. "Kyle, I'm sorry."

"I know. I'm sorry I left everything up to you. Lucas had a weird day, and I didn't feel right leaving him alone."

"About Lucas…"

"Before you finish that thought, I need to tell you something—"

She paused, "Okay."

"Don't," I said.

"Don't?"

"Yeah. Don't finish your thought. I think you made your feelings toward Lucas plenty clear, and I'm genuinely sorry that you feel that way, but our continued friendship depends on you not saying whatever is in your head aloud."

"You don't want my opinion? I'm your best friend. You always want my opinion."

"Not about Lucas. I don't need your opinion about something I've made up my mind about. I love him, and we're going to work things out however we need to do that. I'm not ending it with him."

"So, you're what? You're going to marry the twenty-year-old with daddy issues and a big dick? This is going to be Matt all over again. Why can't you just admit that it's not working?"

I heaved a sigh. "Damn it, Kayla, I warned you. Why can't you leave it alone? It's my life, my relationship. I think you should go."

She gasped. "You're kicking me out?"

"Yes. I'm planning to spend the night at Lucas' anyway."

"They allow sleepovers in the dorms now?"

"Jesus Christ, Kayla. You can't help yourself, can you? Fucking go home."

I stood, ignoring her rant, and tucked clothing into an overnight bag. I opened the bedside drawer and made a show of putting lube and condoms into the bag, even though Lucas had supplies at his house. Childish? Possibly. But it shut her up.

"Fine. I'm leaving."

"Good."

"I'm not cleaning up the mess."

"That's fine. You did all the setup. I planned to clean anyway."

"That's not what I meant." She stared at me pointedly.

When I didn't respond, she huffed, spun on her heels and slammed the front door on her way out. Alone finally, I grabbed enough clothes for a few days, threw any food that would spoil into the fridge and grabbed my keys.

Chapter Thirteen

When my texts went unanswered, I used the spare key Lucas had left under his doormat to enter his apartment. If his mood at all matched the mess, I was in real trouble. His clothes were strewn on the floor and an empty bottle of tequila, spilled salt and a handful of lime rinds covered the coffee table. A container of ice cream had leaked its contents all over a pile of mail.

Guilt-ridden, I wiped up the mess, picked up his clothes and hung them over the chair and tossed the ice cream, tequila bottle and limes into the trash. With a deep sense of dread, I fixed a glass of iced water, rooted around for ibuprofen and searched for my man, praying he wasn't in as bad a shape as I imagined.

I found him on top of his covers, curled in the fetal position and hugging a pillow. The rhythmic rise and fall of his chest alleviated any real concern. With a remorseful sigh, I set the water and pills near his bed, dragged a trashcan closer and covered him with the blanket. After removing my own clothes, I joined him.

My thoughts raced as I hugged him toward me and kissed his neck. He stirred but didn't wake.

I needed another twenty-four — or a million — hours in my happy bubble. I half-wished I'd thought to pack the rose-colored glasses. They'd certainly come in handy. Lucas' skin was warm against mine, and with each breath, my chest ached. The night replayed in my head on a continuous loop. When Lucas had accused me of being ashamed of him, I'd never been so devastated. Ashamed seemed too harsh, but I certainly wasn't proud of what he did for a living either. When confronted with Lucas' job, I had to constantly remind myself that I could love Lucas and not love what he did for a living. No one loved everything about their partner, right? But in retrospect, it seemed like semantics. Whatever part of Lucas found pride in doing porn, whatever caused him to choose that industry for his career, that part of Lucas I needed to understand. And once I understood it, then maybe we had a real shot at forever.

In the morning, Lucas woke me. "Kyle, babe. Let go. I need to piss." He shook me, and I loosened my grip. He practically sprinted to the bathroom.

I sat up, leaned against the headboard and waited for him to return. The toilet flushed, and he turned on the water to brush his teeth.

I heard Lucas rummage through his bathroom. "Shit. Where is it?"

"If you're searching for your Advil, I brought it in here. There's water too."

Lucas returned, appearing haggard. He fought with the bottle cap for a while before he let me help him. I retrieved three pills and handed them over. He swallowed them in one gulp and crawled back into bed.

"Do you want coffee? Dry toast?"

He groaned and tugged the blanket over his head. I took that as a no.

"Come here." I beckoned him with a hand on his hip. He rolled over and laid his head on my stomach, snuggling into me.

I laced my fingers through his hair, which crinkled from the dried product. He'd never looked or smelled worse, and I still fought the urge to kiss him.

He slept it off in my arms for hours. By noon, my stomach protested the lack of food. Lucas stirred. "Sorry," I said.

Lucas rolled away to stretch. "You must be hungry."

"I am. Go back to sleep. I can wait."

Lucas sat up and, swaying slightly, found his bearings.

"Feeling any better? You should drink more water." I reached past him to grab the glass. "Here."

"Thanks," Lucas said meekly and took a careful sip.

"Think you can eat? How 'bout an English muffin?"

Lucas nodded.

"Coming right up." I hopped out of bed and made my way to the kitchen. I fixed Lucas' muffin and a more substantial sandwich for me. I brewed coffee and met him back in the bedroom.

"Do you want it in here or do you want to try to get up?"

Lucas grimaced and let his upper half fall dramatically back to the mattress. Ignoring the theatrics, I placed his food on the bedside table and took a seat on the bed to eat my sandwich.

A few minutes later, he reached for his plate and tried to sit up. "I guess we need to talk, huh?"

"Not now." I picked up his muffin and brought it to his lips. "Eat."

He took the muffin and picked at it while avoiding my eye contact.

"We'll have plenty of time later, because... Lucas, look at me." I waited for him to meet my eyes. "I'm not going anywhere."

He attempted to hide his reaction with a nibble of bread. I returned his smile anyway. "I love you," I added.

"I love you too."

"Finish that and I'll help you shower. We have some homework to do today."

He peaked his eyebrow and took a sip of coffee.

"I realized in all our porn research we failed to get all the perspectives we were asked to."

"But we got a nine and a half out of ten."

"Well, we examined the industry from the perspective of the consumer, the government, the gay community at large, the performers and the studio and site owners."

"Yeah, so who did we miss?"

"Yours, Lucas. I missed yours."

Lucas beamed at me. "I guess that was a pretty major oversight, wasn't it?"

"Yeah. And I had this awesome opportunity to hear about what you love about doing what you do. If only I had asked about it instead of guessing."

Lucas smiled even brighter, "I thought you'd never ask."

"I'm sorry," I said.

"I knew you were trying to figure it out. You probably think it has to do with my mom, don't you? Or being adopted? Some missing hole in my life I can only fill with sex?"

I blushed. *Damn, he has my number.* "Maybe. Is that why you stopped talking about it with me?"

Lucas nodded. "I tried to open up to you about something unrelated, and you kept looking at me like you wanted to fix me. I don't need a daddy to make it better, Kyle. I have a great dad. It's not that deep. The daddy play is just a submissive kink."

I laughed. "I hear Tommy has many kinks."

Lucas smiled. "You watched my scenes finally?"

"No, I want to watch them with you. Matt can be counted among your biggest fans. I think he owns your dildo."

Lucas' face scrunched up. "Yikes. That's weird."

I burst into laughter. "Yes, it is. So, you up for a porn marathon?"

"As long as you don't expect to fuck me. Not a good day to bottom. I feel like a truck hit me."

"I don't see myself getting aroused by your scenes. But I do think I should know more about your sex kinks than my ex does."

"Oh, trust that you absolutely do."

"Then school me in porn from your perspective. I'm ready to learn from the master, and after we've considered this six ways to Sunday, I'll tell you honestly if I can deal with it."

"And if you can't, then I'll stop."

I gasped, "You would?"

"Yes. I need to finish the commitment I made to Case — two more scenes — but if you approach this with a genuinely open mind and it's still a deal breaker for us to be together, then I will stop filming. I can be stubborn too, Kyle. But I want to be with you, and while I love porn, I don't love it more than you.

"In Vegas, Robert suggested they may want me to work part-time on the marketing team. They need help to find new models, and the new ones always need social media brand coaching. There are ways for me to be in the business behind the camera. Case and Robert are talking about starting a cam site in a few years, which will have a full-time marketing person. I have options. *We* have options. I think there's more room for compromise than we've considered."

"You're not giving me much motivation here."

"I don't need to. I trust you want me to be happy, and if you can give me your blessing on it, then you will. And if you can't, it's not because you don't want to. I don't need to manipulate you, and even if I wanted to, it wouldn't work. You'd pretend as long as you could, then we would end. All I really needed was for you to open your mind and try to see it how I do."

I took a deep breath. "It's sort of remarkable how well you get me."

Lucas smiled and batted his eyelashes. "I'm more than a pretty face."

"So where do we start?"

"First, I want to shower with you."

"I thought we were going to dive right in."

"No. The last time we were together left a lot to be desired. I think you brought up my mother during a pretty fantastic blow job. You owe me a do-over."

"I thought a truck hit you."

"I can manage to let you apologize with your mouth on my dick."

"Toppy bastard." I stood, and a hard smack landed on my ass. I twisted to see Lucas' most wicked smile yet. *Obscene.* His smile was still obscene.

"Yep. Now go start the shower and wait for me on your knees. And don't give me any of your crap about being too old to kneel or I'll shove this thing all the way to the back of your throat. Cock worship is done on one's knees. Kill me if I ever get too old to do it properly."

I hesitated.

"Kyle, trust me." Lucas smiled. "Just try it."

Nervously, I obeyed.

I closed my eyes and let the water rain down on me. Lucas slid the curtain aside and stepped in, momentarily interrupting the flow. I shivered with anticipation.

"Good," he praised me. "Now keep your eyes closed and clasp your hands behind your back."

I did, and the tip of Lucas' finger swiped the seam of my lips. "Open your mouth," he commanded in a voice much deeper than his usual tone. I let my jaw fall slack and shifted my weight to alleviate the pain in my knees.

"Good," Lucas said and threaded my hair between his fingers, tilting my head back. The hard, smooth texture of his cock brushed across my cheek. My dick began to respond, although the absurdity kept my head out of the game.

"Lucas...?" I hedged.

"Shh. Do you feel how hard I am?" Lucas asked, and I nodded. "Answer me."

"Yes."

"Yes, what?"

I smiled. It was ridiculous, but I couldn't deny that Lucas being turned on got my dick hard too. "Yes, Sir."

"That's better." Lucas lifted his shaft so it rested on my face. The length of him ran from my chin to my forehead. God, his cock amazed me. It smacked against my face, harder than I anticipated. Then he left it lying there. "God, Kyle, you look so good on your knees for me. My cock is longer than your face. Do you know that? I like looking at it, thinking about how deep into your throat it's going to be." He grabbed my throat and squeezed lightly. "Swallow for me," he commanded and tightened his grasp. "You are going to be a good boy for me and take every inch. It's going to feel like you can't breathe, and your throat is going to spasm like that on my cock. It's going to feel amazing for me, baby. When you start to panic, I want you to think about how much pleasure you're giving me and let it happen. Do you hear me?"

"Yes, Sir."

"Good boy. Do you want to give me pleasure?"

"Yes, Sir."

"Good. Your body was made to give me pleasure, Kyle. Your ass. Your mouth. Every part of you was made for me. Do you understand?"

I swallowed. My cock ached painfully, and the delay was making me even more self-conscious. "Yes, Lucas. Do it." The words, full of desperation and longing, didn't sound like me.

"When I'm ready, baby. Soon. I'm going to take my pleasure from you, don't you worry. But first, you're going to stand up for me and wash me. After you wash me, I want you to lick my abs, because I know how much you love them. You'll cover every inch with your tongue then I'll put you back on your knees."

I unclasped my hands to stand. "Oh, no. No hands, Kyle."

"How can I wash you?"

Lucas smiled evilly and grabbed his loofah by the wooden handle. He poured soap on it. "Open up," he commanded and tucked the wooden end in my mouth.

With considerable effort, I contorted my body to wash him from head to toe. When I finished, he demanded I drop the loofah and squat to take my reward. The water cooled, and Lucas nudged the faucet off while I licked side to side over each ripple. The cooling air engaged another sense in the overwhelmingly erotic experience. My erection returned with a vengeance. By the time he'd guided me to my knees, my leaking cock throbbed and I desperately needed him to use me.

He pushed his way into my gaped mouth and every neuron in my brain fired, commanding me to brace my hands on his legs and slow the intrusion — but I didn't. I peered up at him and opened my mouth wider. I kept my hands clasped firmly behind me. Lucas pushed the tip of his cock into the back of my mouth. My gag reflex kicked in, but Lucas stroked my cheek and reminded me to breathe as he pulled out then eased back in, a slow sensual glide across my tongue and the roof of my mouth.

A few moments later, he moaned loudly and breached beyond my mouth, kicking off violent spasms in my throat. I started to panic but Lucas let me hear his pleasure.

"Fuck. Such a good boy for me. Yeah. That's it." He pumped his hips and clasped my hair to keep me at the right angle. It hurt and was amazing all at the same time. I gagged repeatedly, but he kept going. "That's it, baby. Every time you fight it I get closer to giving you my load."

I tried to suck in a breath but couldn't. My instincts kicked in, but when I jerked back, Lucas held me tighter, using me as an object but lavishing me with praise. "You feel so amazing, baby. Remember you were made for this. You were made to suck my cock. Breathe through your nose for me. That's it. So good for me. God. Do you want it, Kyle? Do you want my creamy load down your throat? You take my dick so good, baby. Yeah. Suck it, baby. Work for it. Show me how much you want it."

And oh my God, his filthy mouth killed me. I wanted to touch myself so badly, but I didn't risk interrupting Lucas' pleasure. I wanted him to use me. I loved being at his mercy and my inability to get release condensed all my pleasure like a tensely coiled spring. I groaned around his thick shaft.

Lucas yanked my hair back sharply and pushed his full length into my mouth. "Now, baby," Lucas barked, and my hand flew to my cock.

My orgasm consumed me like a wildfire, blazing through my body. I gagged violently around Lucas' thick shaft. Gasping, he collapsed over me, braced his arm against the wall, grabbed the base of his cock and unloaded.

"Fuck, fuck, fuck," Lucas chanted, his thighs quaked and he withdrew, squeezing his tip to expel every drop. Despite my aching jaw, I wanted him back in my mouth. I settled for licking what was left of his cum from the tip. He convulsed and yanked my head away by my hair.

"Jesus Christ. That was…" I tried to stand but my knees reminded me I was an idiot. I groaned, and Lucas helped me to my feet.

"Hold on. There is still soap in my crack." Lucas turned the water back on, took his time finishing the cleanup job I hadn't been able to manage and washed his hair.

"Am I forgiven now?" I asked and reached for our towels.

"You're forgiven. Is your throat okay?"

I cleared it to get rid of the raspy quality of my voice, but the pain of my raw throat persisted. "It's fine. Nothing I can't handle."

Lucas shut off the water and dried off. He inspected his cock with curiosity.

"Are you okay?" I asked.

"A little sore spot. I think you nipped me."

"Consider it an occupational hazard."

His amused eyes caught mine. He laughed brilliantly, and I'll admit I was pleased with myself. He shook his head, apparently dazzled by my comedic timing or perhaps from my newly discovered ability to deep-throat, and he pressed a kiss to my chin. Yep, we were absolutely going to figure it out.

Naked, dry and snuggled with me in bed, Lucas teed up the first porn scene. After presenting me a choice, we decided to view his scenes starting with his favorites. He explained he had written a few scene ideas for Case from his personal fantasies, and we were going to watch the first one Case had agreed to film.

"Keep in mind that this is my second or third scene, so don't judge how awkward I was in front of the camera or my bony body. I didn't have this stomach three years ago."

I pouted in genuine disappointment. "But I love your abs."

He grinned and kissed me. "Consider this a 'before' picture."

He hit Play, and I turned my attention to his image in a football uniform. The first few lines he had were cringe-worthy, but I stayed focused as Lucas pointed out all his bad camera positioning.

"Are you this critical of all your scenes? You said it's your favorite."

"It is now. I've developed a new affection for it."

"Why?"

"You'll see."

His scene partner was a man I didn't recognize—considerably older, about my age I supposed—and suited up. He had a dad-next-door kind of vibe. Lucas entered a locker room, where he stripped seductively and ran his hands over his naked body while the man waited outside. Despite his admitted inexperience, there was no mystery to Lucas' broad appeal. His eye-popping cock was even more impressive when contrasted with his leaner, hairless figure.

Lucas exited the locker room, and they exchanged some banter about Lucas' final grade. The teacher threatened to make Lucas ineligible for sports unless he could offer something in exchange. During their conversation, it started raining.

The scene skipped to a room with some flimsy-looking desks. Lucas stood, dripping wet, and ran his hands over the teacher until he had him backed against the wooden table. The man stuttered, checking over his shoulder as though nervous about being caught. They removed each other's wet clothes in typical porn fashion.

"Is this the fantasy then? Is this what I owe you?"

I froze. Lucas twisted to watch me, a huge smirk on his face. Was that…? Did I fumble my way into Lucas' fantasy?

The scene continued. "What's the matter? Can't stay hard under pressure?"

The teacher dropped his pants, and Lucas fucked him mercilessly over the table before giving him a facial. Except for the student-teacher dynamic, it matched Lucas' description of how our thwarted encounter would have played out, and I laughed so hard that my eyes watered.

The scene ended. I slouched until I was on my back and let him climb on top of me. "What did you think?" He pinned my arms above my head, scraped his teeth along my jawline and nipped at my chin.

"I think you're a very naughty boy."

"Yeah, but what did you think of the porn? How did you feel watching me with someone else?"

"I was too busy wishing I hadn't left that damn library. I'm not sure I had time to think about it."

Lucas smiled and let go of my wrists to trace the line of my pecs with his finger. "I have access to lots of costumes at the studio if you ever want me to bring them home and play dress up for you. Say the word. I'll give you a do-over."

"Did you really think I was referencing that scene when we met?" I asked.

Lucas blushed. "Well, you said I owed you, and you do resemble Todd."

"I do not."

"Kyle, oh my God. Yes, you do." He rewound the video and played it again for me until Todd came back on the scene. "See? Same hair, same build, same smile. You could be brothers."

"Okay. A little."

"A little, my ass."

I spanked him and laughed at his surprised jump. He bit his lip and melted me with his aroused, dilated eyes. He so quickly oscillated between confident, punishing top to willing submissive. For Lucas, sex was all about fun. I came to realize the orgasm at the end was just a happy bonus. Sometimes I suspected he'd gladly sacrifice coming if it meant we could keep playing. "So you want me to play teacher or student?" I asked.

"I can switch it up. I love being your boy, you know? But the shower just now? I will be jacking off to that memory for years. We should do that again. Only next time I want to make you eat my ass too. I came too fast."

His confession made me chuckle. "Okay, that didn't kill me, so let's watch another one."

"Are you sure?"

"Yeah. Give me your second favorite."

"Okay. My second favorite has some good news and some bad news."

"The bad news first."

"It's recent. I filmed it after we started dating."

"And the good news?"

Lucas laughed and flexed his abdominal muscles. "You get to see these babies."

I shoved him playfully, and Lucas toppled over on the mattress, laughing. He was hard, but I couldn't get distracted. He clicked Play on the next scene, and Lucas appeared on screen in a dungeon-type room.

I cast a nervous glance his way.

"This is all Tommy, baby. I filmed about six months before I really had his persona down. Remember, Tommy is like toppy-Lucas on steroids."

Apparently, the shower was a preview of his Tommy persona. "Do you love the harness?"

I nodded, a little dumbfounded at seeing all his golden skin crisscrossed in black leather. The harness had a strap that cut his torso lengthwise and attached to a cock ring, which had the duty of keeping Lucas' monster cock hard and upright. "Damn," I said. "That is something."

The scene? I didn't have words to describe it. Lucas put his scene partner, some uber-twinky white boy, in a sling and wailed on his ass with paddles and whips until it flared red. He adjusted the angle, suspended the kid's legs wide apart and fucked his battered ass, denying him any mercy. Tommy used Lucas' shower voice, one that I would forever connect with being on my knees for him. He exploded all over the kid's hole before using his dick to push his semen inside.

"Breathe, babe." Lucas laughed, and I exhaled the breath I wasn't aware I'd been holding.

I shook my head to reconcile what I'd witnessed. Fear chased the arousal out of my body. I swallowed and fought back the instinct to believe my gut reaction — that is what Lucas liked. He wouldn't be happy without slings, paddles, floggers and chains. He was telling me that was what I had to do to satisfy him.

I focused on him and gulped back my first question, which sounded judgmental even in my own head, and I tried a different approach. "So, why is this one a favorite?"

Lucas smiled knowingly, and I wondered if he'd read my mind. "The harness. I loved it. It made me feel sexy and powerful, and it served a dual purpose of covering all the marks you'd left on my body. Well, on my chest, anyway. Did you notice how my back stayed angled away from the camera, even when I wielded the paddle? I had to do it at this angle." He mimicked the motion he used on camera, where he paddled toward himself in a rowing motion rather than the more comfortable tennis swing. "Power exchange turns me on."

"I don't think I'll ever get into whips like that kid, Lucas."

"That kid's name is Cole. He takes my cock better than any bottom I've ever known. He loves submission and being spanked. He likes to feel used. You should see him take two dicks at once. The kid is impressive.

"Before Cole started doing porn, he thought he was dirty. He had all these desires, and people in his life made him feel like he was sinful and perverted because of it. Did you notice his legs? He used to cut himself to stop the desires his family told him were unnatural. Case and Robert turned that kid into a legend. He has a man now, a devoted fan, who worships him from afar. Italy, I think. He's one of the most sought-after twinks in the business because he is one seriously kinky motherfucker.

"I loved that scene because I loved being able to make Cole come undone. And I loved knowing what he felt because you had spent the entire weekend tying me up, calling me boy and making me beg for your cock. Cole even told me to thank you for making me a better Dom.

"I loved that I could take a kid who not even six months ago hated himself for what he wanted sexually and make him fly. But mostly I loved that we filmed it and that it's out there so other kids like Cole can see they aren't wrong or dirty for being kinky and liking what they like. Sex, particularly gay sex, is so taboo, but it doesn't have to be. It's healthy and natural, and I love being part of showing that to other people."

"Okay. Okay." I raised my hands in surrender.

"Sorry. I get a little amped up about this."

"I love your passion, baby."

"Enough to be okay with me filming?"

"I didn't say that. But it's nice to know it's not about wanting to have sex with other men."

"It's not."

"So, there's an obvious question here."

"You can totally paddle my ass."

"Good to know, but that's not what I meant. Were you ever made to feel bad or dirty because you're gay? Certainly not from your parents."

"No, I told you my parents are wonderful."

"So, there is no connection to you deciding to do porn and your mom finding her family. It's unrelated?"

"No, not completely unrelated. There *is* more to the story."

"Will you tell me the whole story, please?"

"Yes. If you promise to listen and not psychoanalyze me anymore."

"I promise."

"Okay. I told you I was a virgin when I started filming, right?"

"Yes."

"Okay. Well, that is true. In high school, I was scrawny and different. I liked what I liked, which didn't exactly jive with the cool kids. I had a habit of taking stuff apart to see how it worked, but I'd get frustrated when I couldn't put things back together. I loved musical theater and being silly and wearing outlandish things. I was just weird...and far less attractive.

"As a junior, I had a crush on a straight boy, and he liked to work out, so I started going to the gym. He was a super competitive macho type and he started monitoring my form, offering to help spot me. Anyway, yadda, yadda, yadda...he wasn't so straight. Just as we started making out, I sort of let go of all the things I wanted to do with him. I shoved my hand down his pants, and he grabbed my dick at the same time. I don't think I said anything exactly, but I'm sure he could tell I was surprised."

"Oh, boy," I said, imagining how badly that might have gone.

"Yeah. Apparently, his competitive streak didn't end with how much he could bench. He basically compared me to a circus freak and berated me, said he wasn't even hard and literally laughed at me for thinking anyone would want to be with me. For years after, nudity terrified me. I refused to go swimming or shower in a public locker room, I'd convinced myself everyone would laugh if they saw me. I couldn't even watch myself while I jacked off. I could just hear him laughing and saying no one would want me. My body embarrassed me, and I didn't trust anyone enough to ask about it. I wasn't out to my parents yet. I thought if I knew my biological dad, I could ask him if it was a family trait to be big down there. So, long story short, I started searching for my birth family."

"Oh, baby. That's terrible."

"The agency that placed me had no record of him. My mother had no known relatives, so my search ended abruptly. I... It was just a really dark time, you know? Everything about me felt wrong—my body, my sexuality, my personality, even my family, to some degree. It felt like no matter what, I would never fit in anywhere—and I stopped wanting to go to school or leave the house at all. I started to scare the hell out of my parents. They took me to a doctor and I was diagnosed with depression and started taking anti-depressants. I had a therapist who helped me come out to my parents, and I don't know if it was the medicine working or just coming out, but things started to get better after that. My parents were so supportive...." Lucas choked up a little and I rubbed his arm. "Kyle, when I told my dad what had happened with the boy, he suggested that I watch porn. He told me that most guys would be thrilled to be gifted with what I had and that I should never be ashamed of how God made me."

Lucas wiped the moisture from his eyes, and the affection and respect I felt for the people who'd raised such a remarkable man swelled ten-fold. Someday Lucas was going to be an amazing father as a result of the example set by Greg and Joann.

"I took his advice and felt so much better about myself and my body, to the point where I stopped taking the pills then lo and behold, I had a crazy sex drive. The doctor thought the medicine might have killed my libido. Around that time, my mom told me she had found her maternal aunt via a DNA test. She asked me if I wanted to try it.

"I was so pumped. I thought for sure it would work as quickly for me as it had for my mom, but it didn't. There were no matches in the database. I got depressed again. Instead of going back on the pills, I decided to create a YouTube video talking about my story, including why I'd started looking for my bio family and my issues with my body. I got this fantastic response, and of course, people began asking to see my dick. Anyway, shortly after that, I started camming and loving all the attention. I began to feel differently about myself and men would reach out to me with their stories. Some of them had body image issues like me, but others had homophobic upbringings or were deeply closeted for a whole host of reasons. But I loved talking to them and turning them on, making them feel better about themselves.

"Robert recruited me to Goldenboys via my cam site, and he asked me if I wanted to film for them. I hadn't had sex yet, so I decided to go for it. And I've gotten to explore my sexuality thoroughly through porn. I loved every opportunity."

"But you never bottomed on camera?"

"At first I didn't bottom because I wanted to save that part of my virginity for someone special. Then, once Tommy Bruiser took off, it was part of his image."

"So, who did you give it to?"

Lucas appeared remorseful. "Evan," he said wistfully.

"I dated a few of the guys I worked with, but they were mostly bottoms. And I always felt like they were dating my penis, rather than me. Evan was the first guy who seemed interested in more, and I was tired of waiting for you."

I chuckled. "Me, huh?"

"I wish I had waited. Evan and I had gone out a few times when I told him I'd never bottomed and was saving it. After that, he pursued me aggressively, and I fell for his flattery hook, line and sinker. He even convinced me to buy my car. It's not even close to what I wanted, but he liked it so much… Anyway, I thought it was understood we had a commitment. He didn't see it that way. We broke up, or I guess I broke up with him. He didn't ever really consider me his boyfriend.

After that, I realized dating other porn models was too much trouble."

"So, besides Evan...?"

"Just you. Before you, I hadn't had sex off-camera since Evan."

"Really?"

"Yes, really."

"How many scenes have you filmed?"

"I think I'm up to close to seventy or so, but some of them have been non-penetrating scenes. I do a lot of spanking scenes."

"And you've had how many partners outside of scenes?"

"Off-camera partners? Five. You were six."

"Wow."

"Wow, good or wow, bad?"

"You've never had sex with anyone outside the porn industry except me."

"You just now realized that?"

"Yeah. You're so good at it, I never thought of how inexperienced you are in boring old relationship sex."

"I don't want boring sex." Lucas tilted his head to the side, and I knew he was concerned about where my head was at.

"Normal relationship sex doesn't always have to involve costumes, role-play and gymnastics," I told him.

"Says who?"

"Says everyone."

"Kyle, what's going on?"

"Nothing. I'm just not sure I can do what you need me to do."

"What is it that you think you need to do?"

"You know. Slings and paddles. Cock worship." My face heated and I studied the pattern of Lucas' comforter.

Lucas scooted toward me and lifted my chin. "How do you feel about what we did in the shower? Tell me honestly."

"It was...okay."

"Just okay?"

"It was embarrassing at first. But I came, so I must have liked it."

"You like being daddy though."

"Yeah. It's different."

"Why? 'Cause I'm younger?"

"No, because it's not..." I answered sharply, and my explanation died somewhere in my head. *Shit.* Why did I have this problem? I got off. Lucas was sexy as fuck when he went all toppy. "I don't know."

"You love to bottom. Is it me?"

"No. It's not like I'm hung up on bottoming and I love that we switch."

"So, what is it?"

"I guess..." I considered my explanation. "I guess I... Look, I'm boring."

"What?" The genuine shock on Lucas' face was reassuring. "Why would you think that?"

"Because, Lucas. Look, I'm trying here, but sometimes it feels like I'm pretending to be someone I'm not. I'm not the guy who gets paddled in a sling. I'm the guy who wakes up on a Sunday morning and wants to rub off together. I like sex, but sometimes I feel like this is unsustainable. At some point, you are going to realize I am not this guy."

"Baby, you are *my* guy. Wanting to mix it up is for both of us. I wish you could see how sexy you are, how amazing I think you are. Sometimes I can't sleep because I'm thinking of all the ways to enjoy your body and to make you come. But that's not because I think you're boring. I could never think that."

"So, if we just spend a day in bed, kissing and cuddling, that's gonna work for you?"

"Baby, don't you understand? Everything you do works for me because *you* work for me. I love you so much. And more than that, I respect you, what you've accomplished, what you still want to accomplish. The way you look at me when we're alone makes me feel like I belong. For the first time in my life, I feel like with you, I'm perfect. Don't you see that? All these years I spent feeling like I don't fit, but with you, I've never felt that way. That's why yesterday… What Kayla and Matt said… All that shit about me not fitting with you, with your friends, with your family. It hurt so, so much, because it kills me to think you would feel like that."

"I don't."

"I know. I knew when you walked out of the library. You saw me, Kyle. I was trying to be Tommy for you, but it didn't work. You knew it was an act and you rejected it. You wanted the real me and I've been trying to show you who that is, slowly, without scaring you away. Come here."

I went to Lucas and fell into his embrace. The relief was palpable. He held me and rubbed my head.

"Hmm, I do believe today is Sunday. Maybe you should tell me about this 'rubbing off together slowly' fantasy."

"C'mere." I pushed him to his back and climbed on top of him. We were both soft, but I shifted my hips up and aligned my cock with his then I kissed him.

With my eyes closed, I let my hips find a rhythm. We moved together in a sensual glide, kissing languidly. I loved the contented sounds that Lucas made as his tongue tangled with mine. I caressed Lucas slowly and touched him like he finally belonged to me. Because he did. I knew him better now, learned how passionate and caring he was. No one would ever love him like I could. They could have his body, but I had his heart safely tucked away, and I wouldn't share it. "Mine," I whispered into his ear.

Lucas bucked his hips sharply, grabbed my ass and rutted. "Kyle, look at me," he asked. I opened my eyes and watched Lucas use my body. He held my face in his palms, his eyes drowning in emotion while he rocked against me, enjoying the unhurried and simplistic pleasure of our cocks sliding together until he came utterly undone in my arms.

At that moment I decided to trust him implicitly, about everything. I would love him like I'd learned to ride a bike — scared, but reckless, without pads or training wheels. If I crashed, my scars would tell our story.

Chapter Fourteen

"This place is gorgeous, babe," Lucas said, awestruck by the breathtaking home we'd rented. Nestled in a remote Oregon community where I'd spent many youthful summers, the cozy one-bedroom house was built to maximize privacy and the expansive views of the lake. We had one last weekend before the fall semester began, and I planned to use it to romance the hell out of Lucas.

I carried our bags to the large master suite, ducked into the bathroom to confirm the Jacuzzi tub and steam room the ad had listed and flung open the room-darkening curtains to expose the view.

Lucas gasped. "It looks like a postcard."

The crystal blue lake sparkled in the sunlight, surrounded by a dense forest of majestic pines. "Isn't this better than going camping?" I asked.

Lucas bobbed his head enthusiastically. "Much better."

"C'mere," I beckoned.

He followed me to the expansive deck that ran along the back of the home. "I love the way it smells here." I inhaled the scent of evergreen, extracted the lounge cushions from the storage box and secured them to the chair, so I could stretch out and take in the view.

"We should look at land while we're here," Lucas said.

I shook my head. "This isn't a house-scouting trip."

"It could be."

"Not yet." I needed to focus on getting through school. "If you like this place as much as I do, we can come back and search when we're ready."

The unintentional slip sent my pulse racing. I thought about it as Lucas joined me in the lounge chair built for one. When he was situated, he gathered my arms around him and gazed back at me. "When *we're* ready?"

The extra time gave me an epiphany. I'd meant it. I wanted Lucas to be a part of the decision, to be part of my future, even a distant one. What good would denying it do? "You said you'd help."

He tensed. "Oh. Of course. I will."

"And if you didn't like it, I would find something you did like."

He eyed me skeptically.

"Lucas, I plan to be with you for the long-term. Of course I would want your opinion on such a significant decision."

"Really?"

"Yes, really. Are you... Do you not feel the same way? You must be worried about it. I mean, when you're my age, I'll be almost sixty."

"I hope your hair turns silver. That'd be hot."

"Lucas, be serious." I turned his chin to see his eyes.

"No, Kyle," Lucas said sternly. "We figured out the work problem and now you've moved on to our age difference. You've seen my parents. There is nothing you could say that would make me worry about it. Let it go. Just be happy."

"I *am* happy," I reassured him.

"Good. Does that hot tub work?"

"Yes, it should."

"Good. I've got ideas." He rubbed his palms together and served up the most mischievous version of his brilliant smile. Ever since he'd taken the part-time marketing job for Goldenboys, he'd been relentless in pitching scene concepts. Lucas was a never-ending font of kink and filth. As the primary beneficiary of his dirty imagination, I couldn't complain, but Case and Robert had encouraged him to be more budget-conscious in his fantasies.

"Oh, I'm sure you do." I teased. "But this isn't a working vacation. No distractions, just us."

"But I get to film us still?" Other than a few recordings of him giving me a blow job, I hadn't allowed cameras. After some negotiation, I'd agreed to change that rule, one time only, that weekend. I regretted leaving the details to him.

"Yeah," I said reluctantly, "if you want."

"I want. So much." Lucas smiled. "I can't wait to see you go all daddy on my ass."

"Are you planning to fuck all weekend? I did hope we'd get out a little. I'd like to hike and kayak, and there are some nice restaurants and fun art galleries in town."

"I've never been kayaking."

"Well, I'll get to teach you then. It's peaceful, especially in the mornings."

"You're such a romantic. I love it."

"Do you? Sometimes I worry. Wouldn't you rather be clubbing and going to bars? I'm okay if you want to go out with your friends without me occasionally."

"I'm never bored with you. I like that you think about more than sex. But this place — a hot tub, secluded lake, Jacuzzi bath, four-poster bed, chairs with no arms… It's like you took me to DisneyWorld and won't let me ride anything."

I chuckled. *Oh, to be twenty-three again.* "I love sex with you, baby, but we need to leave the bubble occasionally. It can't be the only thing that we enjoy together."

"I like our bubble."

"Me too," I admitted. Ever since the disastrous party, I'd avoided my friends. I wanted to wait until our trip was over to fully return to the real world.

"Okay. So, we compromise. We have four days. We spend two doing whatever romantic activity you dream up and two doing whatever I dream up."

"Full days at your mercy? You do know I'm old, right? Unless you packed some Viagra…"

"Would you quit with the 'old' shit. You're a long way from needing pharmaceutical help."

"True, but my recovery time isn't what it used to be. How about I plan our afternoons, and you plan our evenings."

"Deal. What about the mornings?" Lucas said.

"Split the difference?" I said. Lucas grinned his understanding. We'd recently developed an uncanny ability to communicate with grins.

"Excellent. So, couple-ly sex in the morning, followed by perfectly romantic afternoons, we cook dinner together naked, then I get to put my kinky hands all over you."

"Maybe we make time for showers."

"Oh, you can trust my evenings will be making full use of that bathroom." Lucas checked his watch. "It's one-thirty, so we're on your time, baby. What's on the agenda?"

"First, we sit and enjoy the view together." I sighed contentedly as he snuggled closer. "Then I thought we'd check out a local winery, get a few bottles for our stay."

Lucas smiled his approval. "And get you all loosened up. Love how vocal you get when you've been drinking."

I chuckled. "Yeah, maybe that too."

* * * *

On our way to the winery, Lucas gazed out of the window. He'd never been to the area, and I enjoyed watching him discover the beauty of the Pacific Northwest. There was something about the way Lucas reacted to his environment that I never grew tired of. His blue eyes were always at work, observing the smallest of details and formulating new questions about what he'd seen. The way his mind worked — how he approached a new experience with so much openness — was such a novelty to me. I was usually too worried about sounding stupid, but Lucas never hesitated.

"Have you been to a winery before?" I asked.

Lucas shook his head. "Nope, but I like wine."

"We could see if they have a tour. You might enjoy learning about the winemaking process."

"Yeah, that'd be cool. Do they grow green grapes or red?"

"I'm not sure, but it's a biodynamic winery, and their sparkling white is supposed to be really good."

Lucas grinned at me. "You didn't tell me we were having Champagne."

"Well, technically, we aren't. Champagne is a growing area in France. Only sparkling whites from that area are considered Champagne."

"Which region are we in?"

"Willamette, I think. I'm far from an expert."

"So, you want to do the tour, too?"

"Sure."

"Good. Maybe we'll become that couple who holds fancy dinner parties and wine pairings. Does Matt like wine?"

I cast a side eye to him, but he wasn't looking my way. I squeezed his thigh to get his attention. "Where did that come from?"

Lucas turned to me and blushed. "Just been curious about him since the party. He's kind of sophisticated. I guess I figured this is stuff you would have done together."

"No. Matt's more of a bourbon guy. Our first date was actually at a beer and bourbon festival." I smiled because the memory was a good one. We'd spent a good portion of the event checking out other guys together. I probably should have realized then we'd make better friends than boyfriends.

"Oh. That sounds fun."

"And, Lucas…"

"Yeah?"

"I never brought Matt to this lake. I've never brought any other man to this lake."

"Really?"

"Yes. Really." I patted his leg again, and he laced his fingers with mine. He continued gazing out the window, but from the corner of my eye, I could see him smiling to himself.

Lucas was quiet for a few miles. We made the turnoff for the winery and the hilly vineyard came into view. "Wow. This is beautiful."

Smiling, I traversed the curvy driveway to the parking lot. The tasting room was a large red barn and the entrance was marked by large gardens dotted with butterflies. I placed the car in Park and turned to see Lucas snap a picture with his phone. He admired me with a broad grin. "This is freaking romantic as hell. I *love* this."

Lucas clasped my hand as we strolled through the gardens on the way into the tasting room. He took pictures of flowers and begged me to take selfies I pretended to object to. The sun shone brightly, casting Lucas' blond hair with an almost-angelic glow. We arranged to do a tasting followed by a tour. Our guide patiently addressed every one of Lucas' thoughtful questions, but I couldn't have recounted even one detail of her answers. I spent the tour falling even more hopelessly in love with Lucas.

After the winery trip, Lucas drove me, tipsy and relaxed, to the local market and filled our shopping cart with the ingredients we needed for the dinner he'd planned.

"I'm going to grab the garlic and lemons. Do I need sour cream or yogurt for the dill sauce?" Lucas handed me his phone while we waited for the person at the fish counter to wrap our salmon steaks.

I navigated to the recipe's website and double-checked. "Um. Says sour cream," I said when he returned. A phone alert rang in my hand, followed by another, then another then about thirty more in rapid succession. "I'll get it. Here. Your phone is blowing up."

I found the sour cream and returned to see Lucas, open-mouthed and staring at his phone while holding our wrapped fish. "You okay?"

"Um. If I have bad news, would you want to know immediately or wait until we are in private?"

I surveyed the almost empty store. *No. No. No.* This trip would not be ruined by bad news. "Immediately," I answered.

"Ken's interview with me was published yesterday. It's exactly what we discussed. He didn't post your picture, only your first name."

"Okay..."

"But my fans still identified you, and now your picture and full name are all over my feed."

"What? How the hell did that happen?"

"I don't know. I guess we gave too much information. They had your first name and that you work in construction. They know what city I live in and that we go to school together. Maybe someone from our class follows me? The pictures are from us on campus."

"Well, I guess it's not the worst thing that could happen."

"There's more." He cringed.

"Oh God."

"There's security video of us from the library."

"What?"

"I'm so sorry. I guess it's a good thing we didn't actually get naked, huh?"

"Yeah. I guess so." I took the fish and put it in the cart. "Is this all we needed?"

"Babe…"

"It's fine, Lucas. We discussed being more public. I wish it could have been on our terms, but there isn't anything we can do about it now. Can we finish and get out of here? I'm losing my buzz."

Lucas gawked at me but closed his mouth without saying what was on his mind. "Yes. I need some seasonings and the rice."

"Okay. Let's go."

Lucas didn't bring it up again beyond saying he'd posted a message condemning the fans who'd shared my identity. He reported they felt terrible, hadn't meant to upset him and removed their original posts.

Not that it did much good, since the pictures and video had spread like wildfire. Lucas used the inaccurate representations of us to fuel his fury, and by the time we'd arrived back at the cottage, he was more upset by it than I was.

"Calm down, Lucas," I said.

"I feel terrible."

"It's really fine. I think I'm okay with it. I figure it's like being unintentionally outed. At first, it feels like a violation, but then you realize you're set free, and it's not so terrible. Maybe your fans did us a favor. Let's just enjoy these few days, and we'll deal with it when we get back. I'm turning my phone off."

"If you're sure, I'll turn mine off too. Let me text my mom and dad that that's what I'm doing. Otherwise, they'll worry."

"I am. Now, it's six o'clock. We're on *your* time. Tell me what I need to do to make the dill sauce."

Lucas smirked. "First, put this on." He handed me an apron from the pantry. I lifted it to loop the fabric around my neck, but he stopped me. "No, baby. I want that to be the only thing you wear." He winked at me, and like that, we were safely back in our bubble.

The next morning, I lived out the fantasy I'd been dreaming about since I'd booked the cottage. I woke with Lucas in my arms. He shifted his body into me and prolonged the moment of wakefulness with gentle, sensual kisses. He pulled back long enough to touch my face and smile for me. My smile. The one he saved for me alone.

Lucas rose to open the curtain then he left our room and returned with coffee, yogurt and fresh strawberries. We ate together in bed, watching the sun rays dance on the lake.

"This place is beautiful." Lucas sighed, and I popped a strawberry into his mouth and kissed him, smiling uncontrollably while he swallowed the too-large bite.

"I can see us living here," Lucas said and lifted the last strawberry dipped in yogurt to my lips. I licked the fruit and took a small nibble, and he popped the remainder of the fruit into his mouth. The confession took my breath away. I was struck by the realization that I didn't just want Lucas' help. I needed his approval. My dream house wouldn't feel complete if he wasn't a part of it. The feeling was terrifying, exhilarating and horribly addictive—much like everything I felt for Lucas.

"Should we take a bath?" he offered. I nodded. Neither of us had a bathtub big enough for two full-grown men, so we'd never tried before. Lucas jumped out of bed with enthusiasm.

"I wish we'd brought some bubble bath," he shouted over the running water.

I smiled to myself. "Check my toiletry bag." I heard rustling and a squeal of excitement when Lucas found the Lush bath bombs I'd bought for the occasion.

"You're so fucking romantic," Lucas shouted. "Get your ass in here."

I found Lucas in the ginormous tub. The water had barely risen to stomach level and his abs looked sexy as fuck surrounded by the sea-blue water from the bath bomb. "Get in here, lover." He let his legs fall open and I eased myself slowly into the hot water and situated my back to his chest. He used his foot to turn off the water and closed his legs around my waist.

"We need one of these in the dream house,' Lucas kissed my neck and soaped my chest.

I twisted to meet his lips. "Absolutely."

Settling back in the water, I played with his hand and enjoyed the feeling of him wrapped around me. "What else do you want?"

Lucas thought quietly for a minute. I half expected him to suggest a sex dungeon from his porn set or, at the very least, something that would have to be kept hidden from my parents when they came by.

"Can we make sure there is a guest room on the first floor? My dad has started having trouble with stairs this year, and I'd really like to make sure they can visit us. They'd love it up here."

I twisted in his arms and hauled up to kneel between his knees. He peered upward with a reserved smile. His vulnerable gaze spoke to me. It said he wanted everything. The house, the future...all of it with me. He was ready for whatever adventure life had in store for us. I brushed the strands of wet hair out of his face and kissed him.

After our bath, we launched the kayaks the owners kept for renters. I helped him adjust his foot pegs and walked him through how to hold his paddle. With a few corrections to his posture and form, Lucas took to it quickly. Before long we were gliding along the water, enjoying the best the Pacific Northwest had to offer — clean, crisp air and natural forest. Lucas was quiet, but I enjoyed the silence and took pleasure in watching him take in the scenery and knowing that, like me, he was envisioning our future together.

After an enjoyable forty minutes, my arms ached from exertion, and I suggested we turn back. "Can we rest a bit?" Lucas asked and pointed to small inlet edged by cottonwood trees.

I followed his lead, and we made our way to the small shoreline. Lucas plopped himself on the grass, lay back and lifted his arms into a stretch. I smiled, admiring him. "You're so beautiful," fell spontaneously from my lips.

Lucas gave me my smile and laughed. "Back at ya, baby." He patted the grass, inviting me to join him on the ground. He settled my arm around him and rested his head on my shoulder briefly before turning toward the densely wooded area behind us. "Does someone live here?"

"No, this part of the lake isn't available to build on. It's private property though, so we shouldn't linger too long."

Lucas looked at me expectantly, so I elaborated. "Someone owns the land, but they can only use it for water access. This part of the lake has zoning restrictions. There are environmental issues that make it cost prohibitive. You'd have to run utilities around the protected land." I pointed west where a nature preserve had been established for some owl species.

"So, where can you build?"

"Just the stretch where the cottage is. There are probably forty or so undeveloped residential lots on that part of the lake, but I'll probably consider other lakes. Pricewise, this is out of my reach."

"Out of curiosity, what would land like this go for?"

"This land? It's cheap since you are really restricted, but the houses near where we are? You're looking at least a hundred and fifty to two-hundred seventy-five thousand dollars per lot if you want lake and road access."

I laughed at the whistle Lucas let loose. "What would a house like the one we're staying in cost?"

"It's easily a half-million, probably more."

His face fell, and I nudged him. "Why? Were you going to buy it for me?"

With a playful shove, he put me on my back and climbed on top. "Maybe I was. Would you let me?"

"I want to build my dream, not buy someone else's."

"So, realistically, what's the timeline?"

"Um. I'd like to have the land bought in the next five years. Then depending on what had to be done, start running utilities and clearing the land. My goal is to have it be live-in ready and all paid off by my retirement."

Lucas gazed at me, and I sensed the moment my dream became ours. My chest ached with love for him, and again, I wondered how it was possible to feel so connected to another human being.

His broad smile turned playful. I hauled him down and kissed him. I'd swear when our lips touched I could taste the next fifty years of our lives.

"I love you," he shouted, and we laughed as his voice echoed back.

I sat up and hugged him to my chest. "You did it," I whispered in his ear. He pulled back and stared down at me, his eyebrow raised in question. I kissed him sweetly on the lips. "You changed my mind."

"About?"

"You. Me. Everything."

Lucas smiled in smug satisfaction. "Only took me three months. That's not bad."

"And I know you enjoyed every minute." I recalled his words to me after our first class.

"Nah. Thought it be more of a challenge. All I had to do was" — he snapped his fingers — "and you were mine."

I laughed, but he wasn't wrong. Despite all my attempts at resistance, I never did enforce any of the rules we'd agreed to. "Don't be cocky." I tackled him and rolled him on to his back. After climbing on top of him, I kissed the hell out of him.

"Or what?" Lucas asked, his tone just begging for Daddy to come out and play.

"Or I'll have to spank you when we get back."

We played around together, kissing and talking. We stayed much longer than intended. We talked about the house and what we wanted from our future. Our conversation dove deeper than others we'd had. Lucas talked more about his mom and dad, his struggles with depression and some of his past relationships. I told Lucas about the conversation I'd had with Matt and his theory on why we hadn't worked.

"Was the sex boring with Matt?" I could tell Lucas wanted me to affirm his assumption, but since we were being honest, I didn't.

"Not boring, just missing something. I've always had some hang-ups, and I think I could tell Matt wasn't happy. To be honest, his porn-watching used to bother me, and the sexy underwear he kept buying me felt like pressure to be something I wasn't. I didn't realize it at the time, but I think I stopped trying to make him happy in bed because he wasn't giving me what I wanted in the relationship. After a while, it kind of became the way I kept things even—like he wasn't giving me what I wanted, so why would I give him what he wanted. In the end, all it did was make us both miserable."

"Do you feel like that with me?" The concern in Lucas' voice eased my anxiety.

"No," I clarified. "It's different with you."

"Why?"

I thought for a minute. "I don't know. I just want to be sexy for you."

Lucas smiled. "I want to be that for you too. Sometimes if I push you—like in the shower—it's because I don't want us to have boundaries with each other, but I would never want you to do something you didn't want to do."

"I know."

"Good, because I think you're more like me than you think. Someday, when you're ready, I think you're gonna find you love being on the other end of the paddle."

I laughed. "If you say so."

Lucas smiled my smile and pressed a palm to my crotch. "I think one day I could order you to take out your dick right here and stroke yourself, and you'd follow without thinking twice."

"Lucas," I whined and stilled his hand.

"I think you want to be a little slutty with me. I know it gets you hard."

I glanced around. There were no houses in view and no boats on the water in our line of sight, but still, my heart raced. "Maybe," I said unconvincingly.

"Kyle, do it."

"I thought I was the daddy in this relationship?"

Lucas tucked his lip between his teeth and cast an intense stare my way. "Sometimes you should let me be in charge. You may love submission." He removed his hand from my lap and cupped my neck. "I don't need it, but sometimes, I think you might. One day I hope you'll let me give you what you need."

"Maybe," I sighed. If anyone could change my mind, I had no doubt it would be Lucas.

Lucas stood and hauled me up and into his arms. As if sensing the conversation had ignited enough of a spark in my mind, he suggested we head back. We finished our conversation on the deck, sipping wine and sharing everything from our views on politics and religion to pets and embarrassing moments of our youths. I smiled knowing that somehow, no matter how long we were together, being in Lucas' company and talking about everything and nothing — with no rules, no safe and unsafe topics — would always be the best part of my day.

* * * *

The weekend flew by. On our last morning, Lucas woke me up with kisses on my neck and shoulder. I moaned my encouragement. "I love that," I whispered when he kissed the nape of my neck.

"Mm, me too." His erection poked at my hip. I shifted to give him a better angle and he started riding his cock against the cleft of my ass. "Oh, baby. Fuck. Stay right there for me." He buried his mouth into the crook of my neck and rubbed my chest while he used me to get off.

He traveled his hand down my body and gripped my cock, stroking me in time to the movement of his hips. "I love you," he whispered. "Last night was fun, but this is…"

I closed my eyes, enjoying his hand and reliving the last night of our vacation. I'd been riding the edge of tipsy and drunk, but I remembered little bits and pieces—Lucas thoroughly restrained, the paddle, the three orgasms I'd ripped out of my boy before showering him with my cum. Jesus, it had been—

Lucas groaned in my ear moments before the hot spray splashed on my back. His raspy pants towed me to the edge, but a sudden desire kept me from falling over. I wanted to know what it felt like to let go like he had. To just give it all over to him.

"Hmmm. So good." Lucas moaned and rolled onto his back. He yelped as his ass brushed the bed linens. "Damn, this flight today is going to be something else."

I cringed. "Did I get too carried away?"

"Should we watch it and find out?"

"Let's go for one last swim. It might help."

Lucas nodded and climbed out of bed. His ass was still marked with red and purple. He grabbed the lotion and brought it to me. "Please."

He lay on his stomach while I soothed his sore cheeks. It shouldn't turn me on to have my marks on him, but it did. God, he was so sexy when he called me Daddy. Memories washed over me, the ways he'd showed off for me and asked me if he was a 'good boy'. I got hard thinking about it. But the aftermath didn't seem fun at all. "Why do you like this again?" I kept my tone even, but Lucas wasn't fooled.

"I don't love this part. But last night, when you let go for me and took what you wanted..." He bit his lip with the memory. "It's all worth it. That part where you made me go slow, so you could watch yourself fill my ass. My thighs were burning, but the way you kept saying, '*Slower for Daddy*' then when I got all the way down, when you held me there and wouldn't let me move or touch myself. My God, Kyle, I could feel every inch of you inside me."

"You're turning me on again."

"Sure you want to take that swim? We could watch the video?"

"Yeah." I moaned.

"I don't think I can do much," he said.

"You won't have to. Put the video on and grab my phone, would ya?"

Lucas returned and snuggled against me. Facing each other, we pulled the blankets up, so only our heads showed. I lifted my phone high, kissed him and snapped a picture.

I sat up so I could navigate to the Twitter app and sign in to the account I'd created for Bruce R. Lover. The picture was easy enough to attach. I tapped out a short message before hitting the 'tweet' button.

A great weekend spent with my love @TommyBruiserXXX.
#myfirsttweet #allmine

I set the phone down and kissed Lucas. The soundtrack had me rock hard, but Lucas was feeling too playful to get into it. He broke out into laughter every one of the hundreds of times my phone dinged.

Chapter Fifteen

The real world was waiting for us when we returned home. The fall semester began and eroded all my spare time. I worked during the day and had classes every weekday evening, except Fridays. I'd decided to stick with engineering as my major, and since Lucas had finished his core requirements, we didn't have any classes together.

Lucas continued working part-time in the marketing department at Goldenboys and managed a full load of marketing classes. He still performed occasionally, but had reduced his availability, which meant instead of filming two to three scenes a month, he was lucky to get one. He'd supplemented his income with appearances and promotional work, which in addition to working out regularly and the management of his social media accounts sometimes seemed like a job in and of itself.

After my picture stunt, I'd gained close to three thousand followers on Twitter. Lucas said my counts would fall if I didn't post more, so I gave him the password and let him manage mine too. He posted a single nude that I'd taken of him and my follower count ballooned to five thousand. *Thirsty bastards.* After that, I mainly used Twitter to post love messages to Lucas. Lucas wasn't kidding about his straight female fan base. They were very supportive of our relationship, and I noticed they policed his comments and didn't hesitate to let new fans know that Tommy had a boyfriend. This pleased me tremendously.

About a month into the semester, Lucas and I realized we had gone five consecutive days without seeing each other, which we both found utterly unacceptable. After that, I gave him a spare key, and unless he had a work event, he slept in my bed. Within the month, more of Lucas' clothes were in my closet than his own and he started talking about subletting his place, since he was rarely there.

Lucas took advantage of the Columbus Day weekend to do a promotional event at some gay club in San Diego for Playland, the company that sold his toy line. I'd dropped him at the airport and was already missing him when I came home to find Patrick sitting in his car in my driveway.

Surprised, I parked and waved hello.

"Hey, Kyle. Sorry to ambush you when you're just getting home."

"Did you forget something at the party?" I asked, hopeful his unexpected visit was about anything other than Kayla.

He hesitated. "No. I wanted to talk to you about the wedding."

"Come inside."

Patrick shuffled behind me while I unlocked the front door. Nothing about his demeanor left me feeling optimistic. Patrick didn't have body language control. Happy, sad—the man's face was usually a clear window into his mood. He also didn't have much appetite for confrontation. Matt and I had broken up at least three times and Patrick stayed friendly with both of us, refusing to get involved. His sending Kayla in to get Matt the night of the engagement party was a quintessential Patrick move. I couldn't imagine he'd come over on Kayla's behalf.

I held up my bag. "Let me throw this in my room. Want a beer or something?"

"No. No. I'm good."

"Suit yourself." I dropped my backpack on my bed, texted Lucas, grabbed a beer and returned to Patrick. He was standing in front of the fireplace, shuffling nervously.

"What's up, man?" I took a seat on my couch, hoping the casual posture would loosen his mouth and we could get it over with faster.

"So we've been friends awhile, right?"

An ominous start to a conversation if I'd ever heard one. I took a long swig of my beer before answering, "Only about twenty-five years or so."

"Exactly. And I'm getting married. So, as one of my oldest friends, you should be in my wedding. Tracey and I want you in the wedding."

I could have accepted outright, but I had the distinct impression he hadn't arrived at the point yet. "But—" I prompted.

"But Matt is going to be my best man. And this thing between you and Kayla? It's out of control. It's really important to Tracey that there is no drama. I want you in the wedding, but I need you to patch things up with Matt and Kayla."

Matt had texted me that I was a lucky bastard after seeing the library security footage of us on Tommy's Twitter and asked if he could be introduced to some of Lucas' friends. "Matt and I are fine, I think. I'll call him to confirm, but I don't see an issue there."

"And my sister?"

I sighed and took another sip of my beer. "Patrick, I think you should be talking to your sister about it. It's her problem. All I asked her to do was to keep her opinions about Lucas to herself."

"Man, c'mon. Please talk to her. I don't want to exclude Lucas, but—" Embarrassment was written all over his face. And finally, I read between the lines.

"But Kayla's your sister and she doesn't want him there."

"Yeah."

"So I won't go."

"I don't want that either. Can you? Please. For me? Could you try to fix this thing with Kayla? I know she's difficult as hell but you've known us for longer than Lucas has even been alive. If you can't fix it, will you at least consider coming alone?"

"I'll talk to Lucas about it."

Patrick frowned, and I got the sense that that wasn't the answer he'd hoped for. "I'm truly sorry about all this. I've tried to reason with Kayla, but she's dug in her heels. For what it's worth, Tracey and I would like to get to know Lucas better. Tracey's cousin, Simon, really spoke highly of him and it's good to see you so happy. We should have dinner or something."

"Yeah. Okay. Dinner would be nice."

"I'll keep on talking to Kayla, too. I thought if we both did, we might get this all fixed before the wedding. We still have a few months. I hope you understand. I hate being in the middle. I'm just trying to make sure my girl gets the day she deserves. I can't have the focus not be on her."

"I get it. Tracey shouldn't have to worry about a fight at the reception. I'm sorry I lost my temper at the engagement party. It was all my fault."

"Nah. Matt told me what he'd said. Friend or no friend, if he had called Tracey a whore, I'd have flattened him."

I chuckled. "Thanks. But you can assure Tracey it won't happen again."

He nodded, and I promised to think about what he'd asked.

* * * *

With the limited time we'd spent together, I hadn't had a chance to tell Lucas about Patrick's request or about Kayla's radio silence. On a rainy Saturday in late October, I'd woken early to finish a paper for class, while Lucas slept in.

I'd uploaded my homework and hit Submit when I heard Lucas shuffle to the kitchen. "Babe, is there coffee?"

"Yeah. Should still be hot."

"You need a warmup?"

I peered into my nearly full mug. "It's all yours."

"Thank God," he answered. "We're almost out of beans. I'll get some at the store tomorrow."

"There's a list on the fridge," I reminded him and got back the same amused look I had when I'd shown up a minute early for our first date.

Lucas, wearing sweatpants, an old concert T-shirt of mine, and sporting a severe case of bedhead, emerged from the kitchen, mug in hand. "Did you get your homework done?" he asked, sat on the couch next to me and set his mug on the end table.

"Yep. Finished."

"So we have the entire day to spend together." Lucas removed my laptop and straddled my lap. "What should we do?" He grinded on me, his horny smile readily displayed.

"Hmm. I don't know. Why don't you give me a hint?"

He laughed, yanked the shirt from his body, shifted my hand to his abdominal muscles and flexed. Sighing contently, I caressed his hard stomach. "Do you want to work out?"

"No." Lucas shook his head and took my hand, raising it to his mouth so he could suck on my fingers.

"Are you hungry? Did you want food?"

"No." He bit his lower lip, pushed his sweatpants down, freed his cock and thumped my stomach.

"Oh, I see," I teased. "Did you want me to do something about that?"

"Now you're talking."

I wiggled the waistband of his sweatpants down and started to stroke him when the doorbell rang. Lucas collapsed against me. "Fuck. Who is that?"

I shoved him gently from my lap and waited for him to tuck himself in. The bell chimed again, and I opened the door.

"Surprise!"

"Mom. Dad. What are you doing here?"

"I told your dad what good is retirement if you can't take impromptu trips." My mom handed me her purse and proceeded, suitcase in hand, toward the spare room which served as my office and a guest room. She talked a mile a minute about an anniversary party they were attending for some friends.

"Hello, son," my father said, following behind my mother. He held up a small cosmetic case and adjusted the bag he carried his CPAP in over his shoulder. "Your mother's insulin needs to go in the fridge." Without another word, he walked by Lucas into the kitchen.

I turned and stared at Lucas, who sat shirtless on the couch, stunned speechless. I picked up the T-shirt from the floor and tossed it to him. Lucas sprang into action. He'd dragged on his shirt and was smoothing his hair when my dad returned. Seconds after, my mother reentered the family room. They both stopped and inspected Lucas, who faced away from them and adjusted himself, in a desperate attempt to conceal his more-than-obvious dick print. I cleared my throat and Lucas jumped.

"Kyle, who's this?" my mother asked.

Lucas turned a bright shade of red. With an audible swallow, he turned to face them.

"Mom, Dad, this is my boyfriend, Lucas."

"Your boyfriend?" My mother laughed. "Oh, Kyle. Really?"

Lucas and I made eye contact, communicating silently how best to handle the situation. Lucas decided to power through with the ostrich approach, acknowledging neither the fact that my parents had caught him with his hand down his pants or the somewhat subtle slight.

"Mr. and Mrs. McMillan. It's so nice to meet you finally."

My dad shook Lucas' hand with a puzzled expression. "So, sorry. I didn't catch your name, son."

"Lucas Cass, sir."

"Tom McMillan." My dad shook his head at my mother, "Judy, I told you we should have called."

My mother gawked, aghast at touching Lucas' hand after where it had been. Lucas adjusted quickly and returned to my side.

"Well, how was I supposed to know Kyle was seeing someone. It's not like he tells us what's going on in his life. I had to hear about Patrick's engagement from Esther."

Oh, brother. "Mom, I'm sorry. I've been busy."

My mother smiled. "Oh, well. We're here now. Why don't you call Kayla and we'll take you three to breakfast? It'd be nice to see her."

"Um…" I stuttered with a few false starts before Lucas interrupted.

"Didn't Kayla mention she had plans this morning?" Lucas said.

"Huh?" *When did Lucas talk to Kayla?*

"You know. Those plans she mentioned the other day about the work thing," Lucas prompted.

Fuck, he is so good on his feet. "Oh, yeah. The thing. I forgot. Kayla's busy today, Mom. She had to work."

"Oh. On a Saturday? That is a shame. She works so hard. I'll give her a call later. Maybe she'll be free for dinner," Mom said.

Worn thin on the conversation topic, my dad grabbed my television remote, took a seat in the recliner and turned on college football.

"You gonna get ready or what?" my mom asked. "Your dad is hungry."

Lucas stared at me, unsure of what to do. I grimaced, and he nodded his understanding. Apparently we were going to breakfast with my parents.

In the bedroom, Lucas finally exhaled. "Oh my God." He laughed. "That was straight out of a sitcom. Like your parents didn't even notice the half-naked man on your couch."

"I'm sorry about this."

"Don't be sorry on my account. This is going to be entertaining. Why didn't you want Kayla to go? I thought your eyes were going to bug out of your head."

"Um…"

Lucas stopped in the middle of undressing. "Kyle, what's going on? Did you and Kayla have another fight?"

I turned and found something fascinating on the dresser. "No. Same fight."

"She's still not my biggest fan, huh?"

I sorted through a stack of mail, opening each letter like I needed to read all the terms of the credit card offer to throw it away.

"Kyle," he repeated.

I peered up. Lucas' naked body momentarily scrambled my brain. "Huh? Oh, yeah. You could say that."

His raised his hand to his hair, running his fingers through it like he did when he was aggravated. "I did say that. But why don't you put down the junk mail and skip to the part where you tell me what's going on."

I dropped the stack in the trash, sat on the bed and removed my shirt. "I haven't spoken to Kayla."

He sighed heavily. "Well, we've been busy. When was the last time?"

"Patrick's party."

Lucas gasped, "Kyle, that was months ago."

"I know."

"You haven't spoken to your best friend in months and didn't think to mention it?"

"I'm sorry. Kayla wasn't supportive of us, and I've been busy."

He sat on the bed next to me and rubbed my back. "She thought I'd be a fling. Surely she realizes this is more. What's going to happen when your mom calls and invites her to dinner or all the wedding events?"

Might as well come clean. "There's more. But remember you love me."

He gave an exasperated sigh. "What?"

"She told Patrick that she won't come to the wedding if I bring you."

"Seriously? What is her problem with me? You said she was all about you talking to me before we got together."

I shrugged. I had my suspicions, but Kayla wasn't easy to explain. "It doesn't matter. I told Patrick I won't go without you."

"What? How does that help things? Seriously? I hang out with teen porn models, so believe me when I say your friends are immature."

A knock at the door interrupted us. "Kyle, I don't hear the shower running. Are you getting ready?" my mom called from the hallway.

I sighed and dropped my head, while Lucas hastened to the bathroom to turn on the water.

"We'll be out in a minute, Mom."

"Okay. Your dad needs to eat."

"Yeah. Fine. Out in a minute."

Lucas shook his head. "C'mon, silly man. We can shower together to save time."

"Babe, are you mad?"

"No, not mad," Lucas sighed. "But I am hurt that you didn't trust me enough to tell me what was going on."

"I'm sorry."

Lucas led me to the shower and kissed the guilt off my face. "I really am sorry," I said.

"I know." Lucas picked up the soap and ran it mindlessly over his chest. He wasn't sulking exactly, but it was clear he wasn't pleased by my omission or my lack of trust.

"Babe, I do trust you. I was upset with myself."

That got Lucas' attention. "Why?"

"Because I almost lost you that night and I don't know why I kept that truth from you. I guess I didn't want you to think that we don't fit."

"We do fit and Kayla won't ever know that if you avoid her." Lucas lifted my chin. "You know I forgave you before."

"I still feel guilty about it, because I do trust you."

"Do you want me to help with that?" he asked solemnly.

"I don't think you can."

"I could give you a scene."

"A scene. Like a porn scene?"

"No, baby. Like before. I can put you on your knees and give you a punishment. It might help. It did last time."

I thought about it. Earning Lucas' forgiveness had eased my guilt and, more importantly, kept me from obsessing about it. Something I often did. "I'm not sure."

"It doesn't have to be like last time. I can tailor it."

"Can I think about it?"

Lucas smiled warmly. "Of course. It's for you. If you don't want it, it's perfectly fine."

Chapter Sixteen

At breakfast, I learned my parents were attending their friends' party that afternoon and were leaving Monday morning. They'd set their minds on dinner with Kayla Sunday evening, which gave me a twenty-four-hour grace period to either explain to my parents why Kayla and I were not speaking or patch things up. The downside of the truth being my mother's inevitable intervention into the situation. Luckily, my parents' recent cruise dominated the conversation and required only my marginal attention, which was good, because I couldn't stop thinking about Lucas' offer, what his punishment would be and how it would feel to hand over that control.

On the way to the car, Lucas asked me to drive him home, extinguishing my hopes of covertly finishing what we'd started that morning or, at the very least, getting more details on Lucas' scene. The thoughts were not at all welcomed, given our company.

My mother's lousy hip made it difficult for her to climb into the backseat of my truck, so she'd taken the front seat. She peeped back at Lucas, then to me. With a skeptical brow, she asked, "What's the matter?"

My gaze left the road as I searched her face for the source of her concern. "Nothing. Why?"

"You're doing a lot of weird sighing."

I glanced at Lucas in the rearview mirror, and he nodded confirmation with a twinkle in his eye.

"I'm tired. I woke early to finish some homework."

My father coughed, and my mother dug into her purse to produce a cough drop. He took it and put it in his mouth without speaking. I'd never noticed how little my dad communicated. My mother seemed to anticipate all his needs. I wondered if Lucas and I would be like that. "I don't know why you are bothering with the college thing. Seems like a waste of money," my mother said.

I sighed again, that time from actual irritation and not sexual frustration. "It's fine, Mom. I'm going to drop you and Dad off then take Lucas home."

"That's silly. Take him home first. We can wait."

"I need to grocery shop anyway. Is there anything you need? I'll add it to my list."

"Yes. Could you pick up distilled water for your dad's CPAP?"

"I have water, Judy."

"No. Remember the police made us throw it away at the airport because of the terrorists. I don't understand why they'd care about water. There's water on the plane." An image of my mother at airport security arguing with the TSA made me cringe.

"That was a brand-new jug," my dad said. "Kyle, put the game on the radio."

In the mirror, I could see Lucas raise his sweatshirt over his mouth to hide his smile as I tuned in ESPN for my dad.

I dropped my parents off and ran in to grab my grocery list while Lucas moved to the front seat. He appeared shell-shocked, which, granted, my mother was a bit much until you got used to her. She was nothing like Joann, that was for sure.

"Yowser," Lucas said, his eyebrows raised high and expression dazed. "Your mother is a force to be reckoned with."

We chatted about my parents until I was parked outside his apartment.

"I'm sorry. You sure I can't talk you into staying?"

"I hope you don't think I'm bailing on you, but since our plans are shot to hell, I figured I could get the homework I was going to do Monday done today. We'll have time together after I get out of class. I've got a photo shoot tomorrow, and it's probably going to go all day."

"That makes sense. Will you come over tomorrow night?"

"Actually, there are two new models in town. I thought I could hang out with the guys at Case and Robert's and give you time with your parents."

"I know they're a handful, but I want them to get to know you. I'll tell my parents about your work if you need me to."

"It's not that. You can tell them I'm in marketing if it comes up. It's true, and I don't think they need to know the rest. Kyle, were you thinking about what I said in the shower?"

I nodded.

"Do you want me to take care of it?"

I braved a glance. "I'm not sure. Maybe we can try it."

"Take my cock out and suck it."

"What?"

"Do it. Right here, where anyone can see you being a little slut."

"Lucas. Are you kidding?"

"No."

"I can't do that."

"You can and you will. You want to be my slut. I know it's what you were thinking about the whole time we were with your parents. You were thinking about being on your knees and sucking my dick. That makes you pretty slutty, babe."

"I wasn't—"

"You were too. I could tell because your cheeks were red, and your cock was semi-hard throughout the meal."

I glanced around and surveyed the parking lot. It was still early, and no one seemed to be walking about. But we were out in the open. My dick twitched, and I swallowed hard.

"Quit thinking."

I cast my eyes on Lucas and he held my gaze. His voice lowered, and he stroked my hair, pushing my head toward his lap

"Quit thinking and be my good boy. I know you need this, Kyle. Trust me to give you what you need."

I dipped my head and leaned over. Lucas unzipped his pants and held his cock for me. "Suck me in broad daylight. Let me worry about everything. All you need to do is worry about filling that mouth with all this cock and showing me how good you are, how obedient. Your only job is to take care of my cock."

I opened my mouth and followed Lucas' lead. The first few bobs were tentative.

"Do it right, baby. You know how I like it. You don't have to always be perfect. Just concentrate on being a perfect cocksucker. You get to be as slutty as you want to be, and no one can judge you or question you, especially yourself. I'm the only voice that matters right now. Open that throat and take me all the way in."

I closed my eyes and turned off my fears. Lowering my face toward his pelvis, I inhaled his scent and slid down his long rod as far as I could. I choked and fought my instincts to pull back. There was something about the hold he used. It was tight and secure and didn't leave room for doubt. Lucas continued his encouragement and his voice, deep and sultry, distracted me from all my nerves. The never-ending chant of 'I shouldn't' in my mind evolved into 'I have to', and I willed my throat to open. I didn't have the answers, but I trusted Lucas and I wanted my willingness to show him how much. There was nothing I couldn't manage, and as my airway collapsed around his intrusion, I relaxed into the sensation and let him use me. Each time Lucas pulled back and moaned his approval, I got a little braver. My mind went cloudy—a hazy slow churn of fantasies I never allowed to linger in my consciousness sober. Being choked. Restrained. Lucas in black leather. Me—a slutty whore that Lucas could use however he wanted in public.

"Fuck, babe. I'm gonna come." Lucas groaned a long, raspy curse and pushed my head forcefully against his pelvis. He trembled and the pressure against my scalp eased.

"Tell me what you're thinking," Lucas demanded, elements of Tommy still in his tone.

Maybe I was lightheaded, but I didn't scrub the first answer that had popped into my brain. "I'm embarrassed." My eyes went to the gear shift, and Lucas reached for my chin.

"Why?"

Lucas smiled, a warm ray of light flashed above us. I turned toward the light and realized a woman had opened her car door, bouncing the sun rays off her side mirror. If she'd left her apartment even five minutes earlier, she would have seen me. The thought aroused me, and I exchanged a look with Lucas to acknowledge it. "Because I loved it."

"Good. Because you aren't going to like your punishment."

"I thought that *was* my punishment?"

"No, that was for me because all those little frustrated whimpers you were making in the car were turning me the fuck on. Besides, you shouldn't like a punishment. Kyle, I want you to invite Kayla to dinner."

"Lucas," I objected.

"Make the effort to smooth things over. Holding this grudge is crazy. You never know— Maybe she's sorry and too embarrassed to reach out to you. I know you love her. We'll have to convince her that I'm here to stay, and hopefully she'll adjust."

"And if she doesn't?"

"Then you should go to Patrick's wedding solo. I'll make alternative plans. It's a Saturday. I'm sure someone is having a party that night. Case was on me the other day about how I never go to Taco Tuesdays anymore. My friends feel neglected too. Like you said, we can't stay in our bubble forever."

I smiled at him. "I like our bubble."

"Me too," Lucas said.

"I'll call you later, babe." He kissed me and opened the passenger door.

"Hey, Lucas."

He turned back to me. "Yeah?"

"My class was canceled Tuesday. Maybe we could go together?"

"To Taco Tuesday?"

"If you want. I mean, if we must leave the bubble, it'd be nice to do it together — moral support and all that."

Lucas laughed. "Yeah, I'd like that. If you need me at the dinner with your parents, you know I'll be there in a heartbeat."

I nodded. "I'll let you know. I'm going over to Kayla's now. Wish me luck. And thank you for being so understanding."

"Good luck, baby," he said and gave me another goodbye kiss.

Kayla lived in a condominium complex roughly ten minutes from Lucas' apartment. Her car was in her assigned spot. Intense anger coursed through me as I considered what I would say. Deep down, I knew we'd eventually work things out, but it still seemed too soon, and I feared saying something that would irreparably damage our relationship. That thought broke my heart.

I sat in the car with my eyes closed and focused on my breathing. I recalled the ugly words she'd spoken to me. I couldn't remember them verbatim any longer, but the venom she'd used that day had left an impression. Reconciling her fury with the best friend I'd known since we had been fourteen felt impossible. I couldn't help thinking that I had to be missing something.

Kayla had once offered to carry my children. I hadn't even asked. She'd decided I would be a great dad someday and she'd offered. I refused to believe someone who could do something so generous could just make such a mean-spirited, snap judgment about someone I loved. She didn't want me to consider both sides that time. She'd issued an ultimatum. She'd wanted me to choose. Nothing about it made sense. Hadn't she been the one to reassure me I would find my forever guy whenever I wanted to give up? The more I thought about it, the less sure I was that Kayla's issues had much to do with Lucas.

With a deep sigh, I exited the car and used my key to access her building. I paused outside her door, took another deep breath and knocked.

"Kyle," Kayla breathed, clearly as shocked to see me as I was to be there.

"I need to talk to you. Can I come in?"

She flung the door open and moved aside. I took a few steps into her condo and glanced around. Other than the Halloween décor, it hadn't changed. She motioned for me to sit and I did.

I fiddled with my phone then set it on the table. When I peered up, I met Kayla's dejected expression. "So, Patrick told me you don't want Lucas at the wedding, and I agreed to talk to you about that."

"I figured when I didn't hear from you that you're still together."

"We are."

She rolled her eyes.

I sighed. She wasn't going to make it easy. "Kayla, you're being very childish about this situation. We've been friends for a long time, and you've never not tried to get to know someone I'm dating."

"No one you were seeing ever prevented you from talking to me before."

"Lucas has nothing to do with me not speaking to you. He didn't even know until today, and he's the reason I'm here, so maybe you need to stop assuming things."

"So, you suddenly decided after more than two decades of friendship to kick me out of your house and go two months without speaking to me."

"Yeah. I did. I asked you not to badmouth Lucas, but you kept going. You're not an innocent flower in all this, Kayla. You've never had a solid opinion on anything. Everything has always had pro and con, a plus and minus. Except for Lucas, there's no other side there. Right? Suddenly I'm happy and you're absolutely positive the reason I'm so happy has to go."

She recoiled then stood and opened the door. "Then I guess you'd better get back to your little boyfriend. Have a nice life."

I didn't budge, but the niggle of doubt I'd been carrying blossomed into a full-blown suspicion. I had to ask the one question I never wanted to ask. "Kayla, do you have feelings for me?"

"Oh for fuck's sake, Kyle. Get over yourself."

"Well, I didn't think so, but this doesn't make any sense to me. And you said that thing about wanting to have the threesome."

"Like a million years ago. God. You are clueless, you know that?"

"Kayla, you're ridiculous. Stop making me guess. What is your problem with Lucas? Talk to me so we can get past this. I'll go first. I'm sorry I left you to do all the party stuff."

"You think that's what I'm angry about?"

"I have no idea why you're mad, Kayla. You won't talk to me. It makes no sense that this is about Lucas. Why? Is this really about my boyfriend?"

"It's about you ignoring me for your boyfriend."

"What?"

"Um, well, let's see. Since you started dating Lucas…" She counted on her fingers. "I barely see you. When I do see you, you're on the phone texting with him the whole night. You ditched me twice for schoolwork this summer and only later did I discover it was to watch porn with Lucas—"

"Watching porn was my project," I yelled.

Kayla rolled her eyes. "What about my birthday?"

My face scrunched as I tried to recall what I'd gotten her. "Your birthday was in August."

"Exactly."

"I took you to dinner. I got you that necklace you wanted."

She glared at me. And the details of her birthday dinner came into focus. It had been the night I'd gotten drunk and suggested the party. I couldn't remember if I'd even given her the necklace after we'd started planning the engagement party. In fact, I couldn't remember her saying much of anything that night after I'd launched into my Lucas problems. "Oh," I breathed.

"Yeah…oh. The Kyle I know wouldn't have taken his boyfriend to my favorite restaurant on my birthday after telling me he was too busy to go out that night. Then you have the nerve to rub it in my face and talk about him all night when you finally managed to squeeze me in."

"Kayla, I'm so sorry. I swear I bought you that necklace. It's probably still in my truck."

"I don't care about the gift, Kyle. You know I don't. If you were sorry, I wouldn't have to explain this to you. I don't have anything against Lucas, I barely know him. You've made no attempt to change that. The mistake I made was assuming it was because *he* wasn't important to you.

"I don't like you since you started dating Lucas. That's why I don't want him at the wedding. I don't like this rude, self-absorbed person you've become. I don't like that you'd dismissed me from your house. If it weren't for me, you wouldn't have even gotten together with him, yet now my opinion is worthless to you."

I fell back to her couch, awash with guilt. "Kayla…" I pleaded and dropped my head in my hands. "I'm sorry."

She shut the door and joined me on the couch, falling to the cushion as though thoroughly emotionally drained. "Well, that apology at least sounded sincere."

"You know I don't know what I'm doing, right? I've never felt like this."

"I figured. This is generally why I avoid love. It makes you stupid."

"For the record, I wasn't intentionally keeping you from getting to know Lucas. It's been a little overwhelming."

"I want you to be happy."

"I know."

"But that birthday thing? That hurt a lot. Then you suggested a party. You know how hard the wedding is for me. You know how much pressure my mom puts on me to be like Patrick, to want a family and be a good little wife and mother. I am happy for Patrick, but it's been like putting all my decisions in this huge spotlight. Do you know how many comments I got that my little brother is beating me to the altar? Why wouldn't you just throw me a birthday party?"

I hugged her too tight and didn't let her go. "I was an idiot. I had no idea how consumed I've been with Lucas and school." I stroked her hair. "You know I love you."

She started crying, something I hadn't seen her do since high school. "I've really missed you."

"Me too. I hate fighting with you."

"So much that you took a vacation without even telling me. I found out on Twitter, Kyle. It sucked."

"I'm sorry. Truly I am, but you were out of line that night too. This thing with Lucas and me... I need you to be supportive. If you can't be supportive, then I at least need you to be quiet."

She opened her mouth to protest, and I huffed out a warning noise. She closed her mouth and nodded slowly. "I will try." I glared at her because we both knew that wouldn't cut it. "I will. Full stop."

"Okay. So, are we over this now?"

"You take me to dinner tomorrow and you're forgiven."

I froze.

"What? Kyle, I swear if you tell me you have plans with Lucas, I will kill you right here."

"No. It's not that. Tom and Judy are in town. They want to have dinner with us."

"Your parents are here?"

"Yeah."

"Have they met Lucas?"

"Yep." My retelling of my parents' arrival and our breakfast had Kayla howling in laughter, like old times.

When I'd finished, she regarded me again. Genuine sadness had erased her smile. "Is Lucas living with you?"

I bit my lip, all but confirming her suspicions. I couldn't remember a time when Kayla didn't know every mundane detail of my life. She knew when I changed the batteries in my smoke detectors, if I'd gotten a new shirt or if I'd gained a single pound. It seemed unfathomable that she wouldn't know I'd given Lucas a key.

"Yes. Lucas still has his lease, but he's pretty much moved in. He has a key."

"Wow. You and Matt were together two years before he moved in."

"This isn't like with Matt, Kayla. It's so different. I can't even describe how perfect he is for me."

She nodded, and a hint of a smile softened her stone-faced concern. "Is Lucas going to dinner?"

"No. He offered to, but he actually wanted me to invite you instead."

"I'd like it to be for us, if that's okay. But bring him to the wedding."

"Thank you. And if you're up for it, we can grab lunch sometime. You are both important to me. I want you to love him."

She nodded tentatively. "I'll try."

And I knew she would.

Chapter Seventeen

Nothing could have prepared me for Taco Tuesday.

Shortly after my parents' visit, Lucas received word that he'd been nominated for an award. The ceremony would occur the following month, and while he'd previously won several fan-based and industry awards for 'Best Newcomer' and 'Best Top', that marked his first time being recognized for 'Best Performer'. Several other models from Goldenboys and Case had also been nominated in different categories. Lucas warned me, because of that, Taco Tuesday would be rowdier than usual and offered to blow me on our way over. Lucas was right. It did take the edge off my anxiety.

We arrived at Case and Robert's home shortly after sunset. The 'Mansion', while spacious and lavishly decorated, didn't quite live up to its nickname. After being in the business for so many years, I couldn't overlook the quality of workmanship and architectural features that distinguished a true mansion from a cookie-cutter home that happened to be swimming in square footage.

The Everwoods welcomed us in. The musky smell of sweaty boys and cannabis clung to the air. Lucas kept hold of my hand like I was a toddler near a busy intersection as he introduced me to a ton of people, only one of whom, Cole, I recognized. We gathered around a large island where Robert was mixing margaritas.

After two drinks I no longer fought the urge to pace, and we took a seat at the patio table with Case. That lasted a few minutes until a hoverboard appeared, and Lucas shot up and started giving piggy-back rides to his friends on the space-aged skateboard. But every few minutes, I'd catch Lucas doing a silent check on my well-being.

As I watched Lucas, Case eyed me. "Lucas is a great kid."

"Man," I corrected.

Case laughed warmly, small lines wrinkled the corner of his eyes, "Sorry. I met him when he was definitely still a kid."

Case's image of a naive, virginal Lucas was hard to reconcile with the kinky man who'd sucked my dick like a Hoover in the car on the way to the party. "I'm sure."

"In all the time I've known him, I've never seen him this happy."

"He's excited about his nomination."

"No," Case said, "before that. He's always been ambitious, but now he's... I don't know. Focused, maybe? He told me about your plans for Oregon. He asked us if we thought our marketing team could be run remotely."

"That dream's a long way off."

The doorbell rang, and another large wave of models entered the house. Shortly after, Case excused himself to help Robert, and I searched for Lucas.

I located him on the cement edge of the hot tub, his feet dangling in the water. The two occupants, both of whom were naked, doubled over laughing at something Lucas had said. I shored my face to remove any traces of judgment or jealousy.

"Hey, babe," Lucas greeted me.

I smiled as he scooted over to make room. I toed off my shoes and rolled up the legs of my pants while Lucas placed a towel for me to sit on. I eased my feet into the scalding hot water.

Lucas talked to his friends, mostly about the awards ceremony in Las Vegas the following month. Case and Robert were paying for all the nominees to go and bring a plus one. It seemed Cole, who had been nominated in a 'Best Twink' category, was being heavily lobbied by a new model, Jack, to be his plus one.

"Is your boyfriend going with you, Tommy?" Jack asked, batting his eyelashes as though asking for a cookie.

I turned to Lucas. "You taking me to Vegas?"

Lucas bumped his shoulder against me. "Of course, if you want to go."

"Sorry, Jack. You need to find your own man." Lucas' gaze fixated on me, clearly surprised by my willingness to join him. He'd been so delighted to be nominated, I couldn't imagine not being there to help him celebrate.

Cole splashed Jack. "Yeah. Get your own man." Cole beamed at me, and I blushed under his admiring gaze. Lucas and Cole alternated putting Jack in his place. Apparently asking for perks before a single scene had been released was frowned upon. A few minutes later, Jack left the hot tub in a huff.

"Does Tommy call you Daddy?" Cole asked innocently.

I chuckled. "No, but sometimes Lucas does." I took a big swig of my fourth—or was it my fifth?—margarita and swallowed. They went down so much easier now that my lips were numb.

"If you were my man, I'd call you Daddy all the time. I'd like to be tied to your bed so you could take turns on me. Hell, you could do me together."

The suggestion sent margarita flying from my mouth and nose. God, it burned. I used the back of my hand to clean my face. "Um… Thank you? I think," I choked out. "But we um… We don't do that." I coughed a few times and dared a peek at Lucas. He shook with tittering laughter.

Cole puffed his lips out and he rose to his feet, displaying his waiflike, hairless body and prominent erection. "The offer is open." He used my thigh as purchase to lift out of the hot tub, bringing my face within inches of his dick. I averted my eyes back to Lucas, who proudly watched Cole walk away.

He turned back toward me and stared, jaw slacked. Silently, I gauged his interest in Cole's offer, the margaritas having convinced me the topic was worthy of discussion. Then, I remembered Judd Fisher and Kayla's commentary about how I'd rejected the threesome offer without even a conversation. I didn't want to repeat that mistake and Lucas did say Cole could take two dicks like a champ. That wasn't an offer one got every day. "You interested?"

Lucas cocked his head, his nostrils flaring, then shot to his feet and declared, "Well, I'm not nearly drunk enough for that convo," and disappeared into the house.

He returned with two more margaritas and a plate full of tacos and motioned for me to join him at the table.

Lucas' friends were fun, if not a little crazy. Some of them, like Jack, were highly immature and generally acted like a bunch of schoolboys who had just discovered what their dicks could do. Lucas gravitated to the handful that seemed older, content to drink and smoke in moderation, including Case and Robert. I followed him, generously lubricating my anxiety with delicious cocktails while Lucas documented our night for his social media accounts.

By the end of the evening, I'd skipped right over tipsy and landed face first into drunk. I must have fallen asleep because I recalled Lucas nudging me around midnight, informing me it was time to go.

Lucas woke me the next morning with a phone and ordered me to call in sick. I fought him long enough to determine the head-splitting hangover was close enough and made the call.

"No more Taco Tuesdays for you," Lucas said and placed a glass of water and ibuprofen on my bedside table.

"Ugh," I grumbled. "I'm never leaving our bubble again. Bad things happen out of the bubble."

Lucas grinned and forced the pills into my hand. "Take these. Coffee's brewing."

"Sleep," I pleaded and yanked the covers over my head.

I woke again in the early afternoon, having graduated from roadkill to zombie. Lucas was on the couch, watching some property show and typing away on his laptop.

I smacked my lips and ran my tongue over my teeth. "I feel like something died in my mouth."

"Yeah. In hindsight, you probably should have listened to me and stopped before the ninth margarita."

My mouth puckered. "Nine?"

"Don't blame me. I tried to stop you at five. Cole is responsible for six through nine."

"I think I might be too old for Taco Tuesday."

Lucas' eyebrow peeked. "And for Cole's offer?"

I waved him off. "Tequila is evil."

"You're only allowed to drink tequila around me now." Lucas laughed, but his relief was palpable. If I hadn't felt like vomiting, his jealousy would have turned me on.

"How about you go to Taco Tuesday solo, and I'll plan something with Kayla?" I plopped next to him and put my head on his lap, ignoring the hard plastic against my scalp. Lucas laughed, relocated the laptop to the table and stroked my hair.

"Sounds like an anti-date night?"

"Think of it as a 'let's maintain our friendships' night."

He jabbed a finger into my chest. "I still can't believe you didn't tell me it was Kayla's birthday when I suggested dinner that night."

"I can't believe I forgot. It's all your fault. Love makes me stupid."

He pressed a kiss to my forehead and gave me my smile. "You'd better not forget my birthday."

"It's on April Fool's Day. Hard to forget."

"And yours is next month, which happens to coincide with the Vegas trip. Is that okay?" Lucas asked.

"Yeah. Forty-one requires no fanfare."

"It's your first birthday as my boyfriend. I want to do something special."

He was so freaking endearing. If my mouth didn't taste like ass, I would have kissed him. "Dinner and a blow job are fine. Don't go crazy."

He shook his head. "I'll need the distraction. I spoke with my parents this morning and gave them my blessing for Vietnam. They'll likely be gone for Christmas."

I tilted my head and rubbed his cheek. "I'm proud of you," I said. His eyes misted over. "You'll be here with my parents and me, right?"

"I can't wait."

That settled, I relaxed and let him take care of my stupid ass. Lucas recounted his memories of the previous night, highlighting some of my less-than-flattering moments. "Kayla is going to die when I tell her about Cole's offer."

Lucas cracked a smile. "Not sure that's going to help my 'win Kayla over' campaign. Make sure you tell her I'm the one that threatened Cole with a violent death if he didn't knock it off."

Yep, I loved Lucas in green. But I smiled because Kayla was still the first person I wanted to call with a good story. "I will. She's going to be so impressed that I didn't flip out."

Chapter Eighteen

Kayla and I had the first of our 'Tony Tuesdays' after the fall semester ended. We'd spoken on the phone nearly every day but an undercurrent of tension remained that I was anxious to get rid of before Patrick's wedding.

"Two rigatonis, please." I closed the menu and handed it to our server. Ordering our favorite meal in a restaurant that held so many memories was cathartic. I took a sip of my wine and relaxed as our reunion began. "So, we have some things to catch up on. I've fallen in love, been propositioned into a threesome involving double penetration by the twinkiest of twinks and plan to attend the gay adult entertainment awards next weekend. You know, same old, same old. What's new with you?"

Kayla rolled her eyes and swirled her glass. "I'm now Tracey's maid of honor."

"Get out," I cried.

"She and her friend had a falling out. Apparently, I'm the only one that can stand up to a bridezilla, so I got the job."

"Your mother?" I laughed.

"I assume she was the head of the nomination committee."

"So, you and Matt are in charge of the bachelor and bachelorette parties? I'm dying to hear the details."

"Matt's going full stripper I'm afraid. I figured you would know. It's next weekend because his one groomsman was home for the holidays. We aren't doing ours until closer to the wedding."

"Naked women or gay porn stars? Hmmm. Tough call. What are you doing?"

She laughed. "I'm a classy girl. We're doing a bar crawl and spa day weekend."

"Nice. Very Tracey."

She tipped her glass, and I clinked it.

"What else is new?" I asked.

"I got a promotion."

"Oh my God, that's awesome."

Her smile faltered and she hesitated. "It's in Portland."

"What?" I gasped.

"I'm going to take it. It's an Associate VP position."

"You deserve it."

"Well, since I married my career, it's a good thing I'm good at it."

"You're not just good at it. You love it," I said.

"I do. My mom isn't happy."

"It's your life, Kayla. Do what makes you happy."

Her smile returned and she sighed. "Lucas has changed you."

"He has," I agreed.

"For the better."

"I know." I smiled.

"I want to know him before I leave."

"You will."

She aimed her finger at me. "You'd better come visit me."

"Try and stop me."

The rigatoni arrived, and we shared our first and last Tony Tuesday together. Kayla fell into her old habits, advocating both for and against the threesome with Cole.

"Something is enticing about sharing a man with him, but I think it's one of those fantasies that would be best to leave there," I said. "Lucas gets jealous easily. I think he would do anything I wanted, but honestly, I think he'd regret it later. And if it changed things for us, I'd never forgive myself."

She opened her mouth and closed it suddenly. She thought a minute and said, "You're right."

My eyebrows shot up. "I'm right? Can I get that on a T-shirt?"

"When it comes to Lucas, I think you should follow your gut."

* * * *

'Follow your gut.' Kayla's words were front and center in my mind as the Las Vegas Strip grew larger in the window. Lucas squeezed my hand, and my breath quickened as the wheels bounced upon landing at McCarran. My gut told me not to ask Lucas what was wrong. He'd talk to me when he was ready.

"Vegas, baby." Case's voice came from the row behind us, and the Goldenboys contingent let out a collective 'whoop' that made the flight attendant cringe, but Lucas remained stoic. I sent a silent plea to him. *Talk to me, baby. Tell me how to help.*

We piled into the terminal and navigated past the temptation of clings and clangs from the slot machines. Vegas had an infectious energy that could infuse the dead, and Lucas, despite being off, had perked up considerably by the time we'd checked into our hotel.

I set our bags down on the large bench that ran the foot of the bed and fell on the king-size mattress. The place was swanky, with a large bathtub and shower complete with seat, a full-size couch, a desk and not one, but three armless chairs. I wondered if he'd want to fuck against the floor-to-ceiling windows overlooking the Las Vegas Strip. That could be hot. I used the remote near the bed to open the blinds and went to check out the view of the gondolas floating on the water.

"Come look at this," I said to Lucas, but he gave me a distracted nod and stared at his phone, his lip tucked in between his teeth. The fact that Lucas had failed to notice our numerous options for getting busy spiked my anxiety.

"What's the schedule?" I asked.

"My mom is going to call at six. It's nine a.m. in Hanoi." He checked his wrist and seemed unbothered by the lack of a watch.

"That gives us a few hours."

"Okay. But I might miss their call in the casino."

"How about we get some lunch and explore the hotel? I've never stayed at The Venetian. We could do some shopping."

Lucas paced and started unpacking to process his nervous energy.

"Babe, do you want to talk about it?" I asked.

"No. Let's do that. I need the distraction."

I debated pushing Lucas to talk, but he wasn't going to be okay until his parents called. Joann had shared with me that Lucas was always anxious when they traveled, reminding me that Lucas had been orphaned once, so I should never suggest his fear for their safety was irrational. The best I could do was distract him.

Lucas and I ate then wandered aimlessly, weaving in and out of the high-end shops, stopping to say hello to people in town for the awards ceremony from other studios. The real distraction came from the fans. Tommy took over each time someone approached for a picture or autograph, momentarily dulling his anxiety.

"We should head back now," Lucas said, glancing at his phone again to check the time. We still had forty minutes, but I nodded.

The phone rang at six sharp and Lucas' relief was palpable. I excused myself so he could talk to his parents in private. I wandered into Cole and his plus one at the craps table, a man I suspected was the Italian super-fan, based on his heavily accented English and a fat stack of chips. Cole preened like a peacock under his companion's over-the-top adoration, and I saw him through Lucas' eyes—not as an oversexed, vapid twink, but as a slightly-damaged, beautiful soul finally getting his due.

Lucas was waiting for me when I returned to the room. His smile delivered the all-clear I was praying for. "You good?" I asked.

"Yes." He smiled, and I watched the façade crumble. "My mom has a sister." His tone revealed a potpourri of emotions. I rushed to him and held him when tears breeched his eyes and streamed down his cheeks.

"Baby, oh baby." I rocked him, even as he insisted they were happy tears.

He pulled away from me and wiped his eyes with his shirt. "Jesus. I can't stop." He laughed, red-splotchy patches covering his wet neck and cheeks.

"Tell me what your mom said."

Lucas slowly exhaled and wiped away the teardrops clinging to his face. "She met her Aunt Mai and her grandparents, who are still alive. Her mother died in childbirth, which her parents knew when they adopted her, but her birth mother had apparently had another child a few years before her. Her sister's birth father was a US service member who'd abandoned them after the war or died, no one could say for sure. Her mother left that child with an infertile cousin to raise. Anyway, they live in a very rural area, and my mom's trying to arrange a chance to meet her."

"Wow. That's crazy. How do you feel about it?"

"I don't know. I'm happy for her, of course. It's pretty incredible if you think about it." The tears started again, but at least he was smiling.

I nodded and yanked him into my chest. Lucas' sense of well-being was second only to his physical safety in my book. My inability to understand the full breadth of his experience as an adoptee left me powerless. I wouldn't placate him pretending otherwise, so I did the one thing I knew how to do—I listened to him. He told me stories that broke my heart, about a young kid who used to hide in a closet and scream for his mother, who couldn't enter a crowded place without seeking out persons who most resembled them.

While Lucas talked, I conjured up an image. We were in a hospital. Kayla was in a bed, sweaty and exhausted. She handed me a swaddled baby in a blue blanket and, in turn, I passed Lucas his son. The dream was silly. Kayla was already forty-one. I doubted she'd be able to carry Lucas' child, even if she agreed to it. We'd get a surrogate—someone with no ties to us. I didn't care what it cost. I wanted it for him, more than the lake house or the degree. Giving Lucas a biological child became my third, and most important, non-negotiable dream.

Lucas and I ordered a shitload of calorie-ridden foods and spent the evening in our hotel room watching old movies. Well, old for Lucas. I was hard-pressed to put *Sixteen Candles* in the same category as *Casablanca*. Tommy was nowhere to be found, as Lucas snuggled against me and soaked up all the love and attention I could muster until we both fell fast asleep.

The next thing I remember was Lucas shaking me. "Wake up, baby." He was out of bed, wearing workout clothes, his collar wet with perspiration. It took me a few seconds to realize it was morning.

"How long have you been up?"

"A while." Lucas opened the curtain to reveal it was at least mid-morning. "Thought you could use the extra sleep. You've been so restless the last few nights. Did you sleep well?"

I nodded since it was true. Not knowing how to help Lucas had given me a few sleepless nights. Now that we had talked and I understood what all he was processing, I was drained, but Lucas was rearing to go.

"You going to get up?" he asked.

I tugged the pillow over my head as my response and listened to Lucas' mellifluous humming while he went about his morning routine.

"I'm getting naked," Lucas hollered.

A few minutes later, he added, "My cock is out and I'm stroking it."

The shower door opened and closed. Lucas shouted, "Baby, my dick is rock hard. I'm gonna get all soapy and play with my hole."

I sank into the bed and waited him out, stroking myself in anticipation.

A few seconds later, Lucas whined, "Babe, get in here and fuck me."

I chuckled. "You come here and ride my dick."

"Babe—" Lucas begged.

The needy quality of his voice almost ended me. I closed my eyes and pictured him—fingers sliding in and out of his slicked hole. I would be crazy to give in. The day was already going to be long, and he'd be kinky as fuck after the awards ceremony. I needed to pace myself, and that meant starting the day with lazy comfy bed sex, not the back-bending, knee-punishing feat of gymnastics Lucas' shower fuck would involve. That man's imagination would be the death of me.

"Kyle!" Lucas stomped to get my attention. Drops of water listed from his hair down his naked torso before disappearing onto the tented towel wrapped around his waist.

"What?"

"I did abs today." Two fingers traced along the ridges of his stomach, up his chest and squeezed his nipple. He bit his lower lip between his teeth and waited for me to respond.

Damn it. "Take pity on me. I'm an old man."

Lucas' tossed his head back and he fought to stop laughing. His smile faded in an unsuccessful attempt to be seductive. "Fuck me," he said and yanked the covers off the bed. He knee-walked up the mattress until he straddled my waist. I unwrapped the towel like a present. His cock, semi-hard, flopped onto my stomach. I spat on my hand and covered his dick with my palm, pressing firmly. A primal groan fell from Lucas' lips, and his hips flicked forward. I reached up to cup his neck, hauling him down for a kiss as the velvety rod slid over my stomach.

Lucas danced his tongue with mine in between whispered endearments. In full control, he lifted so I could watch his body conduct an erotic symphony. Every moan dripped with need. Every feather light kiss tantalized and teased. He ground his hips on my lap in their own titillating ballet. His quickening breath warmed my skin, leaving goosebumps behind as it cooled.

Slippery fluid spilled onto my belly, signaling a new stage of arousal. Lucas stared down at me, kiss-swollen lips parted and eyes heated enough to melt steel. Reaching behind him, he grabbed my cock and guided it to his hole, nudging the tip and using his thumb on the sensitive spot under the crown. I arched into his touch. "Put it in," I moaned, craving the tight heat of his body.

Lucas reached for the nightstand. Without thinking, I grabbed his wrist and squeezed it tight to still him. I wiped up his pre-cum, added spit and slicked my cock. "I said, put it in, *boy*."

Black pupils eclipsed the blue of his eyes, and he relaxed his jaw. I let go of his wrist and held the base of my cock. The heat of his passage clenched around me and warmth slowly spread through my body as he seated himself. "Good boy," I said and splayed a hand on his abs to keep him upright and still while he waited.

He clenched his muscles, threw his head back and begged me to move.

His cock lifted from my belly, defying gravity. "Ride me slow," I commanded. Lucas lifted and lowered inch-by-inch and simultaneously moved his hips in tight circles. The pleasure flowed in and out, up and down, and pinprick tingles tickled my skin.

"Like that, Daddy?" Lucas asked, then gradually upped the tempo of his movements and opened his mouth like a baby bird to suck on my fingers.

"Yes, baby." I groaned and closed my eyes. "Just like that." He rode me at a pace meant to prolong our pleasure, taking our time to experience every sensation condoms had robbed us of us.

"Watch me." Lucas tilted my chin to the closet to our left. The mirrored doors provided a phenomenal view of Lucas' backside. He narrated our love-making in extravagant detail.

Lust drunk, I held his hips and bucked hard. "Like that," Lucas cried, offering his approval with a breathless, curse-filled prayer. I pressed my back into the mattress and bent my knees, harnessing all the leverage I could muster to meet his pleas for harder and faster. Strobe lights flashed before my eyes, momentarily blinding me, and concentrated the sensations into the intense, almost painful constriction of his muscles around me.

"I'm coming, Kyle. Oh, God. Don't Stop. Breed me. Fill me. Fuck me. Fuck me. *Fuck me*." Lucas tore the orgasm out of me. I convulsed in a full-body spasm that threatened to levitate us right off the bed. His sweaty body collapsed against me, reducing the capacity of my already-burning lungs to fill. I didn't care. I could drown in his body and die a happy man.

Delirious, he rolled off me and landed ungracefully with his legs tangled with mine. "Jesus H. Christ," Lucas laughed and slapped a heavy-hand on my chest. "You are my absolute favorite workout."

"You're going to kill me one day."

Lucas grinned. "You don't know the half of it. Now that the condoms have come off, we are going to relive every kinky, crazy thing we've ever done with an alternate, messier ending."

I couldn't wait.

* * * *

Lucas and I cleaned up and headed out to the Strip, bypassing the pool for the stellar people-watching in the casinos. I got to know a few more Goldenboys and surprised myself with how okay I was running around with Lucas' friends. It helped that two of the other models had brought their non-porn boyfriends.

The evening's agenda started with pre-gaming in Case and Robert's suite. Lucas eased his transformation into Tommy with vodka. Being the wise adult who had learned his lesson, I drank water — until I realized I was the only sober person in a room crammed full of drunk porn stars twenty years my junior. Then, I drank bourbon. *Best. Decision. Ever.*

We made our way to the ballroom for the awards ceremony. The Goldenboys team was seated at two round eight-person tables. I tugged at my necktie and wondered, not for the first time, how my life had led me to a room full of adult entertainers. "You okay, baby?" Lucas placed a hand on my arm and leaned into me. *Oh, yeah — Lucas.*

Dinner was served, and the drinks were flowing. I shook hands with men whose names I would never remember with bodies that didn't seem real. It was a dreamlike world with a cult-like following. Lucas had slipped into his Tommy persona as he worked the room with the same confidence that'd convinced me to follow him to that study room.

The awards were handed out. Cole was the first winner from the table, accepting his award with a touching speech about self-acceptance. His Italian lover—Giacomo or Giuseppe, I couldn't remember—had given a prolonged standing ovation and produced a Cartier box upon Cole's return to the table.

The scene Lucas had filmed over the summer did not win in the 'Best Group Scene' category nor did any of the Goldenboys take honors for 'Best Top', 'Fan Favorite' or 'Best Newcomer'. After a long stretch of losses, Lucas had focused the full weight of Tommy's exhibitionist-loving sexual energy on me. I hadn't had to work so hard to keep an erection under control in public since high school.

"Hey, Tommy. This is you." Case nudged Lucas as the award for 'Best Performer' was announced.

I swatted his hand from my fly. "Behave yourself." His mischievous smile told me he was absolutely *not* planning to obey. I placed a palm on his thigh, squeezed as hard as I could and whispered, "Don't think because everyone is calling you Tommy tonight that Daddy won't spank Lucas over his knee right here."

There. Right there. That was my smile.

"And the winner for best performer in an adult feature is…"

"Tommy Bruiser," the announcers shouted. The entire ballroom erupted with applause. I shot up from the table like Lucas had won an Oscar and hugged him. We shared a brief kiss before Robert swept him into a hug and his friends surrounded him.

He weaved his way to the front, taking the steps to the stage two at a time. I couldn't tear my eyes away from him — under the lights, fed with attention, he blossomed in front of me. I'd stopped trying to figure it out. Perhaps some hole in Lucas' heart was filled by all of it — the semi-fame, the adoration, the porn. Perhaps it indeed was altruistic. It didn't matter anymore, not when the first thing he did was blow me a kiss in front of a room full of good-looking men. My heart burst with pride and love, and that was before Lucas made his speech.

"Thank you so much," Lucas gushed and admired the award while the audience applauded. "Thank you. I want to say a few things. First, thanks to Case and Robert. Working for Goldenboys has been an amazing time. You treat me like family, and I love you both. You're a fucking inspiration."

The Goldenboys tables erupted into renewed applause for their bosses.

"So much has happened this year. I've worked with some wonderful, sexy men, some of whom let me turn their asses bright red. So thanks for that, boys." The audience laughed, and Lucas flashed a brilliant, toothy smile.

"I got into porn because I wanted to make a difference for all the boys like me, for anyone who thought they were weird or different. I wanted to show them how sexy and good their bodies can feel.

"When I started, winning something like this" — he gawked at the trophy — "seemed too good to be true. But now? Now it's time for me to say goodbye to Tommy Bruiser."

The room gasped and Lucas smiled. My smile... aimed right at me. I studied Case, who nodded his confirmation and offered me a toast.

"Tonight, I'm happy to announce my formal retirement as a performer. I'll still be at Goldenboys, working with our awesome marketing team. But there's only one man I want to make feel sexy now, and I'm gonna devote all my energy to making him feel all the pleasure I can for the rest of our lives if he'll let me. I love you, Kyle. You are my rock, my lover, my best friend — and my daddy when I can get you drunk enough. Thank you all for your support. This is truly the best way to end this remarkable ride. Thank you again. Have a great night."

Lucas floated back to me, flushed red from the lights of the stage. I stood, dumbfounded and so damn happy. He was it for me. This was it. Lucas was the one. I wished I had a damn ring.

"What'd you think of my speech?" Lucas asked shyly.

"I think... I think I'm speechless," I said. The table cracked up, and I remembered we had an audience. "Are you sure?"

He nodded. "I love it, but I'm done now. I'll stay in the industry. I couldn't think of anything better to get you for your birthday."

"You don't have to."

"I know. I want to. I want to give you everything, Kyle. I'd do anything for you."

That Las Vegas ballroom could have burned to the ground and Lucas and I wouldn't have noticed. I couldn't stop looking at him, and he couldn't stop looking at me. With just a smile, we said everything that could ever be said. We managed to control ourselves through the last award, which was awarded to Goldenboys as a studio and was accepted by Robert and Case.

Despite the full agenda of after-parties, some of which contained public fucking as the featured entertainment, Robert took us aside and told us plainly we should, "get a damn room."

Lucas agreed it was an excellent idea. The next time we left our room was to catch our flight home.

Chapter Nineteen

The nuptials of Tracey Knowles and Patrick Anderson occurred on a blustery March afternoon roughly a year after I'd met Lucas. The bride, dressed in a figure-skimming floral lace gown, had no reason to worry about the attention being stolen from her. Her hair was styled in an asymmetrical loose updo, secured with a sparkly clip, and her makeup was flawless.

I caught Kayla's attention as she fluffed Tracey's veil outside the small, Catholic church and smiled encouragement. I knew her brave soldier look well. She struggled to keep her wrap positioned and hold her bouquet. Kayla rarely wore any sleeveless tops. She hated her biceps, and the rose-colored knee-length dress did her strawberry-blonde hair and freckled, pale white skin no favors.

When the processional music started playing, Simon and I followed instructions to escort Kayla and Patrick's grandmother, followed by Tracey's mother then Esther and Mitch. Once the family members were seated, Simon and I took our places next to Matt and Patrick.

I stood at the front, glanced around at the elaborate flower arrangements and found my center. Lucas sat in the third row, behind Patrick and Kayla's family. He wore the same pink shirt he'd worn to their engagement party, under a navy slim-fit suit Joann had purchased for him in Vietnam and given to him for Christmas. The pink and navy patterned tie was borrowed from my limited collection. I could personally attest that in addition to looking remarkable around Lucas' neck, the tie looked phenomenal bound around his eyes.

Lucas noticed me staring. He glanced down at his tie and fingered it suggestively and raised an eyebrow. He tucked his lip between his teeth.

Matt elbowed me and whispered, "Would you quit with the eye-fucking already?"

I cleared my throat, straightened my spine and refocused my attention to the bridesmaids ambling down the aisle. When Kayla appeared in the doorway, she met my gaze. I winked at her, and she flashed her brilliant white smile. I couldn't understand what about Patrick's marriage had her racked with angst, but I suspected it threw her own choices into focus. Like Lucas, Kayla always had marched to the beat of her own drum.

In the few opportunities I'd taken to get Lucas and Kayla in the same room together before she'd left, Lucas hadn't thrown himself into winning her over. Kayla would have seen right through that. No, he'd asked Kayla about our shared history and implored her to tell him about our years of friendship in story after story. Every time he positioned himself as the third wheel, and on each occasion, after Kayla and I had relived some obscure memory, a little more of Kayla's guard came down and our bond reformed.

I thought her move to Portland and the distance from her parents had been precisely what she'd needed. In a way, the change would be good for us both. Matt may have had a point about us holding each other back. I doubted she would have considered the promotion if it hadn't been for our falling out and I certainly wouldn't have encouraged her to leave me. I'd missed her terribly the minute she'd left me on the other side of the security line, but we'd fixed what had been broken. Her questions about Lucas and our relationship no longer sounded forced. Her encouragement was cautious but genuine.

The brief ceremony seemed more like Esther than Tracey and Patrick. During the traditional Bible readings and vows, my mind wandered again to Lucas and our wedding. We'd skip the church for something outdoors. A beach? I could see that. Lucas would love something spontaneous like Vegas, too. Anything that didn't follow a traditional path.

My speculation continued during the time that we posed for pictures and made our way to the venue. Lucas waited for me in the atrium with the other guests. Following the introduction of the wedding party, I escorted Lucas to our table in the front of the ballroom adorned with silk-covered tables and elaborate centerpieces of pink-and-white roses. Lucas appeared angelic in the candlelit hall. We sat with the other members of the wedding party and their dates.

"Sit here, Lucas." Kayla motioned to the seat to her left. Lucas stole a glance at me and accepted Kayla's offer. Matt, who had also not brought a date, was to her right. The other place settings were reserved for Simon and his date, a distinguished gentleman named Ron, who we learned was campy after a few drinks.

Ron kept the awkwardness of the table to a simmer with his jokes. "So I hear you're responsible for the trauma inflicted on my poor Simon. Some skinny white girl he could ignore, but you know that sistas gonna earn every penny of their money. He came back from the bachelor party muttering like that guy in *Rain Man*. I had to put him in the shower fully clothed and run cold water over him."

Matt cracked up. "Hey, I'm just the best man. The groom picked the gender and race of the strippers."

Simon slapped him playfully on the chest, and Ron shrugged. "Oh, stop. I did not."

"Oh, girl… You know you woke up the next day and asked me to bleach your eyes, talking about how they were going to strip your platinum status. Next time you are hosting mixed company, I hope you'll at least try to get some big-dicked stud to balance the affair."

The table erupted in laughter until Matt cast a tentative, indecipherable look at Lucas. We'd skipped the bachelor party since it had been the weekend of Lucas' awards ceremony, not that we were itching to go to begin with. I placed a hand on Lucas' knee to reassure him and attempted to diffuse Matt's attention. It wasn't until Lucas searched my reaction that I realized Matt was reacting to Ron's stripper reference and that Matt had sort of a day-dreamy gaze on his face. *Oh, for fuck sake.*

"Matt," I snapped.

Matt whipped his head from Lucas to me, and his embarrassed glow was its own sort of apology.

"Sorry," he mumbled and took a large swig of his drink.

Lucas tossed his head back with glee and smirked. "I don't really dance, Matt, but let me know next time, and I'll send you the strap-on kit that goes with your dildo."

A collective burst of laughter and Kayla's mouthful of wine had half of us reaching for napkins. "Oh my God, Lucas," she howled and bumped her shoulder against him. He beamed at her, and I could sense the affection growing between them.

After that, the table loosened up considerably. Throughout the night, I couldn't have bonded Lucas to Kayla any stronger than if I'd dunked them in Super Glue. Unfortunately, the bonding came at my expense, and Matt was only too thrilled to join in.

"Lucas, have you seen him in project mode?" Kayla asked, sending Matt into fits of laughter.

"You mean 'the face'?" Matt imitated a constipated turtle, and Kayla nodded. "God, I wanted to set the kitchen on fire when he asked me for help on that backsplash."

"I'm not that bad. All I asked you to do was hold the level straight."

Matt rolled his eyes. "You are a perfectionist and you have no patience when people don't meet your high standards. Admit it."

"It's true. In high school, Kyle offered to build the sets for the school play. There were like ten volunteers, and Kyle ran them all off with his perfectionism. He ended up spending hours doing it all by himself," Kayla said.

"Amateurs — all of them. Don't listen to them," I told Lucas.

"Hmmm, maybe I don't want to help finish the garage? You did kick me out of my own kitchen when I dropped the screw behind the fridge."

The table again cracked up, but I'd had enough. "All right. I think we're done ganging up on me. Let's dance, babe."

Lucas hedged. "Uh. I wasn't kidding that I don't dance. Unless you can convince this band to pay rave music and add about two hundred more shirtless men— I can grind with the best of them."

"I'll dance with you," Matt offered, placed his napkin on the table and started to stand.

"Down boy," Lucas ordered. He was smiling, but his tone was Tommy if I'd ever heard it. Matt returned to his seat like he'd had a magnet shoved up his ass. "Kyle will teach me."

I shrugged at Matt. "C'mon, baby." I grabbed Lucas' hand and attempted to explain the simple box step. "One. Two. Three," I counted when he struggled to keep time to the waltz.

Lucas stepped on my foot and cringed. "This isn't working."

I pressed my lips to his forehead. "Don't look at your feet. Relax and let me lead. You keep fighting it. Once you have the steps down, I'll follow you if you want."

"Maybe you should dance with Matt."

"Baby, I'd rather watch you grind half-naked to techno music in a warehouse full of men than dance with Matt."

Lucas shot up an eyebrow and he swallowed a gulp. "Wow, so that's a no to dancing with Matt then."

I chuckled, and the tension left Lucas' frame. He stopped fighting me and started to get the hang of it.

"Yeah, that's a no." I gathered him closer and introduced a turn until we were moving in a natural motion. When the song ended, my mother interrupted and asked me to dance with her.

Lucas returned to the table, grabbed Kayla's hand and led her to the floor. "Think you can handle underarm turns?" I asked my mother. Her eyes lit up with excitement. I'd learned ballroom from my mother, but she was less steady on her feet than she'd been the last time we'd danced. "Is your hip okay?"

"Oh. It bothers me after a long day. But you know I love to dance."

I smiled and led her in one turn, but her face winced as she returned to face me. "Better take it easy," I suggested.

"Lucas seems to be picking it up. He should be leading her though." My mother nodded to where Lucas and Kayla were still practicing off to the side.

Sure enough, Kayla was leading, and I caught Lucas' eye line. He gave me my smile, and my heart jumped. "He's practicing to dance with me," I explained to my mother.

"Well, I hadn't thought of that. That's sweet."

"It is."

"You seem quite smitten with Lucas."

"It's more than that. I love him, Mom. He's everything."

Her eyes widened. "I thought as much, what with including him in Christmas. I can't remember you and Matt spending the holidays together. Did Lucas' parents enjoy their trip?"

"Yes, they did." I updated my mother on Joann and Greg's trip. They'd returned a few days before New Year's. Joann had met her birth sister and her family, which included five children. Lucas had asked me to accompany him to pick his parents up from the airport, and the drop in Lucas' anxiety had been immediate.

The song ended, and my mother wanted to rest. I escorted her back to her seat and said hello to Mitch and my father, who were in the throes of a heated sports discussion.

When I returned to my table, Lucas and Kayla were alone. Simon and Ron were chatting up Tracey's parents and Matt had disappeared.

"You two still trading notes on what an asshole I am?"

Lucas laughed. "No, Kayla was telling me about David. Hot wax? Have you been holding out on me, baby?"

I gave Kayla a dirty look. "Why did I want you two to get along again?"

"Because you love us," Lucas and Kayla said simultaneously, and an unholy partnership was born.

Shortly after dinner and cake, the formal dancing ended. The old people, which Lucas and Kayla insisted did not include me, cleared out, and a deejay began playing contemporary songs made for regular dancing. I mouthed along to the Four Seasons, watching as Patrick and Tracey let loose with their friends and family. Lucas danced with Kayla and surprisingly, my mother, who had stayed behind after my father had called it a night. Everyone was laughing and having a good time. After months of worry, Lucas had not only charmed my friends but my parents too.

I didn't know why I'd worried about our lives fitting together like we were two puzzle pieces that had to connect just so or wouldn't work. We weren't fixed, solid objects. Love and life were more fluid than that. I no longer wondered how to fit Lucas into my life or if I would fit into his. We just flowed along together. *Oh, what a night*, indeed.

The song changed, and Taylor Swift's *Mine* blared over the speakers. Lucas searched me out, flashed his brilliant, knowing smile and beckoned me to the dance floor with a crook of his finger. I joined him and tugged him into my arms. I jumped around, danced poorly and sang along loudly in his ear, serenading him. Confident in my declaration that he was absolutely the best thing I would ever call mine.

Lucas pulled back to grin at me. "You're ridiculous... but I love you."

I shushed him and dipped him back dramatically. He swayed as I set him upright. I kissed him and laughed. "First thing tomorrow we are finding ourselves a better song."

He laughed, shook his head and gave me my smile.

Epilogue

Many years later

On the morning of our tenth anniversary, I woke to find Lucas dancing with a blonde-haired, blue-eyed angel we'd named Norah Joann. She looked exactly like her daddy and was worth every penny, and arguably a million more than we'd paid for the egg donation and surrogacy six years prior. Every time I caught Lucas marveling at her appearance or mannerisms, I fell more in love with them both.

Our home, like our hearts, was busting at the seams. It no longer resembled the showcase I'd once been so proud of. Our framed degrees hung, cock-eyed, above the desk that'd been relocated from the office that now served as Norah's bedroom. The gorgeous maple hardwood had a prominent grape juice stain in front of the stove. The pantry, which had mysteriously shrunk, was covered in Norah's pictures. A wall of colorful plastic bins overflowing with toys now ran the length of the half-wall. After the unfortunate meeting of my stone fireplace with Norah's forehead, we'd wrapped the edges with some Styrofoam contraption that reminded me of the foam, noodle-shaped floats we used in the pool.

Instead of a truck, my finished garage contained four bicycles, one with a ride-along carrier still attached and covered in cobwebs, another with training wheels and ribbons flowing from the pink handles. Two strollers, an ExerSaucer, car seats, a baby swing, booster seats, boxes and boxes of infant-thru-toddler clothes and toys she'd outgrown, and a Barbie Power Wheels' Jeep had joined the lawn mower, weedwhacker and trash bins. I'd suggested we have a garage sale, but Lucas hadn't ruled out adopting a second child and wanted to hold on to them.

I opened the extra refrigerator, smiling with the knowledge that it hid a poorly cut drywall section around the outlet. I still fought the urge to fix it just as powerfully as the day Lucas had insisted his measurement error had given the garage 'character'. I retrieved the apple juice and roll of biscuits with a small laugh at the memory of our first real attempt to do a home improvement project together.

On the way back into the house, I tripped. "Norah," I hollered, muttering a curse under my breath. I softened my tone. "You can't leave your skates in front of the door, darling. Someone could get hurt."

I turned the corner and found Lucas in the middle of the floor, the coffee table pushed to one side. Norah stood on his feet while he led her in a basic box step. "One, two, three. One, two, three," she counted.

"Lucas," I cautioned. He'd staked out the role of more permissive parent early, which didn't bother me, but lately, Norah's hearing had become selective. Lucas glanced up, his expression more remorseful than I'd expected.

He dipped her over his arm and set her upright, spanking her playfully on the butt. "I'm going to help Daddy with breakfast. Go pick up your mess, toots."

Lucas pressed a kiss to my cheek and squeezed my ass. "I would have sent her when we were done. Relax, Daddy."

I rolled my eyes at him. That game had lost much of its appeal once we *were* daddies, which wasn't to say we didn't still engage in some lighthearted nostalgic banter.

"We're out of yogurt because you didn't add it to the list," I said. Lucas chuckled and attempted to kiss the grump out of me. Norah returned, and Lucas dropped his hand to pour my coffee and thrust it into my hands.

"I wanna help," Norah declared when I shooed her away from the stove. Lucas and Norah looked at me. My smile. Lucas' still melted me, but when confronted with the power of Norah's matching expression, resistance was futile.

"Go get the stool from the bathroom," I said.

Meals prepared straight from a box — too often consumed on the way to swim lessons or ballet — had replaced our naked gourmet cooking and wine experiments. Cooking had become a family affair, and Lucas loved to involve Norah, even if cooking with a six-year-old was a million times the mess of cooking with Lucas when he'd first started learning.

Lucas helped Norah drop raw biscuit dough on a cookie sheet and they'd scrambled eggs while I cooked the sausage. We ate together at the kitchen table, with Norah's backpack and coloring supplies shoved to one side.

I glowered at the clutter. Our house had become claustrophobic. "We've got to start hunting for a bigger place," I said.

Lucas wiped up Norah's mouth and excused her from the table. He took a slow sip of his coffee, cocked his head and regurgitated the same answer he'd given me the last ten years, "Why move twice?"

I sighed. My dream house had never matured beyond just that—a dream. Before we had gotten married, I'd worked with an architect to formalize my plans into actual blueprints, and we'd taken a bunch of summer trips to inspect possible lots. But then life happened and, after school loans, Norah's birth expenses and the loss of Lucas' income, we hadn't come close to affording it. I'd been so busy that we were lucky to sneak in our semi-annual trips to visit Kayla in Portland. "I think it's time to bury that dream."

Lucas frowned, cleared the plates and washed the dishes. "When is Rocco going to pick up his slack?"

I laughed, and Lucas stopped the water and glared at me. "It's not an outrageous question."

"Sorry, but the man hasn't been seen in the office in nearly two months."

"You shouldn't have taken that partnership after his heart attack."

"That partnership paid for Norah," I pointed out, and he backed down. He made no secret about his dislike for my boss-turned-business partner. After his medical issues, Rocco had asked me to run the business for him. I'd agreed in exchange for a more equitable share of the profits. When the housing business took a nose dive, I'd taken a pay cut for over a year. We'd survived the crisis, but there was no doubt the business arrangement hadn't paid off like I'd hoped.

"I'm sorry. I just hate how Rocco takes advantage of you."

"I know, and I love you for it."

* * * *

Around five in the evening, Lucas had Norah packed and ready, so Joann wouldn't have to get out of the car. Since his stroke, Joann didn't like leaving Greg longer than was necessary, but any suggestion Norah spend the night elsewhere was met with an adamant refusal. Lucas' list of acceptable babysitters was limited to our parents and, when she was in town, her Aunt Kayla. Not even Case and Robert had made the list, although I suspected that had a lot to do with their pool and would change as soon as Norah learned to swim.

The house was empty without Norah's laughter, but I'd been looking forward to our evening of celebration. I made my way to the bathroom in anticipation of events to come. Lucas' libido had not been tamed over the years, so much as caged. And a kid-free night was the surest way to unleash it.

He rushed me the moment the door shut. "Oh my God. Get naked right now." He used both hands to shove me to the bed then climbed on top of me.

I chuckled and twisted my head to check the clock, "That's got to be some kind of record. We've been alone for less than a minute."

He grinned but continued his quest. My fly came down, followed by a rough yank on my waistband, two sizes bigger than I'd worn the day we'd been married. "A little help here," he motioned. I lifted my hips for him.

He stood and stripped for me. With a slap on my hip, I rolled over. "Your ass is so thick now. I love it." He played my cheeks like bongo drums then pulled them apart for a quick taste. "I've been dreaming about tonight for weeks. I haven't fucked you in months."

"Quit exaggerating," I mumbled into the pillow, trying to recall the last time we'd had sex. The memory surfaced — three days before. I'd sucked Lucas off in the shower when he'd gotten home from the gym. My knees still ached.

"I'm not exaggerating," Lucas said. He trailed kisses up my spine.

I studied him. The tenderness never left us. We'd been through long, dry patches. The weeks I'd spent in San Diego after my dad's cancer was diagnosed and again after his passing. Lucas had broken his leg after falling on some ice three years before. We'd been through countless colds, flu bugs, stomach viruses and an unusually long stretch after Norah had come home. Lucas had been paranoid about her sleeping in her nursery, and I'd refused to have sex with our newborn daughter in the room. That standoff had lasted nearly a month. Other than that, I'd always made sure he never felt neglected sexually, the last residual paranoia I carried about our age difference.

"It's not a complaint, love. I just missed you is all." He bit my butt and murmured, "I missed this."

I rolled over and tugged him down for a kiss. "It has been a while for that, I suppose." I pulled him until he lay on top of me, held his face between my palms and gazed at him. My focus settled on the freckle in the middle of his lower lip that hadn't changed. His eyes had little lines around the corners now. The two days of white-blond scruff couldn't disguise his fuller, less boyish face. His once long hair was short — barely long enough for me to grab onto. Besides my favorite freckle, the only other part of his body that hadn't changed was his stomach, which he worked at twice as hard to keep for me. I could stare at him all day and never categorize all the things I loved about him.

Lucas kissed my neck and chest before returning to my lips. Slightly dazed, he lifted his eyes and studied me. He reached for our lube and waited with a bemused smile. "Seriously. As much as I love your face, I want your ass, Kyle. Roll over and let me get you ready, unless you just want me to shove it in."

Ten years hadn't changed that part of him either and, while I had grown accustomed to his size, 'shoving it in' was still a hard pass where Lucas was concerned — which was not to say my attitude about rough sex hadn't evolved considerably.

"Wait," I laughed and pushed him off me so I could reach under the bed and grab the package I'd stashed there.

"What's this?"

"Open it."

Lucas lifted the lid of the box and gasped. As he stared down at the leather harness and flogger, his eyes brightened and his smile peeked out from around his hand. I pointed to the bedpost where I'd tied the end of the restraints Lucas had brought home over a year before. "Oh, fuck." He pressed his palm to his erection.

I laughed. "Do you still want to?"

"Uh. Yeah. Like fuck yeah."

"Then go change."

Lucas hopped off the bed so fast he nearly slipped, and I watched him put the harness on and struggle to place the cock ring comfortably while he was only semi hard. The black leather transformed Lucas' demeanor. He always exuded sexiness, but like that—crisscrossed in straps that seemed to accent every muscular line of his body—he sent chills up my spine. My body warmed with the anticipation.

"Get on your hands and knees."

The baritone order instantly aroused me. I hesitated only briefly, to nod to the dresser. Lucas crossed the room and flipped on the small handheld camcorder we sometimes used. He palmed it and aimed it at me as I got on all fours.

"Fuck, baby. Look at that beautiful hole." I shivered. He approached me and rubbed his free hand over my ass. I loved the way Lucas saw me through the camera. I closed my eyes and concentrated on his touch while he stroked my skin. His hand fell hard against the skin, and I flinched, but soft strokes lulled me back. Closing my eyes tight, I focused my mind on giving control to Lucas, of letting him own my pleasure, even if it meant scrambling the pain receptors in my brain. Another whack fell on my already-stinging flesh. I rocked back, seeking his soothing touch.

"What do you want, baby?" he asked.

"I want you to use me." And it wasn't a line. I wanted everything Lucas could give me.

"You want to be my slut, baby?"

"Yes." I gulped. Lucas had cultivated my submissive side with close attention to my porn viewing. I still wasn't an avid watcher, but when I did indulge, I definitely had a type. Before he'd retired, Cole had become my favorite porn star—besides Lucas, of course.

"Yes, what?" The crack of leather whipping through the air resounded behind me.

"Yes, Sir."

Lucas' smile sent energy into the room. The hairs on my body stood at attention with the shift in electricity. "That's good, little slut. Tell Sir why I should stuff this pretty hole."

"Because I need it, Sir."

"Show me how bad you need it, baby. Beg me for it."

"Please fuck me, Sir." I twisted my head to gaze at him. The camera was still aimed at my hole as Lucas' cock thumped against it. I pushed my ass back to him. He laughed and stood to set the camera on our bedside table.

"Show me you're worth it."

I rose from the bed and fell to my knees, peering up at Lucas. He laid his cock over my face. He yanked my hair back and, without hesitation, used his hand to swing his hard cock into my cheek. My mouth chased it, but Lucas kept it out of my reach. "That's not how good sluts behave."

I opened my mouth and clasped my hands behind my back. I lifted my face to him, and he spit into my mouth. The spray dripped from my skin and the act settled me further into the role. "Use me please, Sir."

The swift intrusion into my throat made my eyes water. "Fuck. Such a good slut. Yeah. Don't you dare fight it."

I opened wider and relaxed my throat as Lucas' pubic hairs tickled my nose. He pulled back and I gasped for air before his full length filled me again. "Take that cock, baby."

My air choked off, and my body felt lighter. Lucas slapped me and covered me with his spit. Each time, a little more of my neurotic-self slipped away until I was Lucas' perfect whore—a rentboy he'd picked up and taken into the bathroom stall to abuse, a helpless stable boy to a vicious billionaire. The details were irrelevant. I was a fantasy. Lucas' fantasy.

When he finished abusing my mouth, he yanked my hair back and forced me to look at him. My body trembled as I awaited his next move.

"Open up." He cupped my lower jaw and pulled down. With a free hand, he opened the bedside table and removed the O-ring gag and blindfold. He placed the silk tie around my eyes and the leather strap around my mouth and buckled it tight. We'd discovered it was too small for Lucas to fuck my throat with it on, but he loved me in it, my mouth forced open for him. He rubbed his length on my exposed tongue and used a thumb to wipe up the drool. "Get on the bed, slut."

With his help, I rose to my feet. Since I couldn't speak, I thought the words. *Yes, Sir.*

Lucas jostled me, and I let my limbs go pliant as he shifted me and clasped the wrist restraints into place. I lay on my stomach, cheek pressed to the mattress, drool dripping out of the side of my mouth, arms spread and locked into place. Despite the blindfold, I knew the camera was aimed at my face and the knowledge sent a thrill straight to my cock.

The bed dipped and the soft, supple leather of the flogger tails caressed my back. Air whistled from my nostrils as I prepared myself for its bite.

Even with preparation, the stung startled me. The first taste was followed by Lucas' soothing palm. Then he continued until I grunted through the burn and clenched my hole in desperate need. The words filled my head. *Yes, Sir. Please fuck me. Please use me. Please just give me release.*

My ass was on fire by the time he'd finished but I no longer felt the pain. The only burn was deep inside me, a profound longing to have his body against mine anchoring me, to feel the weight of his cock slide between the angry flesh he'd created. I was where I longed to be—where his game took me, untethered from the constant doubts and fears. I was his slut. He was my Sir. He pulled apart my cheeks and teased something against my hole. I lifted my hips in search of some relief.

"Such an eager whore. Look how badly you want it." He unbuckled my gag.

The first words from my mouth were, "Thank you, Sir."

"Tell Sir what you need."

"Fill my hole."

"Which hole, slut? Tell Sir *exactly* what you need."

"My ass. I need to feel that big cock in my ass, Sir. Fuck me."

He circled my rim with his finger, and I moaned. "You're not ready."

Forgetting I was restrained, I lowered my arms. My cock throbbed at the tug of the binds. "Yes, please," I whined. I lifted my hips and humped against the mattress. Lucas' smack reignited the flaming skin on my ass. "Fuck," I moaned.

He pushed my head to the mattress and licked my cheek. "I'm going to take care of my little slut tonight."

"Yes, Sir."

"Just be good and trust me."

"Yes, Sir." Lucas' cock nudged my opening.

Just as soon as it was there, it was gone, replaced by the hot wetness of Lucas' tongue. Since Lucas had discovered the ways to get me out of my own neurosis, he'd brought rimming into our sex life with a vengeance. The sluttier he could make the act, the better. He pierced my hole with his tongue and I moaned in ecstasy.

"Yeah, moan for me." His stern command was honored immediately. "Beg for it."

"Yeah. I want it, baby. Eat my ass."

He went back to work with his tongue, and I yelped as he squeezed the mounds of my ass and pulled them apart to dive in farther. My hips pulsed with need. I could feel my wet hole quiver for him. "Fuck me, Lucas. Oh, God. I'm losing my mind. Sir, fuck me. Fuck me, *please*."

"Fuck, Kyle. So sexy when you beg for me."

"Yes, Sir. I need it. Use my hole. Fuck me hard. Jesus. Put it in, please."

Lucas' cock slammed home so hard that I choked on my own breath. He shoved my head to the mattress and held it there. I felt myself floating as the pain melded into a flicker of pleasure I could grasp on to. I cried out and thrashed against my binds. Awareness of Lucas' punishing strokes flitted away, leaving my head swimming in a warm pool of nothingness. Subspace. Whatever it was called was like a light switch for my brain. Pleasure was the only sensation Lucas allowed me and pleasure was all I felt.

The sensation traveled down my spine and pooled in my balls, giving them a too-full feeling. Too tight. Too hot. Lucas reached up and freed one of my wrists. I clenched around his cock as he rolled me to my side and continued to fuck me relentlessly. "Yes. Fuck," I seethed when the new angle rocked against my spot.

"There we go," Lucas whispered. "You want my load to fill you? You better come for me."

I reached for my dick and stroked but Lucas gripped my wrist and stilled it. "You don't trust Sir to fuck the cum out of you, slut?"

I moaned and my cock throbbed.

"That's a good boy. You take my dick so good."

Lucas drew back and nailed my prostate full on. I yelped as an overwhelming surge of pleasure shot through me. He rocked into me a second time, and by the third, my dick leaped in a dry spasm. A flood of sensations crashed over me, wave after wave, and pulled me under. "There you go. Good, baby. Show me how much you love it."

Lucas' words alerted me to my orgasm as I shook against him. He dug his fingers into my wrist that was pressed tight over my chest. "Yeah," Lucas moaned into my ear, and the force of his orgasm warmed my entire body. We stayed connected, panting and exhausted until I lifted my arm.

"Sorry," Lucas breathed and rushed to untie my other wrist and massaged it. Smiling at me, he reached for his camera. "Fuck, that was something."

"Yeah," I moaned and rolled over onto my stomach. "I need a nap," I sighed, settling into the mattress. I turned to smile at him, our silent acknowledgment of how good we were together.

We cuddled, his back against the headboard with my head on his lap. Laughing, he held the camera in one hand and stroked my hair with the other. His fingertips massaged my scalp, lulling me to a state of complete relaxation. I smiled to myself while our voices played quietly above my head. I'm wasn't sure how much the bedside camera had caught, but the soundtrack alone would make it one Lucas would regularly jerk off to.

Lucas' gentle laughter lifted me from my trance. "What?" I sat upright and flinched with discomfort.

"Nothing. I was just remembering when you told me you'd never like whips as much as Cole and now you're buying them for me to use on you. It only took me ten years to get you to fully embrace your kinky side."

I shrugged. "I never said that."

Lucas smirked at me and leaned to press his lips against my forehead. "It's okay. You can pretend you're still my innocent, slightly sexually repressed Kyle, the man I had to get tipsy to play daddy with me. Next time, in fact, I think we should do that nervous virgin roleplay again, but I want to top. That was hot."

"I wasn't that bad."

"No, you weren't," Lucas admitted. "But I love when you let go for me." Lucas tilted the video screen so I could watch, and I listened to moans and pleas that I hadn't recalled making. I was loud. I was slutty. I was sexy.

The old me would have shirked in mortification, but Lucas had taught me to embrace the messy, fun side of sex. Sometimes we just played with our bodies, but the best times were when he played with my mind. There was something magical about knowing he could transport me to an alternate reality where I saw myself through his eyes. Whether I was the sexiest daddy in the world or his cock-hungry whore, Lucas took me to these places and made it safe for me to exist without embarrassment, without self-doubts, without stigma. "I love when you get me to let go."

After we'd taken care of the most essential part of our celebration, we showered together and dressed for the romantic part of the evening—dinner at a trendy new steakhouse Lucas had dropped numerous hints about trying. I'd made the reservation a month ago and was still limited to a late seating.

The restaurant did its best impersonation of a classic New York City steakhouse. Oversized red leather booths lent a sense of privacy, and bright red roses on the crisp white tablecloth fed the romantic ambiance I'd hoped for.

The tablecloth and orientation shielded the space below the table from view. The fact that I noticed that spoke to the significant influence Lucas had on me over the years. I motioned to Lucas to slide into the booth first and he lifted his eyebrows. The next time we came, I'd be wearing a vibrating plug in my ass and Lucas would stroke my cock under the table the entire night. My pervy boy was getting more predictable as he aged.

We finished dinner well after nine. Stuffed full of the most tender filet I'd ever eaten and wine drunk, I sat back from the table three bites shy of my entire steak. Lucas ordered chocolate lava cake, but I'd tapped out. Eating that late was already hell on my stomach. Damn, I missed my metabolism.

"So, presents?" I proposed, pulling the small gift box from the pocket of my coat jacket.

Lucas beamed and pushed his empty plate out of the way. "But yours is at home."

"That's okay. I'm excited to give this to you." I pushed the box toward him. "Ten years, nine months and sixteen days ago you proposed to me. It was the most perfect, romantic, special day of my life. I still can't believe you found the exact spot we'd gone kayaking on our first trip to the lake and that you and Kayla had that picnic all arranged. To this day, I think it might have been the only secret she's ever kept from me."

Lucas smiled. My smile. He opened the box and gasped at the diamond channel set band that matched the one he'd presented me nearly eleven years ago. "Babe," he exhaled.

"I didn't have a chance to do this, and I wanted to." I stood, kneeled on one knee and took his hand. "Baby, before you I thought of myself as just an average man. For forty years I lived every day thinking that I was happy enough, that life was good enough. Then, through some sort of crazy serendipity, you entered my life and said you'd enjoy changing my mind. And you took me on this amazing ride. I'd followed you that first day in the library, and I will follow you again—today and every day, for the rest of my life. The last ten years you've taught me to think of average as a curse word. Ordinary is an insult to the life we've lived. Would you do the great honor of being my husband for the rest of our lives?"

"Oh, Kyle." Lucas clasped his hand over his mouth. I slid the ring next to his wedding band. "Of course, baby. I love our life."

* * * *

Lucas was quiet on the trip home. He kept inspecting his hand then eyed me, smiling. "I've never regretted a moment of our life, Kyle. Not one second."

"Me neither."

"And I love our sex life."

"Me too."

"Okay, I just wanted to be clear. Even if you didn't let me do all the kinky shit I wanted, it wouldn't matter."

I gaped at him because he was off…jittery about something. "You talk to your mom? Dad okay? Norah?" I asked.

Lucas nodded. "She's having a blast. Mom made ice cream sundaes, and they were watching a movie. Dad was tired because the physical therapist came today. He's doing well with the walker."

We pulled into the driveway and entered our house together, his arm wrapped snug around my waist. I tossed my keys on the coffee table, and Lucas turned on the lights. He returned holding a manila envelope with a red bow and looking a little terrified.

I stared at him, perplexed by the undercurrent of tension. "If those are divorce papers, you're out of luck. You're stuck with me."

Lucas smiled and handed me the envelope. "Open this. It's from Norah."

My lips twisted, "Norah got me a gift?"

"Open it."

I lifted the flap and freed the colored drawing from inside. "Aww. She's gotten so good at staying in the lines. When did she start liking owls?"

Lucas bit his lower lip. "Baby, you might want to sit."

I grimaced. The last time I had to sit for news, my dad's doctor had started throwing around scary words like 'biopsy' and 'malignant'. "Oh my God, you are freaking me out. What is this?" I held up the picture, which, while adorable, did not fit in the various horror stories my brain was working over.

"Just sit and I'll explain." I took a seat while he poured me a bourbon. "Here." He handed it over. He moved to the desk and freed a stack of papers from the drawer. "That's a picture of a Northern Spotted Owl. Have you ever heard of them?"

I shook my head, dismayed. "Did you buy an owl, Lucas? I know we talked about getting Norah a pet, but I was thinking a cat. We cannot have a pet owl."

Lucas rolled his eyes at me. "Let me get this out. I promise to answer your questions at the end. That owl was on the endangered species list eleven years ago. That spot where I proposed. Do you remember? There was a nature preserve behind it."

"Yeah." My answer was as drawn out as his story.

"Shortly after I proposed, I bought that land."

"You did *what*?"

"I found the owner, and I only wanted to buy the spot we picnicked at. He was anxious to get rid of it, but he would only sell me the full acre."

"You have an acre of land in Oregon and you never told me?"

"I was embarrassed. I was young, and it was a romantic impulse. I used almost all my savings. That student loan I took out for the last semester? I sort of needed it because of this."

"You told me you didn't have savings."

"Kyle, I'd done over seventy porn scenes. Of course I had savings. But there's more. Do you want another drink?"

"No, I'm okay. Keep going."

"Tonight you said you'd follow me anywhere. Was that true?"

"Of course."

"Good, because the Northern Spotted Owl is no longer endangered." He handed me a thick stack of papers, survey maps and real estate contracts. I flipped through the papers, pausing at the 'sign here' sticker with my name on it. "I got the approval, appraisal and survey last month. I had a lawyer draw up the paperwork, and once we have it notarized, we'll both own an acre of residentially-zoned Oregon lakefront property, and I want to build our dream house."

"Are you fucking kidding me?"

"No. Are you mad?" He teared up. "I didn't mean to keep it a secret for so long. That year that was so tight. I investigated selling it, but there was no point. Please, don't be angry."

"Lucas, of course I'm not mad." I started crying, too. "Just shocked. I can't believe it."

"There are no utilities, but the lot alone is worth over ten times what I paid for it. I know we could sell it, but I want to do it. I want you to get out of the business with Rocco. He's taken terrible advantage of you. I'm ready to go back to work, and Goldenboys is expanding. They want to move forward with the new sister studio, and Robert offered me a chance to run the entire business. I'd make enough that we can do this, and if you want to work after the house is done, so be it. You can start your own business or, if you're still game for it, we can get serious about adoption and you can stay home this time. All I know is it's time, before Norah gets too far in school. You sacrificed your dream house for me—"

"Norah was for both of us."

He smiled. "You know what I mean. We could have had a family for a lot less money."

"I can't believe you did this."

"I'm so sorry."

"Are you kidding? The only thing I'm mad about is you upstaged my gift. I worked hard on that." I pointed to his ring.

Lucas laughed, tension flowing out of his body. "I absolutely love it, too. So, we can do this?"

"Hell, yes. This is…indescribable. I can't find the words. You leave me speechless."

"That's only fair, because you leave me breathless."

I kissed him and we lost ourselves in the moment. Lucas had made all my dreams come true.

We finished our night making love the way I preferred, slow and sweet, with my body fully enveloped by Lucas'. He wrapped his legs and arms around me so tight that all I could do was rock gently inside him while whispering sweet endearments and placing tender kisses on the curve of his neck. Too soon, the heat of Lucas' release and my name moaned low and breathy in Lucas' sex-drenched voice pushed me to orgasm. Lucas clung to me, panting and insisted on prolonging our connection as long as possible until my spent cock slipped free. I rolled on my back and he followed me, shaping his body along my side. He drifted off in my arms.

Lucas' head was on my chest, and I combed my fingers through his hair, thinking of all the years we'd shared together and all the memories we'd yet to create in our new home. The words I couldn't remember came to me in the middle of the night—ineffable joy. That was what Lucas brought to my life.

I was an ordinary man transformed by an extraordinary love.

Want to see more like this?
Here's a taster for you to enjoy!

Enough
Matthew J. Metzger

Excerpt

He could smell the fire.

He was blind. His eyes streamed. The curling wallpaper crackled and hissed. His skin was burning. The air in his lungs seared him from the inside out. And there was nowhere to go — no escape from the heat, no escape from the orange towers and acrid black smoke, no *air*.

"Ezra!"

The smoke wrapped itself around his teeth and tongue like a grotesque mockery of a kiss, and there was no reply but the roar of hot air and climbing fire. The house was burning. *The house was burning!*

"Ezra! Ez!"

A scream. A piercing scream, like nothing he'd ever heard, but before he could move, the wooden boards crumbled to ash and he was falling, tearing through the shreds of stairs into the inferno, and —

Jesse hit the carpet with a thump and jarred himself awake.

The flat was quiet. The streetlight touched the other side of the curtains with a faint orange light. There was no smoke, no fire, no sound. Nothing.

Jesse dragged himself back onto the bed. The sheets were impossibly tangled and his tank top stuck to him with sweat. His wrist ached in its brace where he'd bumped it, but the panic hadn't quite eased its grip on his heart or his lungs, and he fumbled for his phone, ignoring the pain.

Thank God for speed dial.

The clock on the side said two-fifty-eight, and the phone rang six times before the line coughed and crackled and a sleepy voice, tinged in the early hours with the fading edges of a Welsh accent, mumbled a vague sort of question.

"Ez?"

There was a rustle of sheets. "Jesse?"

"Oh, God," Jesse breathed. The air escaped in a rush, loud and hard. His lungs shook with the effort. "Shit. I just— I needed to check—"

"Jess? What's happened, sweetheart?"

The soft roll of his vowels, the accent entirely muted when he was properly awake, was as comforting as a hug, and Jesse coughed out, "Nightmare," before thinking twice. Ezra was okay. He was okay. It was all okay.

"Oh, sweetheart," Ezra murmured, low and crooning. "Do you want to tell me about it?"

"I need— can I come over? I know it's late and I know you have work in the morning, but—I just—I need—"

"No," Ezra interrupted, and Jesse's stomach twisted violently.

"*Please*, Ez, I—"

"Hey, hey, hey." Ezra cut him off. "Hey, stop, calm down, sweetheart. I *meant* you can't come here. You don't sound okay, not to me, and I don't want you to go out like this, so I'll come to you, all right?"

Jesse exhaled, the twist easing. "Okay."

"You okay if I hang up, or do you want me to put the phone on speaker?"

"Can — speaker," Jesse swallowed against the nausea. He was still shaking, he realised faintly. "I just — I couldn't find you, Ez. The house was burning and I couldn't find you, and I — I need to hear you. You don't have to talk to me, but I need to hear you."

"Okay." The phone crackled again and clunked, and suddenly Ezra's voice was loud and echoing. Soothing. The Welsh hint was fading, and Jesse could suddenly hear him dressing, but he was *there*. "Was it my house or the one last week?"

"Yours," Jesse said. "I was on the stairs, and they gave way, and I woke up. I couldn't find you."

"If my house was on fire, I would probably be in the kitchen having caused it," Ezra said, and yawned loudly. "Make yourself useful, sweetheart, and make up a brew for me? I've not slept long."

Jesse knew better than to apologise. He shrugged out of his sweat-soaked pyjamas and pulled on a pair of jogging bottoms before taking the phone through the narrow hall into the kitchen. The kitchen window overlooked the main road. A police car trailed idly by on the prowl. Phone to his ear, he listened to Ezra swear sleepily at his cupboard, and the soft sounds of those narrow feet padding downstairs.

"Sweetheart?"

"Mm?" Jesse listened to the front door and the heavy sound of the key.

"I'm going to hang up while I drive. You all right for ten minutes until I get there?"

"Yeah," Jesse croaked. His heart had come down out of the rafters, and he could breathe. The streetlights didn't look threatening anymore. He just felt...shaky. Sick and shaky and scared. "Yeah, Ez, I'll be fine."

"Okay. Love you."

The dial tone was immediate. Jesse dropped the phone to the counter and switched on the kettle, staring out of the window and waiting, arms folded against the chill. It wasn't the first nightmare, and it wouldn't be the last. He usually managed one a week without fail, and the injury hadn't helped matters. But they didn't usually involve Ezra in burning buildings. They didn't usually involve losing him.

And Jesse couldn't stomach the thought of losing him.

Which was a bit scary in itself. They'd only met eight months ago. At a gay bar, of all places—the one place where he went to meet sex partners, not partner partners. Jesse had thought the freckled blond with the dark eyes was pretty in the neon lights and had bought him a drink, talked him into a dance, bought him another. Kissed him at the back of the dance floor—and had promptly found himself alone, but with a phone number in his back pocket.

He'd wanted sex. That was all he'd been after. Sex with a pretty guy. But then they'd gone on a date and he'd met Ezra properly, and he was lost. Ezra wasn't just a handsome face and nice legs. Ezra was the world. He was Jesse's world, and it had only been eight months, but Jesse still knew that this was it, for him. Ezra was it. There would never be anyone else like him.

So he stood in a tense vigil at the window, waiting for the faithful little Peugeot 207 to creep around the corner. Waiting for Ezra to come, because there was emotional shock and there was sense, and the two weren't in line right now. He knew Ezra was okay. He knew it. He'd answered the phone. He'd been sleepy and understanding and sworn at his cupboard. He was fine.

But Jesse still needed to reach out and touch him, just to make sure. *Somehow.*

The little blue car was lonely on the three-in-the-morning road, and Jesse propped the door of his flat to creep down the communal stairs and open the main door. Ezra had gotten sort-of dressed, in jeans and an open check shirt, feet shoved into his trainers without socks, and his hair was wild and fluffy, in gleeful disarray, as he locked the car and wrapped himself around Jesse in a tight, warm hug.

Jesse clung back until something creaked, and pressed the side of his face against that wild hair.

"You're all right, sweetheart," Ezra murmured.

Jesse squeezed again until Ezra's grip on the nape of his neck tightened in warning, then he let go and dragged Ezra up the silent stairs by the hand. Concrete stairs. They wouldn't collapse in a fire until the whole building came down.

He didn't say a word until he'd pressed the requested tea into Ezra's hands, locked the door again and bundled them both back to the messy bed. Ezra was equally silent, taking a couple of mouthfuls before abandoning the tea, stripping to his underwear and crawling into the mess to mould himself into Jesse's arms.

"There you go," he murmured lowly, kissing Jesse's encroaching stubble and stroking a hand gently through his hair. "Feel better now?"

"Mm," Jesse pressed his nose into Ezra's neck, tangling their legs together. He could feel a strong pulse in Ezra's jugular. He could feel the rough skin of the bumpy scar on Ezra's shoulder under his fingertips. He could feel the fuzzy mess of Ezra's hair, usually styled and stiff in that messy-but-it's-on-purpose-so-it's-okay manner, now just loose and wild. He could feel *him*. "Thank you."

"Thank me again tomorrow afternoon when I'm grumpy and exhausted after two hours of the Year Nines."

"Okay," Jesse agreed, sliding his arms completely around Ezra's back until he enveloped him. They didn't often sleep cuddled together — or even together at all, between Ezra's eight-to-four and Jesse's shifts — but he needed this. He *needed* it.

"Mind if I go to sleep?"

"No," Jesse squirmed until Ezra got the hint and tucked his head under his chin. His hair tickled. Jesse kissed the top of his head and wished he had the easy grace with language that Ezra did. Wished he could express himself properly. Wished he could talk as easily as he hugged. But all that came out was, "I just needed to touch you."

Ezra said nothing to that, simply shifting until he was comfortable, one arm over Jesse's ribs and the other tucked over his own waist in a casual sort of drop. Ezra was *long* — long limbs, long neck, all willowy lines and bendy joints, and he settled like water into the bulkier, stiffer contours of Jesse's body.

But he fit, and he fit perfectly, and Jesse wrapped him up and held him, breathing in the smell of store-brand shampoo and cheap aftershave until the last traces of the nightmare-induced fear washed away.

It was still a long time before he slept.

PUBLISHING

Sign up for our newsletter and find out about all our romance book releases, eBook sales and promotions, sneak peeks and FREE romance books!

About the Author

Logan Meredith began writing as a teenager when beautiful boys started keeping her company at night. Unfortunately, the voices she heard were imaginary, and their conversations resulted in horrible insomnia. They only let her sleep when she started typing their words down. Thankfully, being awkward as hell and a head taller than anyone else in the school afforded plenty of spare time for writing.

At first, she tried to make them play with characters from her favorite television series or books. She found her lost tribe with a ravenous, crazy group of fan fiction lovers online and started sharing her stories publicly. Then something amazing happened: new characters arrived and started demanding their own stories. Only they wanted their own world to play in and they wanted to find their true loves. So between her day job and making time for her family, she tries to keep up with the demands from her beautiful men for their happily-ever-afters.

A native of San Antonio, Texas, and a graduate of the University of Texas-San Antonio, Logan is an accomplished cross-country mover having honed her skills bouncing between five states. She currently resides in Houston, Texas. In addition to writing, she spends her time reading and re-reading her favorite books, cheering for the San Antonio Spurs, playing Words with Friends, and procrastinating pretty much everything else.

Logan is a proud member of the LGBTQA community and vocal advocate for mental health awareness suicide prevention, and equality campaigns.

Logan loves to hear from readers. You can find her contact information, website details and author profile page at https://www.pride-publishing.com